D1270755

THE WILD WEST:
A WESTERN TRIO

THE WILD WEST:
A WESTERN TRIO

ed. by Jon Tuska

GUNSMOKE

First published in the US by Five Star

This hardback edition 2013
by AudioGO Ltd
by arrangement with
Golden West Literary Agency

ISBN 978 1 471 32132 0

British Library Cataloguing in Publication Data available.

Printed and bound in Great Britain by
MPG Books Group Limited

TABLE OF CONTENTS

Foreword

Jon Tuska

For some years I corresponded with Katherine Anne Porter, and I recall that I once referred to her classic story, "Noon Wine," as a novelette. She was quite taken aback by that inference and explained emphatically that "Noon Wine," like "Pale Horse, Pale Rider" and "Old Mortality," was *not* a novelette, nor was it a *novella,* or any other word derived from a language other than English. "Noon Wine" as many of the long stories she wrote was to be considered a short novel!

In retrospect it was a most apt way to look at a story too short to be a novel—forty thousand words or less—and too long to be a short story. It was a literary form that once was encouraged and flourished when there were numerous fiction magazines published weekly, monthly, or quarterly in the United States, and it is a form at which numerous American writers excelled. Many authors of Western stories wrote short novels, including Zane Grey and Max Brand, and personally I think Louis L'Amour's best Western fiction was written in this form. However, the problem for an editor of a story collection has always been that short novels are too long to fit comfortably into an anthology of short fiction, and, if you do include one or two, it may appear that favoritism is being shown to those authors with the longer stories. For decades, also, book publishers did not like short novels. They were too short to make a book by themselves, and so authors, who wanted to publish short novels in book form that had been written originally for magazines that tended to prefer such a length because the story could be carried in a single issue rather than serialized in installments, were asked to expand their short novels into full-length books. Yet, the truth of the matter is that true short novels do not accommodate being expanded into longer narratives without introducing all manner of sub-plots and additional characters that tend to diffuse the concision and compactness of the original story.

We are fortunate now that these strictures imposed on authors for so many years have been abandoned. Many of the trios of stories by Max Brand published in the Five Star Westerns have sold as well, and in some cases better, than some of his novels first time in book form. The advent of paperback audios from Durkin Hayes have also found a ready market for short novels that can fill a single cassette, or perhaps two, and have in that form met with a strong commercial success. A short novel, after all, is a unique form, and in it an author is able to give the reader more background to the story, pay more attention to the setting, and develop characters with a depth that would be impossible in a short story.

The present collection is the first of a series of books consisting of a trio of Western short novels by different authors. Each short novel is able to stand on its own and perform its function of introducing a reader to characters and situations that are deeply involving, and at the same time each is a story that can be read with pleasure at a single sitting with the satisfying complexity afforded by this more expansive literary form.

Jon Tuska
Portland, Oregon

Riders of the Storm

Robert J. Horton

When Robert J. Horton died in a hotel room in Manhattan from bronchial pneumonia probably complicated by chronic myocarditis from which he had suffered for years, he was forty-four years old. The date of his death was January 19, 1934. Samuel C. Glasgow, M.D., had been his personal physician since August, 1927, and he was attending him when he died. At the time Horton was widowed, and he had maintained his residence in New York City for twenty-one years, although he spent much of his time away from the city, traveling. Since 1920 he had made his living writing Western fiction for the magazine market, primarily after 1922 for Street & Smith. By the mid-1920s Horton was one of three authors to whom Street & Smith paid 5¢ a word—the other two being Frederick Faust, perhaps better known as Max Brand, and Robert Ormond Case. Many of Horton's serials for Street & Smith's *Western Story Magazine* were subsequently brought out as books by Chelsea House, Street & Smith's book publishing company. Although virtually all of Horton's stories appeared under his byline in the magazine, for their book editions Chelsea House published them both as by Robert J. Horton and by James Roberts. Sometimes, as was the case with ROVIN' REDDEN (Chelsea House, 1925) by James Roberts, a book would consist of three short novels that were editorially joined to form a "novel." Other times the stories were serials published in book form, such as WHISPERING CAÑON (Chelsea House, 1925) by James Roberts or THE MAN OF

THE DESERT (Chelsea House, 1925) by Robert J. Horton. It may be obvious that Chelsea House, doing a number of books a year by the same author, thought it a prudent marketing strategy to give the author more than one name. The same practice was followed with Faust's novels which appeared variously from Chelsea House as by George Owen Baxter or by David Manning (Max Brand was the named reserved for Faust novels published by Dodd, Mead).

Despite the fact that Horton claimed New York City residence for so many years, in 1923 he was living in an apartment in Santa Barbara; in 1924 he was in Los Angeles for part of the year and for the rest of it in London, England. Horton had been born in Coudersport, Pennsylvania, of an American father and a Colombian mother, and occasionally he would also return there for periods of time, as he did in December, 1924 and into 1925, before living for a time in Highlands, New Jersey. Later in 1925 his mailing address was in Paris, France. He apparently liked the state of Maine since he would spend long periods there as well, at Oquossoc, Rumford, Rangleley, and Portland.

In the years 1920 through 1922, Horton published a total of fifteen Western stories in *Adventure Magazine*. It was doubtless one of these stories that Walt Coburn was reading, as he recalled in his autobiography, WALT COBURN: WESTERN WORD WRANGLER (Northland Press, 1973). "There were enough mistakes to convince me the writer did not savvy anything about cowpunching," Coburn wrote. "It was only after I had finished the yarn, which had enough plot and character delineation to make good reading in spite of my biased opinion, that I looked to find the name of the author. The story was written by Robert J. Horton, and this surely rang a bell. The author was the same old friend and drinking companion I had known back in Great Falls, Montana. The same Bob Horton who was sports editor for the *Great Falls Tribune*, with a daily column under the byline of 'Sporticus.' I had been completely out of touch with Bob for a number of years, and had no idea he had started writing Western fiction."

Coburn wrote a long letter to Horton, in care of *Adventure*, telling Horton that his cowpunching days were over and that now he wanted to write Western fiction. The tutelage Horton provided Coburn proved invaluable, and it was not long before Coburn himself was having his name showcased on the covers of Western fiction magazines, including Horton's own staple market, *Western Story Magazine*.

However much time Horton may have spent living in the American West prior to 1922, he rarely went there at all after that time. His Western stories are concerned most of all with character, and it is the characters that drive the plots rather than the other way around. It is unfortunate he died at such a relatively early age. Many of his novels, after Street & Smith abandoned Chelsea House, were published only in British editions, and Robert J. Horton was never to appear at all in paperback books. I imagine his name has been generally forgotten, as was also the case with Cherry Wilson. But what follows is one of his short novels I have particularly enjoyed. It was written in September, 1932 at Saranac Lake, New York, and Horton titled it "Storm Riders." Street & Smith changed the title to "Riders of the Storm" when it appeared in *Western Story Magazine* in the issue dated December 17, 1932. It was still the time of the Great Depression, and Horton, as all the other Street & Smith writers including Frederick Faust, had been told he would have to accept less for his stories. In this case he was paid only 2¢ a word.

11

I

"$5,000 reward"

There was no sunset. Stubby clouds scuttled overhead like gray crows. In the north, gray veils unfurled and smothered the low buttes. East to southward the great billows rolled like celestial chariots. Waves of mist swept over the western mountains to drown the sun. Gradually the swirling, gray maëlstrom drew the horizon close about Nine Mile Spring, and the far-flung gold of the prairies was submerged in the saffron hue of a weird twilight. The air hung heavy and too hot for late September.

Bull Pruitt, a mountain of a man on a huge, powerful horse, rode along the dusty road, eyeing the mutable signs of the storm in silent wrath. He fumbled at the week's growth of beard on his face, cursed, and looked at the heavy watch he drew from inside his leather jacket.

"Five o'clock and no spring yet!" he ejaculated aloud.

His horse lengthened its stride at sound of his gruff voice. He drew rein expertly as a shadow loomed ahead. He stared into what seemed a smoky haze, the watch dangling from its buckskin thong as his hand crossed over to his gun and hung there. With a meaningless exclamation he replaced the watch and pushed on toward the trees that had suddenly emerged from the pall of shadow. He glimpsed a gleam of green and the glint of water.

His horse snorted and halted abruptly at its master's touch. Pruitt looked with cruel eyes in which a curious gaze was directed at a man who stood beside the rugged trunk of

12

a tall cottonwood. The man looked up at Pruitt on the big horse with a startled expression.

Pruitt's hand was on his gun as he stared past the man at a notice on the trunk of the tree that appeared to have been freshly posted.

"What's that?" he demanded.

"Part of my job," came the answer. The voice was none too brave; it almost smacked of apology. "I post signs. Thet's a reward notice. I git four bits apiece for putting 'em up."

"*Hrrrumph!* Why don't you find a fence with a lot of posts and make yourself a real stake?" Pruitt eyed the grayish, slight man with the hooked nose intently.

"Cain't do thet. They tell me where to put 'em up. I could find plenty of posts and things if they'd give me fifty cents per to stick a bill on 'em . . . if they give me enough bills." The voice was stronger, mildly resentful.

"Who tells you where to put 'em up?" Pruitt glowered.

"The county seat . . . the sheriff does. Hal Drew ain't putting out more'n he has to, you kin lay to thet." The man cackled.

"Read that notice to me," Pruitt commanded.

The man looked at the notice, hitching his belt, from which hung a heavy holstered gun. He presented something of the appearance of a distorted crow as he canted his head in the half light.

"Cain't read none too well," he said with a smirk, "but it's about some feller thet's wanted somewheres . . . outlaw, mebbe. Feller by the name of Pruitt. There's five thousand dollars out fer him." He squinted at the lowering skies and seemed to sniff the wind.

"Well, now, there you are!" Pruitt boomed. "If you could get an edge on that fellow, you wouldn't have to tack up no

13

more bills. Why don't you go after the big game?" His eyes were flickering points of green in the unnatural twilight.

The smaller man by the tree stared hard at his scornful questioner. "I reckon that ain't in my line," he drawled. "I leave that to the regular trackers. I'm too old fer the rough trails."

"You're just a bit bent." Pruitt sneered, looking at the smaller man's twisted legs. "You've done plenty of hard riding in your day, I reckon." He now contemplated the slightly humped back of the bill-poster.

"I ain't doing any at present, 'cept right aroun' close." The speaker again squinted at the sky. "I reckon one of them ekeenox storms is trying to break loose, stranger." He shot a straight glance at the inquisitive Pruitt.

Pruitt met the look coolly. He suddenly dismounted and strode to the tree, where he read the notice that offered five thousand dollars in cash for his capture, "alive if possible."

"Heh!" He turned suddenly on the smaller man, who had been observing him keenly. "You know what this notice says?" he roared. "They offer five thousand, down south there, for this Pruitt, 'alive if possible!' I reckon by that they'd just as soon have him dead, eh?"

"All I'm thinking about is my four bits per sign," was the other's answer. He looked in the direction of his horse, standing nearby. Next he wet a finger and held it up. "Ain't much breeze yet, but when she hits, she'll hit like the Almighty's hammer, I reckon. I've got to slope along, stranger. I'm through work fer the day."

He peered at the outlaw with a strained gaze. The beard that covered the lower part of Pruitt's face bothered him. He was thinking of the description published in the poster. It fitted this stranger perfectly. But he needed another sign—a sign which he would recognize instantly.

"What's your name?" Pruitt asked.

"Lawton," was the answer. There was no hesitation about replying to Pruitt's questions. The man asked them with an air not unlike authority; he exercised the manner of one accustomed to command.

"Well, Lawton, since you say you're putting up these notices for the sheriff, you must be . . . a deputy or something like that?"

"I'm the constable at Alder Creek," Lawton replied, with his first frown. "Since you're so curious, who're you? . . . I'm asking."

"I'm Bill," said Pruitt with a mirthless grin. "Oh, I'm not dangerous, Constable Lawton, but I'm in a queer situation."

He laughed shortly, unpleasantly, and shot swift glances at the threatening skies. The gathering storm breathed on the gentle rise and fall of a warm wind. It would close and break with the suddenness of a whiplash cracking in the air. It was getting darker.

"I take it this is Nine Mile Spring, all right," Pruitt said. He could see the water that appeared murky in the false twilight.

"You said it," Lawton confirmed. "You riding into Milton?"

"I'm tending to my own business," was the gruff answer.

Lawton said nothing, just stood there looking at the rider, watching for the sign. He was certain this was no other than Bull Pruitt, the outlaw, bandit, and killer described in the circular. If so, his—Lawton's—place was elsewhere as soon as he could get there. Ten years would effect certain changes in a man, but it wouldn't change his eyes much—and it couldn't erase a certain sign. Better than a mark or blemish, that sign, but Pruitt gave no indication of it.

The wind gathered in a gust and shook the branches of the trees violently. A silver light glowed momentarily in the semidarkness. A rumble as of giant wooden blocks tumbling caused the two men to look up. Lightning and thunder protracting its season, a vicious prairie storm was showing its first fangs in the vivid sheetings of lightning and reverberations of thunder. This atmospheric disturbance would be no joke, as both men knew.

"How far is it to town?" Pruitt growled.

"I reckon it's too fur to get there before this thing busts loose, but we better get going . . . if there's where you're heading."

"I didn't say where . . . ," the outlaw began. He was interrupted by a terrific blast of wind that seemed to drop from above, catch them in its vortex, and send leaves, broken branches, and dust whirling about their heads.

Pruitt leaped for his horse but stood still, when he had the reins in his hand, staring at Lawton, who was making for his mount. It was the movement of the man on his legs that convinced the outlaw that he knew him. A name burned in his mind, and he laughed as he swung into the saddle. He motioned to Lawton to ride alongside when the latter was on his horse.

The first violent flurry was subsiding as he held up a hand. "There's no sense riding into town in this," he shouted. "There must be some place where we can wait till the worst of it's over. You know where to go?"

"No!" Lawton called back. "I reckon it cain't blow us offen the road." On Pruitt's face he had detected a glimmer of the sign!

The wind fell away as suddenly as it had burst upon them. The air cooled slightly, and a faint light, virescent to bright green, glowed and died with intermittent flashings.

Both men were struck by this queer freak of the elements. Next a cold blast whipped them, and the heavens exploded with a deafening roar as lightning forked and streaked in blinding chains, and the rain swept in with torrential force.

Lawton's horse reared and plunged against Pruitt's mount. The outlaw could hardly see Lawton's face as wind and rain took his breath and nearly blinded him. But Lawton's conviction and his courage had mounted with the furious onslaught of the storm. He felt certain this stranger, who called himself simply "Bill," was no other than the wanted Bull Pruitt; and, if he were Pruitt, the outlaw would be certain to recognize him sooner or later. Perhaps he already had done so. If this were the case, would Pruitt not be suspicious? Would he not suspect Lawton of having recognized him in turn? If Pruitt were sure of this, the constable's life wouldn't be worth the echo of a thunderclap. On the other hand, the vision of the five-thousand-dollar reward danced before Lawton's eager eyes. He decided to take his chance with the famous outlaw in the storm.

He jerked a hand outward and to the right in a quick gesture. His mouth opened, and Pruitt knew he was shouting, but he couldn't hear what was being said. However, the gesture and the excited look in Lawton's eyes were enough. Pruitt spurred his horse in pursuit of the constable, who was pushing along the road through the trees below the spring.

Pruitt knew the road he himself intended to take led northwest from the main road near the spring, but he was resolved to follow Lawton even if the man held to the main road. Pruitt had had no intention of going to the town of Milton. It was the largest town north of the county seat, which he had avoided. He even considered, for a dark moment, black as the storm, the advisability of shooting down the rider ahead. This evil idea was literally knocked out of his mind as a flying piece of broken branch struck him on the head. He yelled an oath that the wind smothered even as it left his lips, and then saw Lawton veer to the right.

Pruitt's eyes glinted with satisfaction through the rain that was pouring down his face. This undoubtedly was the road he had been looking for when he had run across the constable and had stopped. It led directly through the thick growth west of the spring and was but dimly marked. At present it consisted of two tracks of running water.

The wind lashed the trees, and lightning—forked, chained, and livid flashes—played incessantly while the cold rain drove down. It would have been practically dark but for the angry, continuous play of lightning. The thunder crashes came with such rapidity and spontaneity that they deafened the ear in one hideous roar.

Lawton was lost in the rain, save when Pruitt caught sight of him in the steel-blue lightning. Pruitt had no fear of the storm. With the universe spinning about his head, he was telling himself that, if the constable was, indeed, the man he suspected him of being, he could not allow him to return to town. The outlaw not only would take no slightest chance of being identified and captured; he could not even permit suspicion.

Ahead, clinging to the saddle horn lest he be torn from his horse, the constable was thinking to himself that, if his companion proved to be Pruitt, it would mean—must be *made* to mean—five thousand dollars for himself. Lawton could use five thousand, or five hundred, for that matter. But he must not give himself away; and, above all, he must not risk a draw in the open. He could not dare give his man a chance.

A series of vivid flashes revealed a trail to the left.

Lawton turned his horse into it, with Pruitt close behind, and followed it into a tiny clearing where there were an abandoned shack and lean-to barn.

The storm increased in fury, as if to thwart the efforts of the two men to gain shelter. They had to hurl themselves against the force of wind and rain to secure their horses in the shed. They beat their way to the shack and found it locked. Pruitt threw his whole weight against the door and burst it open. He grasped Lawton and jerked him inside. Then he secured the shattered door, shutting out the whipping wind and stinging rain.

II

"Identities"

For almost a full minute, the two men stood in the center of the room, breathing hard from their exertions, eyeing each other in the lurid light that was punctured by brilliant, dazzling flashes. The small frame shack trembled with the force of the wind. Close about it the tall trees were being stripped of their tinted leaves. Outside, the shrieking of the storm continued unabated, and it was growing colder.

"Somebody's been living here."

It was Bull Pruitt who spoke, and his tone was accusing. It was as if he suspected that the constable already knew this.

"Sure." Lawton nodded, his eyes bright. "A homesteader was here. They called him a nester, and he lit out. I don't reckon he'll be back."

He was watching Pruitt closely as the big man looked

about at table, stove, chairs, bunk, and shelves, and other rude furniture that constituted the usual furnishings of an original homesteader's one-room shack. He wanted to be sure—to be absolutely certain that this was Pruitt, the man he once had known, who also was the man described in the reward notice. The beard bothered him; the eyes were the same. If he could see this man without his beard, or if he could see the sign, that would be positive identification. . . .

Pruitt put a hand inside his leather jacket and drew forth a metal matchbox. He tossed this on the table.

"There's a lamp there," he said pointedly. "Might as well light it. It would be pitch dark this minute if it weren't for the damnable lightning. These furies can't last all night," he added, as if to himself.

"It's liable to last longer'n thet." Lawton snickered as he took the chimney off the lamp and fumbled with the matchbox. "It's getting colder, too. When the thunder and lightnin' quits, it'll settle into a cold rain. Thet's the way it usually is with one of these ekeenox storms up here." He struck a match, lighted the wick, and replaced the chimney, keeping his vigil on the other out of the corner of his eye.

As the yellow glow from the lighted lamp permeated the room, the two stared at each other again. Pruitt's look now was plainly cross.

"You lived up here a long time?" he asked with a deep frown.

"Long enough to see a good many of these storms," was the answer. Lawton's tone and manner didn't appear evasive. To all intent his was the naïve confidence of one long a resident in the locality.

"Where's this Alder Creek you say you're constable of?" Pruitt asked, sitting in a chair near the table and taking out tobacco and papers.

"Five miles up the creek. It ain't a town. Roads cross there. Gineral store, boarding house, and barn, occasional contraband from Canady. I make three hundred or so a year serving papers and doing jobs like today, and thet keeps me. I got a vote, which helps." He winked slowly and bared his yellow teeth in a grin.

Pruitt watched the man sit down and roll a smoke. The skin of Lawton's face was hardly the healthy color of tan or red that might be expected as the result of long life on the range. It was more like parchment, as if it had absorbed at some time—during an illness or otherwise—a pallor that it never had entirely lost.

"You're a hell of a deputy," Pruitt snorted. "How about that liquor at the crossroads? That's against the law, isn't it? Do you wink at that?"

"What're you trying to boss me aroun' fer?" Lawton demanded.

Pruitt smiled grimly. In the steady light from the lamp he had completed his identification of the constable. There were now two thoughts uppermost in his mind. First, he must subtly ascertain if Lawton had by any chance recognized him, and, second, he must try to obtain some information he could use from him. This last might prove impossible without deliberately disclosing his own identity, if Lawton was not already aware of it. As yet, the constable had given him no reason to suspect the latter.

"I don't believe you're what you say you are," Pruitt declared bluntly.

For answer Lawton drew back his coat and disclosed his badge pinned to his shirt. "I reckon thet's good enough for yeh!"

The shack shook with an unusually hard blast of wind. It now was dark outside, save for the lightning play. The table was next to a window, and Pruitt looked to see if this window, or the other at the end of the room, had shades. Both were bare. But Lawton spotted his glances, and his eyes narrowed without the other seeing. They had to raise their voices to be heard above the din of the raging storm.

"You got another of those notices?" Pruitt asked casually.

"I got one more," Lawton confessed. "You seem awful curious 'bout my business fer a ranch hand . . . if thet's what you are." He was scowling faintly.

"I have reason to be curious," Pruitt said quickly. "Let me see the notice and I'll tell you why."

Lawton drew the small poster from an inside pocket of his coat and handed it across the table.

Pruitt spread it out under the lamp and read it closely. As he did so, his jaw clamped shut, and an almost imperceptible twitching of the eyebrows lent an incongruous expression to his face.

This erratic spasm of Pruitt's brows held Lawton's fascinated gaze as in a spell. The smaller man's eyes glittered with fire dots. It was the sign he had been waiting for—a nervous agitation over which the outlaw had no control in that he could not prevent the twitching in moments of intense concentration or excitement. The constable was one of the few who were acquainted with Pruitt's affliction. He doubted if any other man this far north actually knew Pruitt.

With a mighty effort he controlled himself, looking at the lightning flashes that constantly lighted the windows, listening to the cloudburst of torrential rain and the shrieking of the wind.

"You know something?"

Lawton started and looked back at Pruitt to see him

22

frowning darkly, the notice crumpled in his left hand.

"I know it's the worst storm up here in twenty years," the constable said.

"Devil take the storm!" Pruitt exclaimed savagely, bringing a heavy fist down on the table top with a ferocity that caused the lamp to jump. "The description of this outlaw here would almost fit me!" he declared. He flung the poster on the floor where a draft sucked it out of sight under the stove. "That's why I was interested in that piece of paper and in you."

"You're not him . . . not the one thet's wanted, are you?" The smaller man's simulation of startled surprise was perfect.

"I could be . . . if anybody didn't know any better," Pruitt said. "I've seen you peeking at me pretty hard. Do *you* think I look like this Pruitt?"

"Why . . . I . . . can't say I do, Bill," said the constable, to all appearances bewildered but really on the verge of mental panic.

The look in Pruitt's eyes was horrible; it was the red blaze of blood lust. But Lawton managed to stare the outlaw into a less aggressive look and manner. Calling Pruitt by the name he had given to himself also helped pacify him. The twitching of the brows vanished, but the deep-set scowl remained.

"You can't say you do, eh? But you've got a sneaking notion that I do, just the same. Isn't that so?"

"No, it ain't so," the constable flared. He jumped as a broken branch struck the roof with the sharp crack of a pistol shot.

"Nervous, eh?" said Pruitt, who had noticed. "Scared?"

"Why should I be scared?" Lawton asked blandly, his eyes wide.

"You'd be scared, though, if you thought I was that outlaw," Pruitt jeered. "Wouldn't you be scared if this fellow should show up and catch you tacking up bills offering a price on his head?"

"I don't know as I would," Lawton evaded.

"You lie!" Pruitt threw back his shaggy head and laughed.

As Lawton's eyes narrowed, the outlaw laughed harder and harder until the roar of his taunting mirth drowned the tumult of the storm.

"You'd be scared stiff," Pruitt choked. He sobered sullenly. "I'm scared they might take me for this fellow and tie me up a while." He looked searchingly into Lawton's pasty, blank features. "There's plenty of men on the range that description would fit," he continued, "but I'm a stranger, you might say. It's always easier to fit a description to a stranger. Don't you think so?"

"Well, he'd *be* a stranger, wouldn't he?" Lawton pointed out. He was sorry for this retort an instant after the words had left his lips. "I mean . . . he wouldn't be much known, would he?" he amended.

"You mean what you said first, and you were right," Pruitt said savagely. "According to that notice, he isn't wanted up here. Well, I'm a stranger. Now do you get what I'm saying through your head?"

"Sounds reasonable," Lawton conceded with a nod.

"Reasonable enough for the likes of a cheap constable like you to sick the sheriff on me, eh?" Pruitt thundered. "Don't tell me you haven't got that in your head. I can see it in your eyes?"

"Say, have you been drinking?" Lawton asked narrowly.

"Drinking the truth out of your false face!" Pruitt retorted. He leaned his left forearm on the table as the crashing of thunder drowned his voice. "Speaking of faces," he went on presently, "I should think an old bimbo like you, out in the weather all the time, would have a face that was tanned the color of leather, or burned, or . . . pinker."

With the last word he leaned quickly across the table.

Lawton's face gradually grew whiter as his eyes burned into Pruitt's. For a moment, the sense of panic seized him again, but it fled before the realization that the deadly show-down was coming.

"I reckon there's something wrong with you," he managed to say.

"Sure there is," Pruitt agreed. "I don't want to be mistaken for anybody else, because I'd have to answer questions. That's what's wrong with me. I'm guessing I've seen you somewhere before."

He was looking at Lawton steadily, searching his eyes for a glimmer of recognition. But Lawton's gaze was cold, imperturbable.

"That might be," he said. "I'm no stranger in these parts."

"But you haven't lived all your life in these parts," Pruitt said evenly. "I reckon you haven't been more'n ten years in these parts. Now . . . *have you?*"

The question sounded shrilly above the uproar of the storm.

The lamplight might have been shining on wax, so far as Lawton's face was concerned. He knew now, beyond the peradventure of the most remote doubt, that Pruitt knew him.

"I've lived here thirty-six years," he lied steadily.

Pruitt leaned back, an evil smile on his thick lips. "You can't even say it as if you meant it," he said, sneering. "I don't even think you expected me to believe it when you

25

said it. You know I know better. Let's see . . . Florence, wasn't it? Down in old Arizony . . . as you'd put it if you hung onto that whining tang you've affected up here. You escaped from the big stone jug down there about ten years ago. You was so bad you spent most of your time, while you was in there, in solitary. It bleached your face. You haven't ever got back that sweet, pink color you once had. I'll bet they'd be glad to get you back even now."

Still there was no flicker of Lawton's facial muscles. He caught another brief glimpse of those menacing, twitching eyebrows. "You haven't been drinking," he said. "You're crazy."

"And they used to call you Pinky!" Pruitt roared, his lips twisting into a snarl.

Mentally, Lawton went for his gun and shot out both those glaring, mean eyes, glittering with malicious triumph; actually, he sat as if carved in stone—dumb with fearful dread.

The shack rocked as the storm shot a lightning bolt into the trees, and the thunder was like cannon in their ears.

III

"Made-to-order alibi"

As he sat there in the chair across the table from Bull Pruitt, with the fury of the storm hurling itself upon the isolated shack, Lawton's right hand was within six inches of his gun. But he felt that, for every inch of the distance he must cover to draw, the bandit could shoot—a bullet an inch!—before he could get his weapon in action. He found himself wondering—

of all times!—if Pruitt really could be as fast with his gun as his reputation had it. True, Lawton had himself been a gunman, and still was, but even in his prime he never had hoped to be about to cope with a man like this.

Pruitt was looking at him, speculating as to his next move. Lawton could see that in the outlaw's thoughtful, cunning gaze. If Pruitt became certain that Lawton knew him, he would take no chance. He would kill Lawton, drag his body into the brush, hide his saddle and bridle, turn his horse loose to roam the range. It would be days, perhaps weeks, before the crime would even be suspected. Meanwhile, Pruitt would accomplish whatever he had come up north to do. There was a possibility that Pruitt was making for the Canadian line, in which case Lawton might have a chance. But it was too remote a chance to place any dependence upon.

No! There was but one thing left for Lawton to do. He must kill Pruitt. Kill him or wound him so as to incapacitate him. No, it would be best to kill him. Lawton had to seal Pruitt's lips as well as save his own life. For if Pruitt were delivered to the law, he would be certain to recount Lawton's past to the sheriff. And Lawton had been imprisoned for life for murder, before his escape. His victim of ten years ago had turned in his draw and thus received Lawton's bullet in his back. Had it not been for that shot in the back, Lawton might have been freed on his plea of self-defense. Pruitt knew all the facts, but he would tell a story to suit his own ends.

Pruitt had to die. Lawton's whole mind centered on this. In the rumbling reverberations of the thunder crashes he could hear himself explaining to the sheriff. He could explain how Pruitt had come upon him—explain everything just as it had taken place, even to Pruitt's conversation—

and how he had recognized Pruitt from the description on the notice and by his threatening actions. He need not mention that he ever had seen the outlaw in the past. Sheriff Hal Drew would be delighted to turn over the reward offered by the southern counties to him.

Thought of the old appellation of Pinky, by which he once had been known and feared, took Lawton back through the years and reinvested him with much of his former cunning. It could hardly be said of Lawton that he lacked courage, but he possessed the faculty of discriminating between courage and rank foolhardiness. In a normal gun play with Pruitt, he would be facing overwhelming odds. He must play for time; he must resort to every subterfuge, trick, and stratagem to inspire Pruitt with overconfidence; he must catch him off his guard for that indeterminate but brief fraction of time he would need to draw and shoot with absolute certainty. He knew that he would have no second chance.

Bull Pruitt, waiting for Lawton to speak, suspected, in the glow of his own egotism and confidence, that the constable was thinking of the consequences should the sheriff learn his past. He wondered if he could threaten Lawton to advantage, and decided he would be unwise to risk the chance. Lawton would demand a share in such spoils as Pruitt might take in this northern range, and eventually he would have to be put out of the way. He could be of no assistance, anyway.

Indeed, as Pruitt pondered the matter, there seemed little to be gained by bothering with Lawton further. It was just possible Lawton might let some bit of information escape that would be of value. Pruitt had a bold, unlawful undertaking in mind. He could try to learn what he could, or to verify such information as he now possessed, and then dispose of Lawton. But the cruel and sanguinary side of Pruitt's character asserted itself. He was curious to know what Lawton had done with his ten years of liberty.

Lawton hunched forward and peered at Pruitt closely. "You must have come a long way if you're talking 'bout Arizona."

"I've been everywhere that there's plenty of room for a horse to travel in, Pinky," was the growling comment.

"You say you wouldn't want to answer questions. Why, Bill?"

"Huh? Well, I might have been in the same boat you were in once," Pruitt replied craftily. "Now you begin to see why I wouldn't want to be mistaken for this fellow who's wanted?"

"That's right," Lawton nodded. "Was you in . . . in the same place where . . . where you think I was? In Florence?"

"No! But I seen you before and once after you went in. Never mind about me, Pinky. What you been doing since then?"

"I was working cows till I was hurt in a fall. I've been up Alder Creek crossing for years. Kept straight as I could. Somebody up there had to be constable, and they got me the job so's I could get along and pay my bills. You wouldn't want to make any trouble for me, would you, Bill? After all them years? Did I ever do anything to you?" The thin voice had become a whine.

Pruitt was momentarily nonplused. A violent booming of the storm's artillery afforded him time to delay his answer. He caught himself on the verge of feeling soft, and scowled darkly. "How do you know you never did anything to me?" he demanded. "It's been a long time, and people forget. Do you even know who I am?" He put the question as subtly as possible.

"You're Bill, you say. That's all I know. But you say you know me, and that makes me listen hard. I wouldn't want any trouble after all these years, Bill."

Pruitt wondered vaguely if Lawton could be such a fool as not to recognize him. Lawton, as Pinky, had seen him on at least one important raid. He had seen him, too, in an infamous resort on the Mexican border where none but outlaws could circulate with safety. Yet Lawton had not been an outlaw in the strict meaning of the term. He had been more of a hanger-on. Just sneaky enough, Pruitt thought, to make a deal with the sheriff by which he would be protected while turning him, Pruitt, over to the law. The bandit's eyes blazed. He was a fool thus to dally. But he might as well wait until the storm abated. He did not relish the thought of finding his way across the prairie with lightning flashes to guide his way. But he would call the showdown before the end.

Meanwhile, there was one individual about whom he wanted to ask. It would be such a question as could be asked only when he was ready to put the finish to the tense situation. In all that north country there was but one man whom Pruitt scorned, respected, and hated. And he was not sure where this man was located. It was possible that Lawton might know.

"I suppose, if I tell you that I won't say anything, you'll agree to forget this accidental meeting of ours, forget what I look like . . . forget me completely," Pruitt said derisively.

"Sure. I'll agree to that," Lawton said eagerly. "I'm hoping you'll forget about me. I. . . ."

His words were drowned in a terrific crash of thunder. The storm seemed to be gathering its final fury. The wind whistled into the room from beneath windows and door, and through cracks in the wall. Once the lamplight flickered in a freak draft.

"How do you figure I can take your word?" Pruitt sneered.

"I'll give you this!" Lawton cried, flashing his badge of authority. "You ought to know it'll hold me."

Pruitt laughed loudly and scornfully, then flew into a rage as the thunder drowned his false merriment. Suddenly he tensed, and his look froze cold. Lawton's right hand was below the edge of the table. Pruitt came to his feet in a wink. "Bring that hand up . . . *empty!*" he commanded, his own gun darting to the draw.

Lawton's hand flew up instantly, and his face went white as he slowly rose. He was not seized with fear so much as he was dismayed by the thought that he almost had gone for his weapon. Pruitt had moved so fast he hadn't even found it necessary to draw the gun on which his hand now rested. His brows were twitching furiously.

Lawton's lips curled back against his teeth involuntarily.

Pruitt took this as a show of defiance. He might have ended it then and there had not the shack been rocked by another violent burst of wind that momentarily diverted his attention. Then he caught a gleam in Lawton's eye. The latter could not have known it was there. It told Pruitt as plainly as if the information had been shouted in his face that Lawton knew him, had recognized him, probably at first sight.

"You know me!" he yelled in a lull in the crashing thunder.

"Yes, Pruitt, and that's why you should keep your head!" Lawton's face was drawn, his eyes narrowed and bright. His desperate plight left him suddenly cool. Anything to gain time—seconds—minutes, if possible—time and a chance. He knew now he would have to draw, and the overpowering yearning for one clean shot at his adversary flamed in his

31

heart. "I might know something. . . ."

The peals of thunder descended again, brushing aside his words as if he were whispering to himself under his breath. But the ruse stayed Pruitt's streaking hand.

Lawton had raised his hands high when he saw Pruitt's hand hang over his gun and the draw stopped. Now he stepped to the table and opened his mouth to speak. Again the tumult of the storm drowned his words. He shook his head angrily and cursed.

Pruitt relaxed, scowling and drawing a deep breath. He hitched his gun belt below the leather jacket. It was plain that Lawton's manner had tangled the outlaw's thoughts and left him indecisive. But now the renewed fury of the storm was attracting the attention of both. Windows and door rattled, and the upthrust stovepipe, hanging by wires, beat an unearthly staccato on the roof where the rain pounded like the roll of innumerable kettle drums.

Pruitt was merely waiting to ask a question to attempt to learn something from Lawton. Compassion or leniency found no place in his heart. But Lawton had said he might know something; he had said that much when the storm had cut him off. The outlaw was willing to wait and learn what Lawton knew that the latter thought might interest him. It did not occur to him that Lawton was simply playing for time. "What do you know?" he said, when his voice could be heard.

"Enough so it wouldn't pay you to kill me," Lawton replied.

"Do you know if . . . ?"

A gust of soot blew through the room as the inside stovepipe cracked. At the same moment, a branch smashed through the window by the table, and the lamp crashed, spitting sparks and splinters of glass. Darkness came for a brief interval—long enough for both men to draw and crouch back against the wall.

With the first white flash of lightning both fired blindly. Lawton dropped on his left hand and right knee. He fired again with the next flash, and Pruitt's gun blazed with a hail of lead.

The frail shack was trembling, shaking, swaying—it seemed—with the terrific force of the wind and driving rain. The room suddenly was blue—white—green! A tremendous flame burst into it, and Pruitt felt himself hurled against the door, which broke into pieces before his weight. He was on his face in the mud, every muscle and nerve pricking him painfully, an avalanche pouring down upon him, his eardrums splitting with an explosion that seemed to tear the very world apart.

It seemed hours that he lay there, stunned, before the pricking sensation subsided into numbness. He might have dozed. He rolled over on his back and sat up loggily, dazed. His hat was gone, his jacket split open. Ahead of him burned a sullen red glare. The shack was on fire!

With this sight came the realization that the shack had been struck by a lightning bolt. A spray had hurled him through the door, torn his clothes, stunned him. But he was alive. He gibbered aloud as he felt of himself to make sure he was whole. The lightning was still flashing, and now it inspired him with terror. It would not miss him a second time! He slipped in the mud getting to his feet, staggered, stepped on the hard metal of a gun, and picked it up. Then shrill laughter came from him. Lawton must be dead. If he hadn't stopped a bullet, he must have been in the way of the lightning. The rain was putting out the fire, but there must have been enough of a blaze to sear the body.

"Perfect!" Pruitt croaked in exultation. "A made-to-order alibi if I should ever need it." He stumbled and slid in the mud toward the shed where the horses had been left. Both animals had broken away. They had snapped their tethers in fright when the lightning had struck so close.

Pruitt staggered about the small clearing, whistling for his mount. He flung up an arm each time the lightning flashed, and cursed horribly. His nerves jumped as he almost ran into the shadow that was his horse. The left rein of the bridle was broken, but the knot held to the right rein. He quickly tied the reins together and climbed into the saddle.

With a last look at the smoking shack, he spurred his horse and rode cowering in the saddle beneath the lightning, through the trees, and swung out into the road. He galloped madly through the storm, gradually recovering control of himself. He didn't realize, however, that he was riding on the main road to Milton, the town he had intended to avoid.

IV

"At Milton"

The spreading western fringe of the storm hit the town of Milton at seven o'clock, more than an hour after it had centered its forces on Nine Mile Spring. It was more of a hard, cold rain, here in town, with less wind and only intermittent bursts of thunder and lightning. But it drove everyone from the streets and plunged the town into Cimmerian darkness, save for the stabs of yellow lamplight from windows.

At nine o'clock Mel Davitt was in the living room of the

home of Sylvester Graham, president of the Bank of Milton, with Virginia Graham, the banker's daughter. Sylvester was in the library, as he called his home office and study, leaving Davitt and Virginia to their own devices in the warm, spacious living room. Davitt was standing in the center of the room by the table on which burned a shaded lamp. His was a tall, straight figure, lithe and muscular. His features were clear-cut, his complexion a light bronze, his eyes gray and bright and roving, with a bewitching sparkle and subtle shadings of expression. He was dressed in a becoming double-breasted gray suit with white soft shirt, dark-blue tie, and the inevitable black riding boots, highly polished, with their ornate tops hidden by his trousers. He presented an immaculate appearance thus, at total variance with his usual range attire.

Virginia was seated on a lounge, looking at him thoughtfully, with now and then a glimmer of admiration in her hazel eyes. She was not infatuated with Davitt, not in love with him—so she told herself—but she was more than merely interested in him. It wasn't the man in him that fascinated her and frequently clouded her eyes; it was the nature of his business, vocation, or avocation—whichever way one wished to look at it—that had caught her fancy and stimulated her imagination. If he were just a rancher's son. . . .

Mel Davitt spoke in a low, vibrant voice. "In a way this is an event, Miss Virginia. I'm glad there's a storm raging outside. I seem to think better when there is some kind of a disturbance. You have caused me a great deal of annoyance lately."

He emphasized this astounding statement with a wave of his right hand, in which a cigarette poised between the first and second fingers. But he also smiled, and, when he smiled, he was handsome in more than an ordinary degree.

35

"Annoyance?" said Virginia in surprise. She didn't know whether to laugh or frown.

"Yes," he said soberly. "I've been thinking too much about you lately, which has bothered me. Since you are the beautiful, although sensible, subject of my thoughts, I have to put the blame where it belongs." He stepped gracefully to the fireplace and tossed the cigarette end on the blazing wood.

Virginia now gave way to soft laughter. She enjoyed talking to Davitt because he amused her without being silly, entertained her, thrilled her with his personality, impressed her sometimes with an unexpected alertness and keenness of serious thought. But, even as she luxuriated in mild merriment, she sensed that he was more serious this night than usual.

"All right, I'll take the blame," she said, with a smile.

"And that's quite a responsibility," he answered, standing again at the table. "Since I came up here last spring and danced with you, before going out and putting an end to the career of that no-good Crow, you've been very kind to me. You've loaned me books and met me on common ground, despite the fact that our positions . . . in society . . . are not the same. But you've done something else, Virginia, without realizing it."

The quality of his tone caused the girl to flush slightly. She could think of nothing to say and looked away from him. He leaned his right hand on the table, and she could not resist glancing at it with a faint shiver. It was a strong, well-formed hand, like that of a great pianist, and she had reason to know that it could move almost with the rapidity of the lightning that was flashing in the windows.

"I'm turning over a new leaf," he announced.

"A new leaf!" Virginia was genuinely astonished. "Why,

36

you haven't been so bad . . . that I've heard of, anyway."

"Oh, I don't mean morally," he said a bit impatiently. "Miss Virginia, I'm giving up my present . . . er . . . occupation."

She stared at him. "You're quitting . . . ?" She left the sentence unfinished in her confusion.

"Exactly." He nodded. "And there's no I-want-to-be-a-hero stuff mixed up in this announcement. It's why I said tonight was something of an event. I'm going to tell you why I am quitting."

He sat down beside her on the couch. They could hear the banker clearing his throat in his best professional manner in the next room. It had the effect of bringing stern reality to them.

Davitt smiled. "I think your father invited me here to dinner tonight because he wants to talk to me. I have an idea as to what he has to say. That's why I want to talk to you first."

"Father never forgets his business," the girl murmured.

"And that's one reason why he never can forget mine," Davitt said quickly. "Virginia"—he lowered his voice—"I've fallen in love with you. I was suspicious that it was going to be in the picture the first time I saw you. I've studied you. You're not just beautiful, and sweet, and lovely . . . you're a regular and sensible girl. This combination of all these characteristics is rare. I'll bet you've never been told this in quite this way before."

She looked at him out of wide, clear eyes, her lips parted.

"I've got you thinking . . . which is good," he told her, smiling. "I'm talking my best. All I know, outside of range work and what experience has taught me, I've learned out of books I've read. In that last, as I said, you've helped me. Now we'll get right down to cases and lay out the cards."

He tapped his knee and looked into the fire as he spoke, only now and then glancing at her face to assure himself that she was listening intently. Virginia was more interested in him than she ever had been interested in a man in her life, although he couldn't know this.

"I was born on the southern range," he said quietly. "I've worked cattle and done 'most every kind of ranch work. How I got into the game I'm in doesn't matter so much as the game itself. I'm a trailer, a manhunter, a range operative . . . whatever you want to call it . . . and my game is catching outlaws, bandits, and rustlers, or putting them out of business. I've got a reputation, and about half that reputation is as being a gunman. I've made considerable money. I've been so lucky, we'll say, that I'm well off. Now I'm quitting the game cold . . . here, now, and tonight." He looked at her as he finished.

"Why are you quitting?" she asked.

"There you are!" he exclaimed. "That's the hard part to tell you. There are some who haven't got much use for me, because of one thing or another, who'll say I decided to quit while I had a whole skin. That isn't true. There are others who say I've made my pile and that's why I'm through. That isn't true, either. I'm getting sick of the game, for one thing, and, for another, it sets me out apart and makes me too . . . what is it? . . . conspicuous. I've even been called a killer."

He spoke the last sentence in a bitter tone with a grave look in his eyes.

"Is this . . . are these the only reasons you're giving up the game?" Virginia heard herself asking.

"No!" He leaned forward to look into her eyes. "I'm also quitting because of you. A man with my reputation cannot make love to you, Virginia. There's always the specter of a gun, of fighting, of the danger trail about me. I know what your dad would call the money I've made. Perhaps you call it that yourself. In a way it makes me an outcast."

"I wouldn't say that, Mel," she said quietly. "The range is certainly better off for losing the characters you've rid it of. The law has to be enforced."

"Yes, but a sheriff is in a different position than I am," he pointed out. "He's a man of substance, elected to an office. I'm called in on tough cases as a trailer and gunman. My six-gun can be hired. That puts me in a different light. I can see it every day in different ways." His face was white under his tan as he spoke. "I've quit," he said. "The trail has led me to you. I'm going away for a year. Then I'm coming back and . . . just to see."

"But why go away?" the girl asked. "And what about your partner?"

"You mean Buck Granger? He was my assistant, not actually my partner. There's a distinction there, too, that the range understands. I convinced him I was through. He knows me well enough to believe me. He's gone off to the Snowies. He has a girl up there, and, unless I'm mightily mistaken, he's going to marry her."

"But why go away?" the girl repeated.

"To give these people a chance to forget," he replied.

"But they won't!" she exclaimed softly, putting a hand on his arm. "Don't you see that, if you go away, people won't know where you are or what you're doing, and, when you return, it'll bring everything back fresh in their minds?"

He looked startled. "But I've quit," he said stubbornly.

"Then quit right here . . . stay right here, I mean," Virginia told him eagerly. "Let Sheriff Drew spread the word that you're no longer an . . . an investigator. Do something else. In a year, people won't be thinking of you as a gunman or anything like that."

He took her hand between both his own, patted it, looked smilingly into her earnest eyes. "I told you that you were a regular girl, Virginia. But have you forgotten that I told you I love you? Don't you see why I can't stay? I can't stay, for both our sakes, to put it bluntly. Here!"

In a moment, he had her in his arms. He kissed her, and her lips lingered against his for a moment.

"No man would kiss you like that and not really love you, Virginia," he said slowly. "I'm not sorry I did it, and I'll never forget it."

To his surprise, the girl's eyes were deep wells of glowing light. She smiled at him faintly. He realized she was not angry.

"You are not very practical in your love-making," she said, with a wistful note in her voice, "but don't forget that Father is in his study and is liable to come in here any minute."

"There's the rub," he said ruefully. "Even if you . . . if you wanted to. . . ." He faltered and smiled boyishly. "Your father will be pretty mad when I tell him what I've told you."

"Then why tell him?" Virginia asked, favoring him with a sly look. "At least, why tell him right away?" she added hastily.

"It's only fair. I wouldn't practice any deceit with him."

"Mel Davitt, I've never thought of you just as a trailer and a gunman," the girl said earnestly. "I've always shuddered when I've thought of your extraordinary ability with a six-gun, but I was brought up right in town when it was awfully tough. I've been away to school and all that, but I've never forgotten my heritage. I'm range stock myself. Even after Father started the bank here, Mother and I spent most of our time on our ranch. She died the year after we came to town. I've had Father to look after, and he's changed a lot. He . . . but no matter, I didn't hold your business against you, but I'm glad you've given it up." Her last words were spoken so softly he scarcely heard them above the noise of the storm that partly filled the house.

In a moment, he had taken her hands again. "Virginia, do you mean I've got a chance?" he asked eagerly, his voice tremulous. "Please . . . don't make it harder for me to. . . ."

She put a warm hand on his lips to stop his speech, and he kissed it.

"I'm not saying . . . anything," she whispered. "Remember you're taking a year to. . . ." She stopped in confusion, her cheeks blooming faintly like pink roses.

"To win you!" he exulted. "Now, that's a go!"

"It may not take a year," she bantered, "and it might take forever . . . or not at all. Oh, I don't know what I'm talking about!"

"But, Virginia! Tell me," he pressed. "I *have* got a chance, haven't I?" Their faces were so close together he could scent the perfume of her hair.

"You're young, and I'm young," she said, looking away. "I expect to love some man someday, and if he asks me to marry him, I will. But he won't win my love by heroic exploits, nor by any spectacular means. He must be sound of mind as well as of body. There must be substance to him." She looked at him slyly, then laughed nervously.

"You mean you won't marry any gun-toting trailer," he said.

"I mean I'm crazy," she said, smiling. "I'm always crazy when it storms!"

"Then I wish it would storm hard enough to make you so crazy you'd marry me straight off!" he blurted. He grinned as she tossed her head and raised her pretty brows.

41

"Sound of mind and substance! You got that out of a book," he accused.

"Sounds a little too educated, doesn't it?" she flung at him.

"You don't take me seriously," he complained.

Her manner changed instantly. "Perhaps I really take you *too* seriously," she told him soberly.

They were sitting close, looking into each other's eyes, when a sound caused them to look quickly toward the door into the hall.

Sylvester Graham was standing in the doorway of his study, looking at them.

Mel Davitt rose immediately. The girl busied herself arranging her hair. She tried to conceal her confused irritation. Davitt looked coolly at the banker, whose expression was void of any suggestion of emotion, and wondered how long he had been standing there.

"Before you go, I'd like to see you a minute, Davitt," said Graham in his concise, business-like voice.

"That might as well be now," Davitt said wryly.

"But you're not going yet, Mister Davitt," Virginia put in sweetly. "Father isn't in a hurry, I'm sure."

"No, whenever you're ready," Graham said dryly. He spoke to the two of them, but looked at Davitt as if the words were meant for him alone.

"If you please," Davitt said to the girl, and walked toward the study.

A crash of thunder drowned Virginia's voice as she called him back softly. She watched her father close the door to the study after Davitt had entered. She clenched her hands and pressed her lips tightly. Then came the tears.

V

"A quarrel"

The banker motioned Davitt to a chair and seated himself near him. Sylvester Graham stroked his close-cropped mustache as Davitt eyed him questioningly and appraisingly. Graham was known as a hard-fisted businessman, conservative but with an eye for healthy profit. He had called Davitt north on his first case in that country when the Bank of Milton had been robbed.

"I wouldn't want my daughter to learn the subject of our conversation," said Graham pointedly. "You understand?"

"You needn't worry about me," Davitt replied easily.

"But that's just what I am doing. I have eyes and a certain amount of perception, Davitt. I also realize that Virginia is an attractive girl."

"I agree with you there," Davitt said with a nod.

"I mean she is attractive . . . not merely because she is beautiful and has a charming personality . . . but because she happens to be my daughter," the banker explained with a thin smile.

"So far as I'm concerned, you can leave that last part out," Davitt said coldly. "Miss Virginia is attractive to me because of her own charms and for no other reason. What you've just hinted comes mighty close to being an insult, Graham."

"I don't want to insult you, so get that out of your head," said the banker in a vexed tone. "I'm not forgetting that I was responsible for you coming up here in the first place.

43

You got that Crow outlaw, cleaned out the rustling north of here, and did several other important jobs. I give you proper credit. But these things were strictly business, and you made money."

"Sure I made money," Davitt agreed. "You don't object to my making money, do you? I've got a pretty neat stake in your bank alone. That should be taken into consideration."

"Yes, yes, I know," said Graham irritably. "But . . . ah . . . it's. . . ."

"I know what you're thinking," Davitt interrupted. "You're thinking it's blood money. Would you rather have the crew that's been working up here back on the range at large?"

"No, no. I'm not thinking about the money at all, Davitt. But I expected our relations would be strictly on a business basis."

"Well, they are, are they not?" Davitt asked, an amused twinkle in his eye. "When you invited me here tonight, I supposed you had some business to talk over with me."

"But you come here when I don't invite you," Graham said bluntly.

"Oh, I see," Davitt purred. "You don't like it because I come to see Miss Virginia. Is that it?"

"You've made it much easier for me," the banker replied, raising his brows. "You've guessed my attitude in the matter exactly. I asked you here tonight to see if . . . to make sure. . . ." He checked himself with a frown. It was different talking to Davitt here in his home. He lacked the sustaining environment of his office at the bank. As a guest, Davitt was altogether too presentable, so much so that he would have made a much more favorable impression if Graham hadn't been prejudiced.

"You were watching us out there?" Davitt waved a hand

in the direction of the living room. "Listening, perhaps?"

"I'm not an eavesdropper," Graham retorted testily, "but I can't help seeing what takes place right under my own eyes."

"Let me tell you something before we go any further, Mister Graham," said Davitt coldly. "I had occasion to tell your daughter tonight that I love her and. . . ."

"You *what?*" exclaimed Graham, looking incredulous.

"I told her I loved her, and I told her I intended to tell you," said Davitt stoutly. "I've something else to tell you. I've quit playing hide-and-seek with outlaws, quit being an investigator, manhunter, gunman, and all the rest of it. I'm going away for a year."

The banker stared at him as if he doubted his ears. Then his face hardened, and a grim smile played on his lips. "You told her that, too, I suppose. You thought that would make it easier for you . . . that is, you thought it would please her?"

"It pleased her," Davitt affirmed. "But I didn't quit the game I was in for the mean reason you think. For one thing, I'm tired of it."

"Did she believe this?" Graham asked skeptically.

"There's no use trying to talk nice to you, Graham," said Davitt slowly. "You've got it in your head that I'm out to win Virginia any way I can. So I might as well tell you that I am out to do that very thing . . . by fair means." His eyes sparkled with the fire of determination as he said this.

"You mean you want to marry my daughter?" Graham asked narrowly.

"I want to win her love," Davitt replied boldly.

"You realize, I suppose, that she's all I have?" said Graham. "The only human I really love?"

"I can't help but know that, Mister Graham," said Davitt

sympathetically. "I . . . of course, I know that." He shifted uneasily in his chair.

"You know, too, that I know very little of you?" the banker persisted.

"My life and record is an open book for you to look into any time you feel like it," Davitt said. "I know what you're getting at. You don't think I'm good enough for her." His tone was brimming with resentment.

"Do you blame me?" asked Graham with disconcerting frankness.

"No father ever thought any man was good enough for his daughter," Davitt parried. "I may think, or know, that I'm not good enough for Virginia, but I'd hate to have any-body else tell me that."

"Then we won't talk about it," said Graham coolly. "The point now is that I object to your attentions to Virginia. That's telling you straight."

"And what about Virginia?" Davitt asked mildly.

"I think she'll see things my way," Graham replied crisply. "It's natural for a girl to become infatuated with a spectacular . . . er . . . character such as yourself. Wait a minute! I'm not saying anything against your character. But I don't think Virginia knows what she's doing, if she's given you any encouragement. Has she given you any reason to think your . . . er . . . feeling might be returned?"

"I refuse to answer that," said Davitt shortly.

"Then she hasn't!" Graham cried triumphantly. "Under the circumstances, I think you should respect my wishes in the matter."

Davitt found himself wondering if the girl were listening at the door. No sooner had the thought assailed him than he felt disgusted with himself for allowing such a conjecture to enter his mind.

"I respect you as Virginia's father and a responsible businessman," said Davitt frankly. "I think you should play fair."

Graham eyed him speculatively. "You say you intend to go away for a year? Do you intend to come back at the end of a year?"

"I'm not prepared to answer that question, either." Davitt's face went white, but he kept back the hot words that were on his tongue. He felt that Graham would stoop to questionable means to influence Virginia. It was unfair competition. "Suppose I do stay?" he flared.

"In that case I'll tell Virginia frankly that you refuse to go because you're afraid of my opposition. I'll show her the ridiculous side of it. I know Virginia far better than you do, and I know how to talk to her. It won't be long before I'll have her laughing at your preposterous presumptions. She is a sensible girl."

There was something in what Sylvester Graham said. Mel Davitt, famed manhunter who had faced death calmly and emerged from a score of gun encounters with notorious outlaws, was losing his grip on himself in this verbal clash with Graham. The youthful look disappeared from his face; the sparkle and gleam in his eyes hardened to a steel-blue.

"You'd use your wily tongue as a weapon behind my back," he accused in a tone that made the banker shift his gaze uncomfortably. "What you've just said makes it impossible for me to go away. I'm declaring myself, Graham. I want Virginia, and I'm going to have her!" He had unconsciously raised his voice until his last words fairly rang.

Graham touched a finger to his lips in caution as his face darkened with anger. He was not accustomed to having a man defy him.

"Have you ever thought there might be someone else?"

"I don't think that needs an answer," Davitt returned curtly.

"The sons of several reputable ranchers are close friends of my daughter," said Graham casually. "They have property and . . . position. Ahem! Have you asked Virginia if . . . ?"

"I haven't asked her anything along the line you're hinting," Davitt broke in sharply. "I don't intend to ask her, because I don't care."

The banker's temper got the better of him. "You think you're the kingpin, eh?" he said sarcastically. "I knew you were a man-killer, but this is the first time you've put yourself in the rôle of a lady-killer!"

Davitt leaped to his feet. "I don't have to take that, even from you!" he cried. "You're not only insulting me, but you're insulting. . . ." He regained control of himself just in time to leave what he had thought to say unfinished.

Graham rose from his chair. "No man can talk to me like you have," he said grimly. "I ask you to leave my house, and I forbid you to come here again!"

"That's the showdown!" cried Davitt. "But we're going to get an even start. I'll tell you the big reason why I've quit the game that gave me my reputation. I quit it because it's too dangerous! Now call me a coward, and I'll forget your years and knock you through that window!" Davitt's jaw was squared, thrust out, and his eyes were flashing with the heat of his emotion and speech. "Do you know *why* I say it's too dangerous?" he thundered. "You think you do, but you don't. Do you think it was easy for me to get Crow? Do you think it was just in a day's work to put the rest of the rustlers and outlaws I've gone after out of business? I took smoke from all their guns! Every one of them drew down on me. There's always an element of luck in a fast gun play. Falter for the length of time it takes to wink an eye, and you lose.

"So far, I reckon I've had the luck on my side. I make no bones about it. And I've been fast enough . . . sure enough . . . not to lose. The next time I might not be so lucky . . . nor so fast. There's always a next time. I couldn't ask your daughter to marry me while I was high-trailing. Sooner or later I'd take a trip and wouldn't come back. I couldn't go into business, or buy a ranch, when I didn't know but that my next case would be the last. That's what I mean by danger. I've got to stay in the game or get out of it. If I stay in it, I cannot ask anyone else to depend upon me. I can't take a chance on leaving a wife and maybe children. I can't risk leaving property to go to wreck and ruin. I've got to get out of it in order to live the life I want to lead. That's why I've quit."

Sylvester Graham's face was hard, his eyes cold with an inscrutable expression. "What you say is true, Davitt," he said firmly, "but that does not alter my determination to keep you from my door."

"Then I'll make you play square!" cried Davitt. He stepped quickly to the door and opened it wide.

Virginia had heard Davitt's ringing words. She was standing by the table in the living room and crossed the hall into the study as Davitt beckoned.

Graham, momentarily taken aback by this unexpected development, galvanized into action immediately. He took Virginia by the arm. "Come upstairs," he said.

"But, Father, what's the matter?" the girl asked, resisting his effort to draw her away.

"There's something I have to tell you," Davitt said quickly.

"You'll not say a word to her!" shouted Graham hoarsely. Then the last vestige of control left him. He stepped away from the girl and struck at Davitt.

Virginia screamed as Davitt caught at her father's arm and sent him spinning into an armchair. Davitt stood over the banker, his face white.

"That was a mistake," he said through his teeth. "Calm down!"

"You . . . you threaten me . . . in my own house?" Graham gasped.

"I'm protecting you from making another mistake," Davitt said calmly. "It might have been better if I had let you hit me." He stepped back as Virginia came to her father's side.

A gust of wind shook the windows, then died, leaving stillness in its wake. The harshness of the storm was abating. The lightning had ceased, and the thunder was rumbling faintly from a distance.

"I'm not going away, as I intended, Miss Virginia," Davitt said, looking straight into the girl's troubled eyes. "Your father will tell you I'm afraid to go. That isn't so, but you can judge for yourself. I told him everything I told you tonight. No one can blame him for getting excited. That's all this amounts to. Now, I reckon I'll be going."

Graham sat up straight, but not a word passed his lips.

"You told Daddy?" The girl was flushing. She stepped back so she could look at the two of them. "I had reason to think the trouble was over me," she said, biting her lip. "Are you very angry, Father?"

Graham remained silent. He merely glanced at her, his face drawn and stern.

Virginia Graham looked bewildered. Davitt's eyes were luminous. Then all three started as the sharp reports of guns sounded from the direction of the main street, which was but a block from the house.

VI

"All for a hat"

Bull Pruitt had ridden the better part of an hour before the storm began to diminish in volume. Since it was moving in a southwesterly direction, and he was riding almost due west, it took him this length of time to reach its western fringe. He realized that he had been shocked by a spray from the lightning bolt, but his nerves were recovering rapidly from the jerkiness the shock had caused. He was thinking clearly again.

Pruitt had come north on an important mission. He had a job in mind which, he expected, would yield him a stake that would enable him to cut up into Canada and rest from his lawless activities for a long time to come. He had looked forward to this job on the north range for months, even years. But the pickings had been easy in the southern counties and below the Montana boundary. His latest exploit in the south had involved a killing, and he cursed his luck because the reward notices in connection with this already had been sent out and were being posted in this very county where he intended to work. But Pink Lawton would post no more of them.

The outlaw had been depending upon his horse and the flashes of lightning that illuminated the landscape to keep to the road. He had known for some time that he was on the main road, that he was headed for Milton. His first objective, however, as far as the business he had in mind was concerned, was a ranch several miles to the northwest on the Cross River. But a foolish coincidence was causing him to

51

continue on toward Milton.

He had lost his hat when the bolt had hit the shack near the spring. He had been on the point of turning back to the shack several times, but it seemed foolish to do so. He was certain he had lost his hat in the quick moves he had made after the branch had crushed through the window, putting out the light. It certainly had been precarious and tricky, shooting, in the blinding flashes of the lightning. He could not recall much of what had taken place after the lamp went out, because everything had happened with incredible swiftness. It seemed as though the world had ended and begun anew between the ticks of a clock. Pruitt took out his watch and read its face by a desultory flash. Seven o'clock. The watch had stopped when Pruitt had been thrown through the door by the striking bolt.

The incident of the lost hat bothered Pruitt a great deal as he wiped the rain from his face with a wet sleeve. While there were no identifying marks in the hat, the outlaw hoped, nevertheless, that it had been destroyed. Its loss placed him in a curious predicament. He had to have daylight to find the ranch on Cross River, for he had never been there before and had only a description of the place in his mind to serve him as a guide. But a hatless rider would be spotted and remembered by any who might see him.

Of all the times in his life, this was once when Pruitt did not wish to appear conspicuous in any way. But any rider he might meet would at once notice the absence of Pruitt's hat. He could explain easily enough that he had lost his hat in the storm. He could say that lightning had struck near him and had thrown him off his horse. He could prove it by his torn clothing. But it would mark him, cause whoever might see him to remember him, perhaps interfere with his plans to execute a daring robbery in this section.

Pruitt swore futilely as he rode at a moderate pace. His small pack was intact on the rear of his saddle, but it contained no spare hat. Nor did it contain any substitute for the torn leather jacket he wore. He had to have another hat and a coat or jacket. He might get these at the ranch he intended to visit, but he might also be seen on his way there. He could not expect to get to Milton before the stores closed, and, even if he did, he would attract attention to himself by going into a store hatless. Nor could he go into one of the drinking or gambling resorts hatless without being unduly noticed. Queer how a simple thing like a hat could cause so much trouble.

As he rode out of the full force of the storm, Pruitt allowed his horse to choose its own pace, which was little more than a walk. His first heed must be paid to obtaining a hat. He couldn't hold someone up and take a hat—just any hat would hardly do, for that matter. It certainly had to be a reasonable fit. It also had to go with Pruitt's range attire.

Time and the ferocity of the storm passed, and finally the outlaw saw the faint lights of Milton blinking in the misty rain. The logical manner of getting a hat, under the peculiar circumstances, suddenly struck Pruitt with harsh humor. He rumbled with short laughter. He must steal one without being seen. He must break into a store and steal a hat and jacket. The importance of securing these articles of apparel loomed larger and larger in Pruitt's mind as he swung off the main road to enter Milton stealthily through the dripping trees.

Bull Pruitt had been in Milton but twice in several years. He had hurried through on a forced trip to Canada when the new hotel was just completed. He had come back through several months later when the Bank of Milton had just moved into its new building. By these buildings and the

53

famous Blue Bottle resort he could easily enough find his way about the town. Both these visits had been surreptitious, and he was acquainted with the back streets and alleys. Indeed, sly and darkened travel was in line with Pruitt's business.

He had reached Milton as the storm was betaking itself southward, with less brilliant flashes of lightning and a mere muttering of thunder. But the rain still was falling hard. He experienced no difficulty in making his way to the rear of the buildings on the north side of Main Street. The bank was at one end of a block at the other end of which was the hotel. Stores and a café were between. It still was too stormy for anyone to be abroad, except in case of unusual necessity.

Pruitt made his way to the rear of a general store in the office of which a lamp burned dully. It was quiet, save for the incessant patter and drum of the rain on roofs and streets, the swish of the wind in the trees, and the distant roll of thunder. From the under side of his pack, Pruitt drew a tool. Leaving his horse in some trees, he jimmied a rear window of the store with swiftness and ease that bespoke long practice. He let himself into the store quickly. He had no difficulty groping his way to the section where men's hats, clothing, and furnishings were segregated. He groped about the shelves and selected the quality of hat he wished by its feel, and it was not difficult to try on two or three and secure his size. He would rub it in mud and let the spatter of rain erase its appearance of newness. From a rack he took a light Mackinaw of the proper fit. Since he had no intention of molesting the office, it was not probable that the loss of the hat and Mackinaw would immediately be discovered. For that matter, the injured window might not be noticed for some time. And he would get rid of the apparel as soon as possible.

"Made to order," he muttered to himself gleefully, as he started back toward the window. Retracing his steps, he had to creep past the light shining from the open door of the office and the glass partition.

He had just entered this beam of light when a key rasped in the lock of the front door, and the door swung open to the accompaniment of a startled cry. Pruitt had donned the hat and the Mackinaw to facilitate his movements—put them on right where he had found them—and now he leaped past the office door toward the window by which he had entered.

The store rang with the sharp reports of a heavy gun, and red tongues of flame licked at the darkness near the open door. The wind came in with tremendous force, hurling objects of ornament and pieces of merchandise about.

Pruitt, cursing with the thought that he should be detected in a common burglary, was almost at the window that he had left open, thus creating a draft through the store. A piece of cloth or some other article from a show-counter display struck him in the back, and he whirled, drawing his gun.

At this moment, a final flash of lightning lighted the store. Pruitt saw a man running down the aisle from the front. He didn't know him, but suspected he was the proprietor, come to make sure everything was all right after the hard onslaught of the storm. The man fired again as Pruitt went through the window. Then the outlaw realized that the storekeeper might be able to give a good description of him. He stood just outside the window and shot twice before running for his horse. There was no further sound from within the store. Pruitt got through the trees and started straight north, where the first stars were breaking from the retreating storm clouds.

For several moments, Sylvester Graham, Virginia, and Mel Davitt stood in the banker's study and stared at each other. Graham appeared to be the most concerned; Davitt was calm, merely lifting his brows. Virginia was the first to speak.

"It must be that tough outfit from the Payne ranch, shooting for fun," she said. "They came in from the ranch, and they usually celebrate by heaving a lot of lead." She had reverted naturally to range idiom.

"I don't think so," said Davitt, looking at the grave face of the banker, who seemed to have forgotten the hot moments just passed.

"How do you explain it . . . at this time of night and in the rain?" Graham asked in an apprehensive voice.

"Oh, it isn't your bank," Davitt answered with a smile. "If anything important inside there was bothered, your new-fangled alarm would be clanging itself hoarse. The only way robbers could take the bank's money would be with you or somebody inside to open up for them without setting off that alarm." He smiled more broadly as he thought of how the famous Crow had held Graham up in his own bank for the only robbery in its history. His smile vanished as he thought of how he had finished Crow.

"I wasn't thinking of the bank," said Graham unconvincingly. "What do you think it was?"

"The first shots," Davitt explained thoughtfully, "were fairly distinct, as if in a partially confined space. The next were smothered, as if they were fired inside a building. The last two were sharp, as if they were fired in the open air and fairly close at hand. The last two shots seem to have settled

56

it. It might have been a running fight through a building. It might have been a raid on one of the resorts. It might have been an interrupted robbery. A bunch of cow waddies would empty their guns, if they were having fun in about the same place and add a flock of yells. We're just starting to hear shouts now."

"Aren't you going to see what it's about?" Graham demanded.

"Why, no," Davitt drawled. "The regular law is well represented in this town. I understand the sheriff is here today himself."

"Didn't Sheriff Drew appoint you a special deputy?"

"Sure he did. But that was for special work. I'm giving him back that special star tomorrow. I'm going to buy a ranch and settle down. I've never taken a hand in small plays." The last was said grimly, with a hint of bitterness.

"You're going to buy a ranch?" the banker blurted blankly.

"Sure. I'm going to buy a nice place for two reasons. I want to take up stock raising, which I've always been interested in, and I want to assume a substantial interest in the community."

At this, Virginia put a hand on his arm and smiled at her father.

"This interruption in our . . . say . . . misunderstanding," Davitt went on, "was timely. There is disorder in the town. The law must be enforced to assure peace and security to citizens like yourself. But because I've gone in for the heavy duty, you might say, I'm spectacular and a character. I shall not offer my gun for sale again."

Graham was nonplused by this array of sound logic. "I don't think your occupation is dishonorable," he said. "It is merely that I don't approve of your attention to my

57

daughter for personal reasons. That should be sufficient for Virginia, at least." He looked swiftly at the girl.

"I told Mel . . . Mister Davitt, before he came in here to talk to you, that he shouldn't go away," Virginia said slowly. "I'm glad he isn't going."

Graham's look was angry again. "I won't talk any more about it now," he flared.

"Here are visitors!" Davitt exclaimed, as quick steps came up the porch.

Virginia hurried to the door, her father following her. Davitt stood in the hall as a girl and a young man came in.

"Why, Georgia!" Virginia greeted smilingly. "Did you come over from the dance?"

"Sure we did," said the youth for her, taking the girl's raincoat. "We passed trouble on the way, too. Did you hear the shots?"

"Yes, yes!" Graham exclaimed. "What was it, Jay?"

"Robbers!" the youth cried excitedly. "Somebody broke into Moss Harley's store. Moss went over to see that everything was all right and caught him . . . or them. They shot it out, and we heard men yelling in the street that Moss was hit. Maybe I'd better go over. They may need riders."

"I wouldn't bother, if I were you," Davitt put in. "It's a pretty bad night for a posse to do much good, and there's plenty of riders in town who're not escorting pretty girls."

"That's right," Virginia added quickly. "You stay and look after Georgia. Oh . . . ," she turned to Davitt. "This is Jay Chester, from the range north of here, and Georgia Buxton, from her father's ranch up on Cross River."

"It gives me my first real smile tonight to meet them," Davitt said with a slight, graceful bow.

"Are you the famous Mel Davitt!" Jay exclaimed. "I'm

proud to meet you." He offered his hand. "You could solve
the trouble *pronto!*"

Sylvester Graham made an impatient gesture. "We're all
visiting in the living room tonight," he snapped out.

VII

"Pruitt's plan"

Bull Pruitt fled northward as fast as his horse could safely ne-
gotiate the soggy prairie. He knew that by cutting off to the
northeast he would encounter the main road that led north to
Cross River and beyond. The ranch he proposed to visit for
his own nefarious purposes was the first ranch on the left
when he should hit the river. He didn't know about the road.
He had visited this ranch but once, and that had been five
years ago. To the best of his memory, the road to the ranch followed the lower, or south, bank of the river. He remembered
the river—really little more than a wide stream or creek—was
lined with cottonwoods, alders, willows, and brush. It would
be easy enough for him to hide if he reached it before dawn, as
he intended to do. He was in a worse predicament than when
he had merely been without a hat. For now any rider meeting
him would remember and be suspicious when he heard of the
store entry and shooting in town. It seemed to Pruitt that
every coincidence of a possible damaging nature had been
against him since he had arrived on this range. He cursed into
the failing wind and resolved that his business in this locality
would be finished in less than twenty-four hours.

At all times dangerous, Pruitt was doubly dangerous
now. He would eschew meeting a chance rider merely to

avoid killing him to still his mouth about the stranger seen riding north after the robbery and shooting. Pruitt wondered if the storekeeper were dead, hoping that he was. He reloaded the gun he carried in the holster on his left.

The northern sky was now swimming with white-fire points of starlight. The wind was dying, and the thunder was an occasional faint grumble far to the southward. The rain had ceased. But it was wet, sticky, spongy going underfoot, and Pruitt nearly shouted aloud with satisfaction when he felt and heard his horse's hoofs on a hard surface. The road stretched northward in the starlight, the ribbons of rain water in its tracks silvered and gleaming. No trouble to sight an approaching rider a considerable distance away, and Pruitt would certainly be more alert this night than any chance rider.

He halted and listened intently at times for sounds of the pursuit he did not fear. There was one man, however, whom he believed to be in this country. If he should appear, there would be no alternative but swift action with a gun and a burst of speed into Canada. *Pooh!* Pruitt figured the law of averages—something he always had relied upon and never had fully understood—would protect him from more hard luck. Still, there was always the outside chance. He would have felt much more at ease if he had known what had taken place in town after his departure.

The sheriff himself had been one of the first to enter the store after the sound of shots had attracted attention. He had taken charge immediately. Moss Harley, the storekeeper, had been seriously, perhaps fatally, wounded. He had been shot in the side and in the neck. The latter wound had paralyzed his speech, and a vague scrawl he made on a piece of paper before losing consciousness could not be deciphered by anyone. He had been carried to his house at the doctor's orders.

Sheriff Hal Drew's next move, after convincing himself of the storekeeper's condition, had been to order deputies out to station volunteer posse members about the outskirts of the town and to search the town thoroughly for robber suspects. It was, in his experienced mind, plainly a case of disturbed burglary.

After this, with the assistance of two store employees, he began an examination of the establishment. All the lamps were lighted. The open window was discovered first by the draft it created. There were wet marks on the floor where rainwater had supposedly dripped from the robber's soaked clothing. But others had already walked about, leaving trails of rainwater. The sheriff ordered the others out, with the exception of his assistants.

He now turned naturally to the office. The safe was the logical target of a robber. The sheriff had seen to it that no one went into the office ahead of himself. But there were no streaks of water, no damp spots on the floor. The safe was closed and locked. None of the desk drawers had been tampered with, and not even the papers on top of the desk had been disturbed. The sheriff looked puzzled, as everything proved to be in order. There was not the slightest indication to show that the burglar had been in the office.

Sheriff Drew straightened with a light of comprehension in his calm gray eyes. "We'll search the store to see if anything is missing . . . anything at all," he announced.

With the two store employees the counters and stock were speedily inspected. Nothing appeared to be missing. But in the men's section the sheriff saw a blot on the floor.

"Hand me a lamp," he ordered.

Holding the lamp low, he found the damp imprints of

riding boots and little pools of water.

"Harley didn't wear riding boots, did he?" he asked.

"Of course not," replied one of the clerks. "He wore broad soles and low heels. He often complained because he was on his feet so much."

"Then the robber was here," said Drew, pointing at the footprints. "Do you see anything missing here?"

The clerks looked at the coats, hats, and other apparel, and shook their heads. They could not remember if anything were missing. It would require an inventory. They were both bewildered and excited, and, in that frame of mind, nothing seemed to have been taken.

"Then the thief .ran over there to hide!" Sheriff Drew cried. "Look at those prints of riding boots on the floor. A pair of shoes such as Harley wears never could leave an imprint like that. Moss Harley probably . . . must have discovered him . . . and then the shooting started. The burglar was discovered before he had a chance to steal anything. An experienced thief wouldn't shoot unless he had to, so Harley must have shot first. The thief shot to get away or conceal his identity." The sheriff ceased speaking and stared thoughtfully at the two clerks, who nodded.

"He needn't have shot just to get away," the sheriff added. "He could have made the front door and gotten out easy. Harley's no marksman. Those riding boots and what's happened . . . or the way it happened . . . make me think it was some cowpunching amateur."

With this expressed conviction, Sheriff Drew concluded his investigation in the store and ordered it closed up for the night.

Bull Pruitt favored his mount on the ride north, but reached Cross River before daylight without having seen another human abroad. By now the sky had cleared in all directions, and the moon was out. When the outlaw came to the river, he found a road leading along the south bank but none on the north. The one road was fairly well-traveled, and he took it. The first ranch he came to was the ranch he sought. He saw cattle, and a fence shut off the river. When he saw a faint light, he suspected the house was across the stream. The light came from that direction. It grew larger and brighter as Pruitt rode cautiously. When the lighted window came in sight, with the black hulk of the house about it, Pruitt saw the gleam of water. He cursed as the road turned to the right and he came to a gate on the bank where the trees were cleared away on both sides. He dismounted and led his horse through, then closed the gate.

It was the house he was seeking, all right. He recognized the windmill to one side. He didn't like the looks of the ford, for the stream had been swollen by the heavy rain. He couldn't risk calling out—and he had to cross the ford, anyway.

He had put the stolen Mackinaw on over the leather jacket, and this tended to bind his arms, which would be a handicap if he had to swim. He took off both Mackinaw and jacket, intending to carry them. On second thought, he threw the torn jacket into the rushing stream. He had intended to discard it in any event. No one had seen him wearing it save Pink Lawton—and Pink was gone.

Pruitt secured the Mackinaw to the saddle horn and likewise secured his boots, so he would have freedom for swimming, if it should be necessary. The dark, flowing water appeared ominous in the shadows of the trees, with weird, subdued lights playing on it from stars glimmering through the branches and from the soft yellow gleam of the lamplight.

He mounted and urged his horse into the water. All his precaution and fears proved unwarranted, for horse and rider crossed swiftly to the opposite bank. Pruitt's legs and feet were wet. He laughed softly to himself as he put on his boots and the Mackinaw. The luck had changed, he thought as he chuckled. He had kept the gun dry by putting it inside his shirt.

He walked his horse to a clump of trees near the front of the house. As he approached, he recognized the rambling lines of the structure. He tied his horse in the trees and stole to the lighted window. He peered into the living room and saw a man asleep in an easy chair before a fireplace in which a blaze still smoldered.

"Old Buxton himself," Bull Pruitt croaked in a hoarse voice.

He looked quickly about. There was nothing—no sound, no movement—to indicate that anyone was abroad save himself. He estimated, with uncanny accuracy, that it lacked an hour of dawn.

But he did not take a chance on rapping on the window, nor trying to raise it. He slipped noiselessly around to the courtyard in the midst of the ranch buildings. He went first to the bunkhouse and heard no sound. The barn was dark. He walked back to the house and tried the rear door. It was not locked. He turned the knob and entered softly, closing the door behind him. Next he was in the living room, with Allan Buxton asleep in the chair before him. He gazed with a sneer on his lips at the pudgy, placid face of the snoring man.

Peace and comfort—that was the phrase that framed itself on Pruitt's lips, but was left unspoken. His eyes flashed dangerously, then filled with a cunning light. He shook Buxton by the shoulder till the rancher sat up, awake.

"That you, Georgia?" Buxton mumbled, rubbing his eyes. "I stayed up, but I didn't think you'd come back till the storm was over."

"The storm is over," said Pruitt sharply. "You better snap awake and see who your visitor is, Bux."

The sound of the voice caused Buxton to start and sit up, wide awake. He peered up at Pruitt and started to his feet, but desisted in his attempt to rise when Pruitt pushed him back into his chair.

"Easy, easy," Pruitt cautioned. "Work careful this time, Buxton. I'm not just hurrying north or south. I came here to see you special. Are you waiting for that girl of yours? Where is she and when will she be back?"

Allan Buxton was blinking as his normal senses returned after his heavy sleep. He did not care to tell Bull Pruitt that his daughter, Georgia, had gone down to Milton to the dance with Jay Chester. He smothered an artificial yawn.

"It's you, Bull?" he said, as though angry because he had been disturbed. "Why didn't you pile into the bunkhouse? Don't talk so loud or you'll wake up the whole house."

"All right, Bux," Pruitt said more amicably. "I got pretty wet plowing through that ford of yours. I'll dry my feet at the fire while you make some coffee and get me something to eat." He pulled off his boots while Buxton stared at him with a bland expression.

"There's still hot coffee on the stove, I reckon," Buxton said in a growling voice. "I'll get you some and some cold meat and biscuits. It's all I've got this time of morning. Did you put your horse up, and what brand is he wearing this time?"

"Put him up yourself," Pruitt snapped out savagely. "He's out in those cedars in front. Leave him fixed so I can get away fast, if I have to. For once, Bux, if you're wise, for your own good get busy fast."

"Are you being chased?" asked Buxton in evident alarm.

"What if I am? I've been chased before, haven't I?" returned Pruitt.

"But Bull, you've never been chased to my place," Buxton said in a worried tone. "You wouldn't want to be caught here, would you?"

"For your sake, I wouldn't," Pruitt snarled. "Heat that coffee, feed my horse, and get the grub in here. I've got to be out of sight by daylight, you fool."

"How'd you get so wet?" Buxton asked curiously as he rose.

"Riding through your damned ford!" the outlaw exploded. "It . . . but I told you that. You ought to be fat enough off the gang that stops here going to and from the line to build a bridge."

"But I have a bridge," Buxton complained. "Been opened two months. Cost me plenty, too . . . more'n I could afford. It's just above where you turned down to the gate, if you came that way."

"I didn't see no bridge, nor no road to a bridge," Pruitt retorted crossly. "I'd forgotten a lot about the road, anyway. But I got across, and maybe I'm chased, for all you know. If I'm caught here, I'll spill the works on you, Buxton. If I get dried out, get my horse taken care of, and something to eat, I'll be hid by daylight. And I'll put real money in your pocket . . . not just enough for a safe stop, like the tinhorns you put up here, but a real chunk of dough. I'm a fool if you don't need it."

"I can use it," said Buxton quickly. "I'll set the coffee on to heat, take care of your horse . . . in the cedars, you say? All right. And I'll have you fed and on the run in no time."

"Then hop to it!" Pruitt exclaimed, with a curse.

Buxton hurried away. Pruitt heard sounds in the kitchen, then the soft opening and closing of the rear door. Buxton was following instructions to the letter. Pruitt guffawed, and his eyes glowed evilly. *Buxton better do as he was told,* Pruitt thought rapidly. He wondered if Buxton knew Pink Lawton. Both Buxton and Lawton had come to this range from the south, but from widely separated parts of the south. But Pruitt had covered *all* the south. He decided not to mention Lawton. He decided, also, after a struggle in his mind, not to mention the burglary and shooting in Milton that night. But he would lay the law down to Buxton in such a manner that the latter would be sure to do as he told him.

Pruitt dozed in the chair Buxton had occupied, his feet and legs a proper distance from the hot embers, his wet boots far enough away from the heat to dry slowly without burning or warping dry. He roused with a start, his hand leaping to his gun as Buxton touched him on the shoulder.

"Heh-heh," Buxton snickered. "Just as fast to draw as ever."

"I may have to be faster than ever," Pruitt growled. "I mean, if things don't turn out right."

He turned to the coffee and food that Buxton moved close to him on a small table. He began to speak between bites and swallows.

"Horse all right?"

"Quart of oats, plenty of hay, and not too much water," Buxton replied.

Pruitt nodded in approval. "Listen, Buxton, I'm not up here on a getaway, you might say. I'm here on a job, and you're the son of a coyote who's going to help me put it over. It'll make money for both of us, understand? And then I leave the country for Canada and points distant. I don't expect ever to come back, understand? With this job you get

67

rid of me and make money, see?"

"What kind of a job?" Buxton quavered suspiciously.

"The Bank of Milton!" Pruitt exclaimed hoarsely. "Big money!"

Allan Buxton's face went white, and his whole body trembled as he dropped into a chair. In a flash he thought of his daughter, Georgia, and her sweetheart, Jay Chester, now down in Milton. He thought, too, of Sylvester Graham, with whom he had built a moderate but substantial credit at the very bank Pruitt proposed to rob. He thought of his undercover activities at his lonesome ranch near the Canadian line—activities that he had gradually been giving up. He wished, almost, that he had killed Pruitt, dozing there in the chair. But he feared this notorious outlaw as he feared no other man. There were reasons why he couldn't give him to the law.

"What . . . what do you expect of me?" Buxton managed to ask, his strenuous thoughts whirling like a maddening maelstrom in his head.

Pruitt gulped down the coffee and quickly consumed the balance of his food. He wiped his lips with the back of a hand and leaned back to roll a cigarette, waving away a cigar Buxton offered him. He lit the cigarette, his eyes glowing brightly.

"You've shipped your beeves," he said. "How do you stand at Graham's bank in Milton? I know you bank there, because it's the only bank close enough to do business with. How much has the old skinflint got against you?"

"Eighteen hundred dollars is all," Buxton replied, surprised. "I've cut down on stock and loans, and paid some. I'm not in bad shape, you might say, if we get a decent winter and don't have to feed too early or too much."

"Yeah?" The outlaw sneered. "You'd rather keep on

owing this fellow than to pay up, eh? And you don't want to tell him that you've been cracking the boys a hundred dollars a head to hide 'em when they was hitting for the line, or back, with posses at their heels . . . eh? You want to be a stockman in full rights, isn't that so?"

"You tell me this when I've helped you yourself," Buxton breathed, his eyes narrowing. "You're squealing?"

Pruitt's gun was out so quickly that Buxton tipped in his chair and fell over backward.

"Don't say that again!" Pruitt hissed, as Buxton clambered to his feet with beads of sweat on his forehead. "Now! Will you listen?"

Buxton turned up the chair and dropped into it weakly. "Keep the gun out of it," he said.

"The gun's going to be in what I've got in mind, if you're not in it!" Pruitt growled. "This is a last chance with me, Buxton. It's going through like clockwork, or I'm going out, and, if I go out, I'll take certain parties along with me . . . one of them is you."

If ever a renegade spoke from the bottom of his black heart, it was Pruitt this minute—and Allan Buxton knew it. Buxton decided that, after all, it was up to him to protect his own life and his daughter's future. But he resolved that beyond a certain point he would not go, even if death engulfed him.

"Let's have the proposition," he suggested in a normal tone.

"Now you're showing some sense," said Pruitt with a twisted grin of satisfaction. "After all, you didn't do anything bad down south. I just happened to know you and ran across you again up here. More'n you have kept hide-outs for men on the high trail. It isn't such a terrible disgrace, unless . . . you're found out. That would be bad in your case." He paused, looking at Buxton's flabby, washed-out face.

"What I'm . . . what we're going to do has to be done within the next twelve hours," he continued grimly. "I'm going to take the Milton Bank for what I can get . . . which'll be plenty. Don't say you won't help, Bux, because you're my only chance to pull this job easy. There's some other things you don't know, but you can bet that, if you fall down on me, you'll stop a bullet. If you don't stop a bullet, you'll be in so bad you'll probably throw one into yourself of your own accord." His taunting laugh echoed dully, menacingly, in the big room.

Pruitt dug a roll of bills out of a trousers pocket. "You got any money?" he asked.

"Sixty dollars," Buxton grunted.

The outlaw peeled off a sheaf of banknotes. "Here's five hundred," he said crisply, handing them to the astonished Buxton. "You're to go to Milton this afternoon, catch old Graham, and drag him to the bank *after* regular banking hours by telling him you want to pay five hundred on your note and get a new note. He'll do it, all right. You can manage to slip the catch on the door as you go in. I know you're slick enough to do that. And that's all you have to do. I'll do the rest. All I need is to get into the bank when the whole force isn't there. You go right ahead with your business with Graham and, when I appear, just do as you're told and keep your mouth shut. You'll get your cut of winnings, besides getting the five hundred, and nobody will have a reason in the world to suspect you had a hand in the robbery. You'll be fixed. You won't never be bothered by me, and you can turn down the high riders. After all, Buxton, this is a mighty smooth and safe proposition. It shouldn't be necessary for me to threaten you." Pruitt's eyes glowed with cunning.

"I never expected to put in on a deal like this," Buxton mumbled, staring at the dying fire with gleaming eyes so Pruitt couldn't see.

"And the beauty of it is that it's a sure shot!" Pruitt exclaimed in triumph. "I'm going to let you go in same time as I do. Nobody knows me there, but get any idea of double-crossing me out of your head. You can't do that without me making you a party to the business . . . if I don't get a chance to spray you with a Forty-Five. You've turned some tricky dollars, Bux, and nobody knows it any better than me. You might as well turn a flock of 'em at one crack and quit. Now listen and. . . ."

For twenty minutes, Pruitt went over the plan carefully, omitting no detail, intimidating Buxton, and finally convincing him that it could be done. In the end, Buxton had no alternative but to agree to help.

Pruitt exchanged the new hat for an old one that Buxton hadn't worn in months. He secured an old coat. He explained he needed these as a disguise. Then, with a packet of food in his pockets, he rode away just as the gray film of dawn was silvering the eastern horizon.

He took a trail on the north bank, instead of crossing the river, and sought a few hours of rest in the shelter of the trees. He could depend upon Buxton's misleading any chance posse.

Buxton had been chopping some wood as Pruitt left. The outlaw thought he still was hearing the sounds of the axe when he rode into the dim trail. But the sounds of the axe had stilled as Allan Buxton spied his daughter, Georgia, and Jay Chester ride in from town across the bridge. What Pruitt had mistaken for chopping was the beating of hoofs.

And both Georgia and Jay caught a glimpse of Pruitt as he plunged into the timber.

VIII

"Davitt in charge"

At eight o'clock in the morning, two hours after Georgia Buxton and Jay Chester had arrived at the Cross River Ranch, the sun was shining all over the north range, the breeze was balmy, and there were no traces of the terrific storm save for the swollen creeks and rivers and the pools of water rapidly evaporating in depressions in the prairie and the roads. It was a freshened landscape.

Milton was bright and sunny, drying out fast, so far as the elements were concerned. But no mere time of day, as the saying has it, was being exchanged between the agitated inhabitants. At no place was this human turmoil more conspicuous than in the office of chief deputy in the "holding jail," as it was known. It was known by this cognomen because it was merely a detention place where malefactors were detained before appearing before the justice of the peace, serving a ten-day sentence, at most, or being sent, otherwise, to the county jail at the county seat.

When in Milton, Sheriff Hal Drew made his official headquarters in the chief deputy's office in this jail. The sheriff was in this office this morning. With Moss Harley, the storekeeper, hovering between life and death, the doctor frankly pessimistic as to his patient's chance of recovery, and the whole town stunned by the futility of the shooting in which Harley had been so seriously wounded and the burglar had escaped, there was ugly talk, grave reasoning, and general uncertainty. Sheriff Drew was mad all through.

No trace of the wanton marauder had been discovered. The promiscuous shooting still appeared foolish and unnecessary on the face of it. Nothing had been found missing in the store, and the sheriff still held to his opinion that entry had been forced and the miscreant who had shot and fled was an amateur. Only nominal posses had been sent out on the main roads.

Yet within the hour, another development had arisen that overshadowed the tragedy staged in town. It concerned the sheriff more than the local shooting. A duly appointed constable had been found in an abandoned shack near Nine Mile Spring, apparently struck by lightning, but under circumstances that were suspicious. His body had been seared by the fire that had raged in the shack until being put out by the heavy rain. He had been identified as Mike Lawton of Alder Creek.

Two cowpunchers, passing along the road near the spring in the direction of Milton, had spied a horse, saddled and bridled, in the light timber. Because of the saddle on the horse, they had looked closer and had seen the broken bridle reins. This had showed that the animal had broken away, and further investigation had revealed the ruined shack and the body. They had brought the body into Milton and had reported to the sheriff. Just after listening to their stories, the sheriff had learned from the undertaker and coroner that the constable might not have died from the lightning shock but from bullet wounds. On his desk, the chief deputy had the badge, gun belt with its cartridges, gun, and hat of the dead constable, and a wad of water-soaked paper that had miraculously escaped the freakish ravages of the lightning.

So Sheriff Drew walked the floor and swore, while thinking so hard it must seem that his head would burst.

Besides the sheriff, the chief deputy, and the two cowpunchers who had discovered the body, Sylvester Graham was in the little office. The banker had come because of his interest in the shooting of a fellow townsman; he had stayed, astounded, after this new disclosure.

At a point when silence reigned in the office, save the sheriff's impatient pacing, the door opened, and Mel Davitt, bright and cheerful, entered. He noticed the tense looks of those present, felt the charged atmosphere, and was about to withdraw when the sheriff and Graham both called to him abruptly: "Come in!"

Davitt turned with a hand on the doorknob.

"I came to see Sheriff Drew," he said coolly, nodding at that official. "If he has a minute to spare."

"I hope you're going to help solve what's happened," Graham blurted, his face reddening.

"I told you what I intended to do, last night," Davitt retorted with a frown. "May I see you privately?" he addressed the sheriff.

"Sure," responded Drew gruffly. He waved the chief deputy and the two cowpunchers out. Then he looked askance at the banker, who hadn't moved. "Is it all right for Graham to stay?" he asked. "He's always had a great interest in civic affairs."

"I intend to have a considerable interest in affairs around here from now on, Sheriff," Davitt said curtly. "I'm quitting my business of manhunting. I came here to tell you of this and to hand in my special deputy star." He drew the badge from a pocket and put it on the desk.

The sheriff's face darkened as he lost his temper. "Throwing it back at me in time of trouble, eh? I tried to help you when I could! You accepted that badge in good faith, did you not? If you didn't, I'll throw it out the window!" He grasped the badge as if he meant to carry out his angry threat.

"Just a minute!" Graham exploded. "I've recommended to the sheriff that he request your assistance in these two cases," he told Davitt suavely.

"But I'm not and never have been a county officer," Davitt pointed out with a blank look. "My work has all been special . . . and I've quit it." He now was looking at and talking to the sheriff. "I'm going to buy a ranch and . . . er . . . settle down."

The sheriff, taken aback, merely mumbled, nonplused.

"I think . . . if the sheriff asks you . . . you might consider to help in this case, as . . . in the capacity of a citizen," Graham said.

Davitt gazed at him queerly for a moment, then faced Drew.

"If the sheriff asks assistance, I'll do what I can. But without pay. Merely as . . . a citizen." He smiled faintly.

Sheriff Drew sat down at the desk.

"I've never asked you to help in county affairs," he said. "But, since you've given up, as you say"—he glanced quickly at Graham—"your special line, I might ask you in your rôle of citizen . . . and promise none of the county's money in pay."

"Go ahead, Sheriff," Davitt said cheerfully. "What's up . . . besides the idle rumors I've heard?"

Banker Graham actually smiled.

"I don't know what you've heard, but here are the facts as I have them officially, so far." Drew nodded, cleared his throat, and proceeded to tell Davitt all he knew of the entry to Moss Harley's store, of which Davitt already knew most of the surface details, and finished with a careful account of the circumstances surrounding the finding of Constable

Lawton's body in the wrecked shack near Nine Mile Spring after the storm of the night before.

Graham looked expectant when the sheriff had concluded.

Davitt glanced at the exhibits on the top of the desk.

"Have you got Lawton's watch?" he asked crisply.

"Why, yes," stammered Drew. He opened a drawer and brought forth the dead man's timepiece.

Davitt took it, glanced at it, shook it, and listened with the back of the case pressed to his ear. Then he smiled vaguely. "Put out of commission at seven o'clock," he said. "That must have been when the lightning bolt hit him, for there is no identification on the case or crystal to indicate it was struck by a bullet. At seven o'clock the storm must have been at its peak at Nine Mile."

"Why do you say that?" the sheriff asked with a new note of respect in his voice.

"Because that watch stopped when Lawton was struck by the bolt," replied Davitt, his eyes lighting with interest. "Let me see what else you have there."

Graham now was watching him in sheer fascination.

Sheriff Drew handed over the gun and gun belt. The latter had been burned by the lightning.

Davitt examined the gun carefully, broke it, took out an empty shell, regarded its casing critically, looked at the loaded cartridges in the belt, and dropped the empty shell into his pocket as he addressed the sheriff. "Lawton didn't have a loaded shell in his gun when he died," he said slowly. "He must have shot the gun clean during the storm, or maybe shortly before. He wouldn't be one to go around with an empty gun, would he?"

"Of course not!" Drew exclaimed. "He was an old-timer . . . came up here from Arizona. He never carried no gun for an ornament."

"Then he wouldn't fire at the lightning, or thunder, or a shadow . . . not six shots, Sheriff," Davitt purred. "He fired those shots, if he really did fire them, at someone or something which was molesting him. He didn't have a chance to reload the gun before he was struck down . . . by those bullets you say hit him, or by the lightning. There was someone else there."

"Go on," the sheriff said excitedly, while Sylvester Graham found it hard to subdue the light of admiration in his eyes.

"What's that dried-out, crumpled piece of paper there?"

"Found on the floor," Drew explained, handing over the exhibit.

Mel Davitt opened it carefully. "Why!" he exclaimed. "This is a reward notice for one Bull Pruitt!"

"Lawton was posting them," the sheriff explained. "He had regular places out there in the middle of the county where he put up posters for me. They were notices like this, sheriff's sale posters, notices of election, and so on. A batch of these came in several days ago, and I gave him a bunch to put up. This Pruitt named in this poster pulled a killing down near Bozeman. He's never worked his way up this far, but he's supposed to be bad medicine. If I'd run across you lately, I'd have asked you if you knew him."

"I've run across him," growled Davitt. "I seem to have met most of the worst ones at one time or another." He was carefully reading the indistinct printing on the crumpled paper that had been thoroughly water-soaked. He put it back on the desk.

"Save it," he said laconically. "There were other posters in his pocket?"

"No. I reckon he was down that way posting 'em . . . the boys said there was one up at the spring . . . and this was the

77

last he had. Evidently he threw it away in the shack."

"Why should he?" Davitt asked sharply. "He got so much apiece for putting them up, didn't he? Well, then, he could have found a place to stick this last one and make an extra fee, couldn't he? And, if he wanted to throw it away, why should he crumple it up, like he was mad, before he threw it away?"

"Maybe the lightning did it," Drew ventured.

"Nonsense," Davitt scoffed. "It isn't even scorched. Somebody else clenched that notice in a powerful hand and flung it aside. Did this Lawton have any enemies down there . . . anybody who might follow him to the shack in the storm to kill him?"

"Not a soul I know of," declared the sheriff vehemently. "He was so mild-mannered that I thought this was about all the work he was good for."

"That leaves a clear suspect," Davitt smiled calmly.

"What's that!" the sheriff exclaimed, half rising in surprise.

"Just as I told you, Drew," said Graham complacently, "Davitt could figure this out in no time."

"Thanks," said Davitt dryly. He noted skeptically that the banker's attitude seemed to have changed overnight. "But I haven't figured this out at all," he said with a smile. "I'm merely guessing. In the books they would call it the process of deduction." He grinned at the sheriff."

"Whatever it is," growled the sheriff, "it's an idea."

"Seems logical to me." Davitt shrugged. "There was shooting in that shack during the storm. Lawton wouldn't have kept on firing after he'd hit himself once. But his gun is empty . . . all bullets fired. There must have been another person there, shooting, too. You must send a man up there to try to find bullet holes made by shots that went wild.

Send him at once. Dig out the bullets. I don't reckon there was cause or reason for Lawton to try suicide."

"Not on your life!" Hal Drew exclaimed. "Lawton had had that job for eight years. I knew he was square. He only wanted to make a decent living, which he was doing."

"That's right," Graham affirmed. "He had a moderate savings account with our bank."

"A man came along who didn't like those notices," Davitt said gravely. "He . . . well, who would be the one who would like it the least? The man advertised for, of course . . . Pruitt! I'm guessing Pruitt came on him when the storm started. They took refuge in the shack. Pruitt asked to look at that last bill. He must have suspected that Lawton recognized him, because *anybody* could recognize him from that description. He was on his way north after his trouble in the south, and Nine Mile is directly on the north and south trail. A road from there leads to Alder Creek or to Cross River, just this side of the Canadian line. I'd be inclined to think Pruitt shot it out with Lawton in the shack. He couldn't let a man . . . a constable . . . run around telling folks he'd seen a man who looked like Pruitt, could he?"

"By George, no!" the sheriff ejaculated. "I'll have my man look around to see if there's any sign that a horse beside Lawton's was cached there, too, and for anything else he can find."

"Now you're taking hold," Davitt complimented. "I've got some more fool ideas." He smiled. "I think they shot it out by lightning flashes. This Pruitt is dynamite with his gun, and in a steady light he would have knocked Lawton off the first time he fired. But here we have a gun with all the cartridges exploded."

"Surely was a lot of promiscuous shooting," Drew frowned. "But what you've said is certainly enough to work on."

"I've got more in my head," said Davitt, gazing at Sylvester Graham. "Several times in my career, it has been a matter of outguessing instead of outshooting. I'd rather outguess than outshoot, any day."

Graham squirmed in his chair uncomfortably. "I've always given you credit for being more than a tough-riding gunman," he said.

"And I'm not riding in this case," Davitt pointed out. "I'm serving our sheriff to the best of my ability as a private citizen."

Sheriff Drew was regarding them queerly. "What's the matter?" he asked. "Have you two had another flare-up?" He looked at the banker suspiciously. "Wouldn't be surprised if it was over Miss Virginia," he conjectured.

Davitt laughed loudly, while Graham scowled.

"Perhaps we'd better stick to the matter in hand, which is strictly business," the banker told the official crisply.

"I guess I deduced the matter right on the head," Drew smiled. "Well, the two of them could do a lot worse than hook up together!" Then, sobering, he looked questioningly at Davitt. "You say you got more in your head?"

"More guessing," Davitt affirmed. "But look here. Doesn't it seem queer that this popping off of Lawton and the burglary and shooting here in town should happen on the same night, during the same storm?"

"Jumping Juniper!" cried Drew, leaping to his feet. "You mean this Bull Pruitt was responsible for both jobs?"

He was much excited, and Graham was leaning forward eagerly with his hands on his knees.

Davitt waved a hand. "Don't get heated up," he warned. "It's just a supposition. But the shooting at Nine Mile occurred about seven o'clock, and this business in town about five hours later. A man could easily ride from the spring to town, even in a storm, in five hours. And a man who knew the country none too well could get confused in the storm and take the road west instead of the poorer road north. Isn't that so?"

"He'd be more likely to take the best road, under the circumstances," said Graham wisely.

"He might've changed his mind and decided to come to town after what had happened at the spring," Drew put in.

"Now you're thinking," Davitt said, smiling. "If our reckoning is anywhere correct, Pruitt, or whoever it was, might have been heading for Milton in the first place. Or he might have changed his mind." He stared thoughtfully. "Look here, Sheriff," he said suddenly, "it was no amateur who jimmied that window. I've inspected the marks left by the tool. Three of them where they'd do the most good. The man who broke into Harley's store knew what he was doing, how to do it, and he did it in quick order when the wind and rain drowned the sounds of his work. Harley chanced along at midnight, just in time to catch the intruder at work, and scared him off. I heard the shots myself. The first were muffled, as if they came from inside the building. The last two were sharp and clear, like they'd been fired outside the window."

"Maybe Harley saw him before he could get in," said Drew. "No . . . there were wet marks inside."

"The outlaw shot Harley as he was leaving, because Harley had got too close and the outlaw was afraid of Harley giving too good a description. Now do you see the force of my feeble reasoning?"

"Nothing feeble about it," Graham said frankly.

"But where would he go?"

"Ah! That's for you to find out," Davitt said, rising. "He had all the north ahead of him. The storm was clearing up there . . . as we could see from here. The south was still stormy. I reckon he'd hit for the best ground for his horse to run on. North, in my opinion."

"I've already telephoned and sent some men up there," the sheriff said.

"You'll never get Pruitt, unless it's by a trick," Davitt said gravely, "or by still-hunting him."

"Why don't you go out after him?" Graham suggested slyly.

"Too much risk, as I told you last night," Davitt said with a smile. He addressed the sheriff, saying: "I'm not riding the hard trail or matching guns with any bandits. I'm settling down, you might say, and intend to buy a stock ranch."

"And we'll be mighty glad to have you on our voting list," the sheriff boomed enthusiastically. "I'll have to keep a tight hold on my political wires, or they'll be making you sheriff." He offered his hand while Graham started at his last words.

"I've got plenty to work on," Drew continued, "but I may have to call on you again . . . as a citizen. Any objection to your keeping this special's badge . . . for now?"

"Sure not," said Davitt, pocketing the badge. "So long."

As he walked up the sunny street toward the hotel, he was surprised at the many cheery nods and greetings. He didn't know the word had been passed around that he had taken charge of the case.

IX

"The wrong gun"

When Mel Davitt entered the lobby of the hotel where he had made his residence for some six months, save when he had been out working on cases, he was met by the affable proprietor, whom he knew but casually.

"Howdy, Mister Davitt," the proprietor greeted. "Have a cigar?"

"I'm always suspicious of greetings which have a cigar tied to 'em," Davitt said bluntly, rolling a cigarette.

The hotel man passed over this rebuff lightly. "I just took a tangled-up long-distance call from the Snowies for you," he said, beaming. "The man on the other end was . . . you remember that cowpuncher who worked with you this summer?"

"Buck Granger," said Davitt with some interest.

"That's him." The other nodded. "Well, he couldn't wait for you to come in, but he had an urgent message. Seems he went up there to see a girl named . . . let's see . . . ?"

"Polly," Davitt broke in, with a show of annoyance. "I can't remember her last name, although I believe it was Peters, or. . . ."

"Guess that was it," agreed the local man. "He said her last name didn't amount to much at that time because at noon she would be Missus Buck Granger, and for you not to leave town, because they would be here tonight on their honeymoon, and they want to see you."

"Oh, is that so?" Davitt exclaimed. "Well . . . maybe it's a

83

good thing." He looked about vaguely.

"So I thought I'd have sort of a wedding dinner for them," said the man, rubbing his hands. "Granger's got friends here, including yourself, and I thought I'd set a table for eight or ten. We don't have many newly married couples, and the hotel will stand the expense. Don't you think that's a good idea?"

" 'Bout the hotel standing the expense? I certainly do!"

"Do you think you could get away from your present case long enough to come to the dinner?" the hotelkeeper asked anxiously.

"I have no present case," Davitt snapped, pushing past the man. "Of course, I'll come, and I'll bring a guest, most likely."

Davitt went to his room, agitated because the town evidently had assumed that he had taken over the troubles of the night before. Now that he was about to become a property owner, he didn't fancy the idea of having his former calling brought up continuously. He had been unable to prevent its becoming known that he would consider the possible purchase of a stock property, but he disliked the thought that an element of a political nature had entered into the rumors of the last few hours. He had learned from various sources that he was even now being mentioned as possible sheriff material. This was an honor Davitt didn't invite.

But Davitt did a lot of thinking about Sheriff Hal Drew's predicament in trying to solve the two serious cases that had come under his jurisdiction during the duration of the storm the night before. He took out the empty shell he had removed from the gun that had been found in the cabin. He remembered it was an important clue, something upon which he had based his deduction of that morning. He slipped it back into his coat pocket and pressed his lips with another weighty thought.

There was no doubt but that he had become head over heels in love with Virginia Graham. And, despite the objection of Sylvester Graham, he meant to win her, have her, and keep her for his own. He had kissed her twice the night before. That wasn't enough. He intended to kiss her a thousand times again!

He was a very different Davitt from the manhunter all outlaws feared. He wondered, idly, if Pruitt knew he was in the country. For Pruitt would be a more formidable foe than he ever had met. In the depths of his mind, however, he believed Bull Pruitt already was safe in a hide-out in Canada. He shrugged and went down to his dinner. He had a ranch or two he wished to look at. His was a different business at present, he told himself.

As Davitt came out of the dining room after his meal, he saw an elderly man he knew to be a hand about the stables and gardens of Sylvester Graham's house in town. This man approached him in a casual way.

"Miss Virginia wants to see you as soon as possible," the man said without looking at him directly.

"Tell her I'll be right over," Davitt said in an aside.

They passed so quickly that no one would have been aware that a message had been transferred. Davitt was thrilled. Here was an element of mystery that appealed to the ever-present youth in him. While Georgia Buxton and Jay Chester were preparing to leave, and Sylvester Graham had relaxed his frowning vigil early in the morning, Davitt had been able to take abrupt and somewhat affectionate leave of Virginia Graham. Now she was sending for him. Could the summons mean a tryst of personal importance?

85

Davitt managed to leave the hotel casually and to walk slowly through shaded side streets to the Graham home. Virginia opened the door for him as he came up the steps to the porch. Her face was momentarily radiant, then sobered as she asked him in and led him into the study where the tempestuous scene of the night before had taken place.

"Listen, Mel," she said soberly, closing the door behind them. "I sent for you because . . . well, Georgia Buxton is back again, and she's told me some queer things. Jay Chester told her to see you, but she came to me first. I thought she had better tell you here. Father has had dinner and gone back to the bank. I . . . ," she broke off in confusion.

Davitt was anxious and all attention as he saw the girl was upset. He led her to a chair, and his concern showed as he spoke.

"You were right in sending for me," he told her earnestly. "You must *always* send for me first, if there's so much of a hint of trouble. Georgia must have told you something to disturb you, and I think it would be best if you let her tell me . . . in your presence, of course."

"I'll call her in," Virginia responded quickly. "I wouldn't have sent for you, knowing you've quit trailing, as you call it . . . but both Georgia and Jay are good friends of mine, and this may have something to do with what happened in town last night. It all might involve them, I mean." She flashed him a look of pleading, and a few moments afterward brought in Georgia.

The young girl was flushed and nervous, and appeared embarrassed, until Davitt quickly put her at ease. The girls sat while Davitt stood by the table, smoking.

"It's about something strange that happened this morning . . . early . . . and about Father," Georgia said, twisting a

86

small handkerchief in her pretty hands. "I think. . . ." She hesitated.

"Just tell me about it," said Davitt in a quiet, friendly tone, "and let *me* do the thinking."

"I believe the man who broke into the store was at our house before Jay and I got there at daybreak this morning," Georgia blurted.

Davitt gestured with his cigarette. "That wouldn't be so strange, Georgia. Cross River would be right in his path if he rode north."

Virginia saw by his eyes, however, that he was most keenly interested.

"Jay told me to see you," she said simply.

"Where's Jay?" Davitt asked.

"He's following the man," the girl replied.

This brought Davitt up with a start. "Tell me everything as quickly as you can, Georgia," he said rather sharply.

The girl looked at Virginia, who nodded encouragement.

"Jay and I started home early this morning when the weather cleared," Georgia explained, talking fast to have it over with. "When we reached Cross River, where the road to our ranch forks off west, Jay saw something that looked like a man's back in the water. He got off his horse to investigate, and found it was a torn leather vest or jacket which some man had discarded. There was nothing in the pockets, but Jay said it didn't look as if it had been in the water long. He tossed it into some brush, and we rode on.

"When we got to the place where the old road drops down to the ford we used to use before our bridge was built, we saw the gate open. Jay went down and said there were fresh tracks that showed that a rider had crossed the ford after the rain. We thought that was strange, because every rider who is familiar with our place uses the new bridge a short distance west of the ford. He fastened the gate securely, and we rode on.

"As we were crossing the bridge to the ranch house, we caught a glimpse of a rider dashing into the old trail on the north branch."

The girl paused, looking at Virginia.

"The rider who crossed the ford might have discarded the leather jacket," Davitt mused. "What did this man look like . . . the one you saw that was riding away from the house?" He bent his eyes searchingly on the girl.

"He was big, broad-shouldered. He had some beard, and, from the one peek we had at him, we thought he was middle-aged."

"Did you ask your father about him?" Davitt asked quickly.

"Yes, and Father was mad." The girl looked directly at her questioner for the first time. "He said the man was a hand from another ranch who'd stopped there because he saw the light in the big room burning. Father said he'd been sitting up all night, waiting. We sometimes have strangers stop in the bunkhouse overnight or so on their way north or south. But Jay thought, if this man was from another ranch as Father said, he would know about the bridge and wouldn't bother to ford the river."

Trouble now swam in the girl's eyes.

"Do you have very many strangers stop at your place?" Davitt asked absently. He was aware that fugitives had regular stopping places near the Canadian line, but he didn't wish to say anything that would indicate he might be suspicious of Allan Buxton.

"Quite a few," said the girl. "But not so many stop now as used to stop. Father took down the Buxton Ranch sign that used to be at the main road." There was appeal in her eyes.

"Why, I don't seem to find anything so strange about this," Davitt said easily.

"But there *is* something strange about it!" Georgia exclaimed. "I found a new hat in the living room. It had some caked mud on it, that's all. I keep track of all of Father's things, and, when I asked him about it, he said it was one he'd bought the other day. If he had bought a new hat, I'd know about it. But he hasn't bought any new hat, and this one isn't even his size. What's more, it had Moss Harley's store's name in it!"

"Even that might be accounted for," Davitt soothed.

"Oh!" cried the girl, clenching her palms, the tears starting. "I just know inside of me that the stranger was the store robber! He rode north and stopped at our ranch, and I'm afraid he'll get Father in trouble. Father wouldn't talk. Said he'd been up all night, and he went to sleep. Said he had to come down here to Milton this afternoon. I saw where he got a lunch for somebody. Maybe the man threatened him."

Virginia was patting the girl's hands now, and Davitt's face was serious.

"Your father isn't going to get into any trouble," Davitt said sternly. "You can depend on me for that. I wouldn't mind seeing the hat, though," he reflected.

"It's here!" cried Georgia. "I brought it with me."

"I'll show it to you," said Virginia, rising.

"In a minute," Davitt cautioned, with a nod at the other girl. "You say that Jay is following this stranger?"

"He followed him far enough to learn that he didn't take the north road," Georgia said. "And he didn't take the south road. Jay rode back to the ranch to see me, and told me to get away and get word to you somehow. I got away easy enough and rode down here as fast as I could. Jay's gone back to trail the stranger."

Davitt's brows lifted. "All right. You just stay here," he said. "You can ride back with your dad." He started out the study door, beckoning to Virginia.

In a minute, he had the hat Georgia had spoken of in his hands. He examined it carefully.

"I'm taking this with me," he said shortly. "Keep the girl here and keep her quiet. And if young Jay shows up, send for me. Meanwhile, don't say anything to *anybody*."

He put the hat under his coat.

Virginia put a hand under his arm. "Do you think it might be . . . serious?" she asked anxiously.

"Never can tell," was Davitt's reply.

"But . . . you're not going out on the . . . the trail, are you?"

"No." Davitt smiled. "I don't think it'll be necessary."

In a few minutes, he was closeted again with Sheriff Hal Drew. Drew was examining the hat.

"Find out if it was in Harley's stock last night," Davitt was directing. "Remember you said you saw wet tracks near where the hats and men's things are? I'll wait here for you. It might be Pruitt lost his hat in the storm and stopped here for another so's not to look strange riding around without one. He might have taken a coat, too, and thrown away that old leather jacket. He might have gone straight to Buxton's hide-out for a reason. Go ahead, Drew, and remember this is *your play!*"

Hal Drew went out with the hat, and almost from this moment events moved with the flashing rapidity of the streaking lightning that had illuminated the storm.

The sheriff had hardly left Davitt alone in the office when the chief deputy came hurrying in with an air of excitement about him and his eyes eager.

"Where's Drew?" he asked.

"Gone out for a few minutes," Davitt answered. "I expect him back soon."

"Well, you know all about this," said the man, leaning on the desk. "I'm just back from the Nine Mile shack. Went out there with one of the men who found old Lawton. We rode like we were afire. We found half a dozen bullet holes. Three near the door, one through the stovepipe . . . what was left of it . . . another in the floor near the stove, and we found this slug of lead almost intact in the grate."

He handed the bullet to Davitt, who examined it critically.

"What's more, the door had literally been knocked off its hinges and smashed proper, like a heavy man had crashed through it."

"That's news," said Davitt. He appeared now to be in charge. "Any sign of more than one horse having been there?"

"The cowpuncher who went with me says he is dead certain that two horses were hitched in the lean-to barn and that they both broke away. Part of the hitch rail was broken."

"That explains how Lawton's horse broke away. The other man's horse must have broken away, too, and he found him. We've got dead-sure evidence two men were in that shack, and both shooting. I reckon Lawton was murdered." His words fairly snapped with the old thrill of the hunt. "You've accounted for half a dozen bullets, and Lawton had three inside him. What else?"

"The shack is a wreck and partly burned. Here's another slug I picked out of the wall with my jackknife."

Davitt examined it. "Both are Forty-Five slugs, as you can see," he said. "Therefore, both guns were Forty-Fives.

Listen. Did you ever buy any Black Brand cartridges up here?"

"No," said the deputy. "We get S and W and others, but no Blacks."

Davitt drew the empty shell he had slipped into his pocket—a shell from the gun found in the shack. He took the gun and belt out of the drawer.

"This belt was on Lawton, so we can be pretty sure it was his," he pointed out. "Notice the shells. Every one of them is an S and W. See?"

"Sure." The mystified deputy nodded. "That's natural."

"But look at this empty shell," Davitt said, handing over the shell he had taken from the gun. He now broke the gun gently. "And read the heads of the empty shells in this gun found in the shack."

"Holy smoke!" the deputy exclaimed. "They're Black heads!"

"Not the same make as Lawton had in his belt," Davitt said. "The shells in this empty gun are all of a different make than the shells Lawton carried. There were two guns. One was found, and the murderer carried away the other. He also carried away his own gun belt, of course. It's my opinion that the murderer carried away the wrong gun. I think this is not Lawton's gun at all. In some way, during the confusion of the storm and the crashing of the lightning bolt, the guns became mixed. This is the outlaw's gun."

"Dog-gone!" the chief deputy exclaimed. "You're no manhunter. You're a natural-born detective."

"I am when the clues are as plain as this," Davitt remarked. "That gun was, I think, a give-away. Now keep this under your hat. The afternoon's getting on, and maybe we'll have work to do. I'm taking an interest in this . . . that's all, remember. Do you want to take an order . . . or suggestion from me . . . to save time? I guarantee the sheriff will back up the order."

"Sure." The deputy nodded. "You're a better man at this kind of work than the sheriff. . . ."

"Don't ever say that again!" Davitt interrupted sternly. "All the credit in this affair . . . if there should be any . . . will go to the sheriff and his force, understand? Fair enough, then. Don't talk to anybody. Go out and raise the toughest posse you can get together. A dozen will do, but twenty would be better. Have as many rifles . . . *rifles,* understand? . . . in the bunch as possible. They can think they're going out to hunt the man who shot Moss Harley. They can think anything. Have them ready to take a short trail in half an hour. Can you do it, chief?"

"Watch me!" the deputy exclaimed as he went out the door.

Davitt let him go and sat examining the gun and shells until Hal Drew entered. The sheriff nodded at Davitt and put the hat away.

"It was stolen last night, all right," he said grimly. "It was the only hat of that style and size left in stock, one of the clerks remembered. There were marks on other hats which showed they had been pawed over, and a pile of Mackinaws had been rumpled. Looks like the thief broke in to get a hat and took a Mackinaw, too."

"Then threw the worn and torn leather jacket he had been wearing into Cross River this morning," Davitt said. "The stranger who visited Buxton's ranch up there at dawn was the robber, and the robber probably is Pruitt."

"I'm not so sure about that," Drew said. "Why the gun and shells?"

"Your chief deputy came back busting with information and boiling with energy. I listened to what he had to say,

93

checked up on a few points, and took the liberty of sending him out to raise a posse to save time. Now I'll tell you about how the hat was found, the fugitive up at Buxton's, and this gun business. Then I'll step out of it, Drew, because I want to be in the background."

Sheriff Hal Drew and Davitt then spent half an hour in close conference.

"Now we know everything and, maybe nothing, except that the bandit who shot Moss Harley hit for Buxton's ranch." It was the sheriff who said this.

"And that Buxton is coming to town," Davitt said.

"Since this fellow changed his stolen hat, and probably the coat, I won't have a thing on him, unless I can prove he had a gun fight with Lawton," Drew said, scowling.

"Unless he should prove to be Pruitt."

"Maybe we're doing a lot of guessing. Why didn't you tell me about this gun matter and the shells this morning?"

Davitt laughed heartily. "Because I didn't want to make out that I was too wise in front of Graham, for one thing, and I wanted to think it over and hear the news from the shack. Damn it . . . I'm not sure yet!"

A persistent knocking was heard at the door of the office.

"Come in!" cried Drew impatiently

The door opened, and Jay Chester appeared, looking singularly boyish as he took off his hat. He gazed steadily at Davitt.

"Speak up, Jay," Davitt invited.

"That fellow is heading down this way along the creek."

Davitt got quickly to his feet as the chief deputy also entered.

X

"Davitt's hunch"

Bull Pruitt, unaware that he had been seen leaving the ranch after his meeting with Allan Buxton, secreted himself in the timber along Cross River to the east of the road at a point where he could observe any who should pass north or south. He smoked and rested. Finally he slept for the first time in thirty-six hours. It was while he slept that Georgia Buxton cut across the prairie on her fast ride to town.

He awoke, sitting up, cursing, and reaching for his gun. But he quickly attributed this to nerves and natural caution. The sky was mellow with the soft light of late afternoon. A breeze whispered in the tinted leaves. His horse was standing quietly as though waiting, the wind ruffling its mane. The stream was flowing smoothly, its lowering water clearing rapidly.

There was nothing whatever to cause him to suspect that he might have been seen or watched. He looked at the vast stretch of empty plain, at the dusty ribbon of road, undisturbed by any moving thing.

He took out his packet of food, and, as he ate, he went carefully over his plans. If he knew Allen Buxton at all, the man wouldn't try to cross him. He knew of too many wanted men that Buxton had shielded for a cash reward. Although Buxton was better off than he had suspected, Pruitt thought the man was still a gambler and as much in need of money as ever. He thought, and he thought—and the bank job looked perfect!

When he had finished eating, he saw the trailer of dust kicked up by the team drawing Allan Buxton's buckboard. Buxton was driving to town as directed, alone. Pruitt caught up his horse and started. He rode along a creek that flowed south toward town from the river.

At dusk, Pruitt cut out from the trees along the creek above Milton and spurred for town. A speedy arrival, a quick finish to the business at hand, an immediate escape to the security of the Buxton Ranch was his plan. So preoccupied was he with his schedule that all other thoughts were banished from his mind.

The crashing report of a gun rocked him in his saddle as a bullet fanned his face. Two more reports came in quick succession, and a slug of lead tore through his hat. He looked back to see a number of riders bearing down upon him, spreading fan-like. A posse and rifles!

Pruitt raised his hands high, holding the reins in his left, but did not check the speed of his horse. His thoughts were whipped into a turmoil. Was this a posse in search of the robber of the night before? To be caught in such a mess! Time was what counted. Buxton would be going to the bank with Graham, and Pruitt was due to enter the bank shortly after they went there. He might charge for the shelter of the trees on the outskirts of the town, a short distance ahead, but not with rifles in the game.

"Keep 'em up and keep riding," came the sharp command from just behind him.

The unexpected roar of guns had shocked him; now the voice startled him. Next moment he was cool, his cunning mind alert to the emergency—not the prospect of being seized as the invader of the store and possible killer of the storekeeper, but the possibility that he would not be able to get to the bank in time. He was prepared to make a break for the trees at the last moment, but the posse closed in on him, surrounded him, and he was forced to halt.

It was nearly dark, and Sheriff Hal Drew leaned from his saddle to search the face of the captive. There was the possibility of a mistake that would make him appear ridiculous. Identification should be at least reasonably sure. He saw nothing but a general resemblance in the captive's appearance to the outlaw known as Bull Pruitt—a resemblance which might easily be imagined. Drew was inclined to be cautious. He knew nothing of the outlaw's affliction and mistook the twitching of his brows as a sign of fear. Pruitt, so he thought, would show no such fear.

"Where you from?" the sheriff demanded.

"From up above," Pruitt answered in a whining voice. "If you fellers think I'm heavy with money, you're mistook. I guess you stopped the wrong man. I'm just a cowhand with what little is left of my summer's wages."

When desperate occasion required, Pruitt could be a good actor. His bearded face, his slump in the saddle, his assumed attitude gave a certain credence to his explanation. His cunning implication that he mistook the posse for a band of outlaws was simple.

"You know we're not after your money?" the sheriff scoffed. He didn't want to play any of his leading cards ahead of time. At the moment, this stranger neither looked nor acted like the notorious outlaw he sought. "I'm the sheriff of this county."

Pruitt lowered his hands.

"I'm shore glad to hear that . . . if it's true," he announced in an undeniable tone of relief. He peered at the sheriff in the rapidly failing light. "You look like one of them fellers. I'm going into town with a hundred and ten dollars to spend, if I have to. I'd rather double it." The last was spoken wistfully.

The outlaw could see that Drew was by no means sure of his catch. But he was just as sure that the sheriff would hold him for investigation. Under the circumstances, no sheriff would release him. He could only play for time and a break. He had to make a break. Buxton and Graham might be headed for the bank this minute!

"Where were you working up above, and what's your name?"

"I was with the PC outfit, and my name's Davis. I've got a Conway check to prove it."

That was Pruitt's chief alibi—for just such an emergency. There was such an outfit in the north, and Buxton had given him a check he had cashed for a 'puncher by the name of Davis. The 'puncher hadn't been able to endorse it because he couldn't write his own name. But Buxton was used to taking chances with signatures.

If this were true, and the sheriff could see no reason why it shouldn't be in view of the fact that the captive would have to back up his statement, it was a poser for the official.

"Say, you looking for somebody?" Pruitt blurted eagerly.

"I guess I'm looking for you," Drew announced. "I'm taking you in, anyway."

"Then let's go right along," Pruitt said. "I'm hungry and thirsty. But there was a couple of queer-looking riders I circled back a ways." Time—time—it was almost time!

Sheriff Drew suddenly laughed harshly. "That cinches it," he said sternly. "All your alibis are stiff ones. If you've got a PC check, you stole it. You made a fool move by doubling back here after the trick you turned last night. I've got you so cold I even know who you are, and your name isn't Davis, nor anything like it."

He swung down to take the gun in Pruitt's holster, and the sudden move caused his horse to shy. A second horse moved. It was the single moment of confusion with attention momentarily directed from himself that gave Pruitt the break he sought. He took it in a flash, spurring his horse through that narrow gap, spurting into the trees in the darkness before the rifles could be brought into play and before, indeed, the posse members were sure it was he who had bolted.

The posse was dashing toward the trees when Drew halted them.

"Scatter outside!" he commanded. "Scatter so he can't leave without being seen! In town he's the same as caught!"

Mel Davitt had taken Jay Chester with him to the hotel. He didn't wish the youth to be further involved in the business of catching the fugitive. Whether the robber was caught or not, whether he should prove to be Pruitt or not—Davitt considered his own part in the business as ended. The posse was quite likely to locate and capture the man Jay and Georgia had seen at the Buxton ranch.

Davitt was thinking of the prospective arrival of his erstwhile associate, Buck Granger, and his bride. He had made sure the proper arrangements were being done for the dinner that night. He intended to ask Virginia Graham to go. He dressed while talking to Jay, and it was just dark when they prepared to go to Sylvester Graham's house. As they left the room, Davitt told the youth to wait in the hall a moment while he returned to his room. An impulse that he could not resist prompted him to put on his gun in a shoulder holster.

They arrived at the Graham house shortly afterward and found Georgia Buxton there with Virginia. While Jay and

Georgia were talking, Davitt told Virginia about the dinner.

Her eyes sparkled as she agreed to accompany him later.

"Where's your father?" Davitt asked, noting the study was deserted.

"He's gone to the bank with Allan Buxton," Virginia replied. "Some business or other. It's always business and the bank."

"When did he go . . . how long ago?" Davitt asked quickly.

"Why . . . not very long ago. Buxton came for him. . . ." The girl's face appeared anxious as she saw Davitt's eyes light queerly.

Davitt was thinking in lightning strokes—the suspicion that the robber of the night before was Pruitt; the fact that this man had fled to the Buxton ranch; the possible connection between him and Buxton; the outlaw's proximity to town, as believed; the arrival of Buxton; and now Buxton and Graham in the bank after dark.

Davitt got his hat quickly.

"What is it?" the girl asked. As she made to touch Davitt's arm, she felt the hard metal of the gun snug under his left arm. She started back. "Mel . . . you don't believe . . . what is it?" Her tone was insistent.

"It's nothing," he told her calmly, "except that I'm roped and tied by . . . precaution. I'll be right back."

He hurried out the door before she could speak again. Davitt fairly ran, to the accompaniment of his whirling misgivings. He saw the light from the window of Graham's private office in the rear of the bank. Precaution, fiddlesticks! Would he never get over . . . ?

Somewhere horses were running in the darkness, their hoofbeats drumming on the wind. Davitt turned in behind the bank. A shadow moved, and his gun came out with the swiftly rippling smoothness of rustling silk. It was a tethered horse. Davitt leaped to the rear door of the bank. He tried the knob of the door and found it unlocked. He slipped in silently while a voice came to his ears weighted with fearful threat.

"Now step out there and open that vault as I say, Graham. And you, there, sit still. I'm ready to drop the two of you at the first sign of a false move. It's the old story of money or your life, gents, only this time it's two lives. Step, Graham!"

"Put up your gun first," Graham said in a heavy voice. "It makes me nervous to see it."

"I'll put it behind my back while I count three. . . ."

"Make it four, Bull. Be generous!"

The words, clearly spoken, cold and sinister, stung Pruitt into a stony stare of incredulity, looking at nothing but feeling that presence behind his back.

Graham's eyes had leaped with the fire of hope. Buxton started in his chair, his face white.

"Now keep that gun down, Pruitt, and turn around," Davitt ordered. "You're covered for keeps."

Pruitt turned slowly, his brows wriggling and twitching so that they gave to his face a hideous expression that was augmented by the red flames of anger in his eyes. He recognized Davitt.

"No man can be sure of shooting straight by lightning flashes, Pruitt," Davitt said coldly. "You emptied your gun at Lawton out in the shack and only hit him three times."

"That was enough, wasn't it?" Pruitt said with a sneer. "He was an escaped felon from Arizona, if you only knew it." He still held his gun. He would kill this man-trailer!

"No man can shoot straight with another man's gun, either," Davitt said, his gaze locked with the outlaw's. "That's why you couldn't kill the storekeeper last night with two shots. You didn't have your own gun and didn't know it. You carried away the wrong gun from the Nine Mile shack after the lightning struck. It's Lawton's gun you're holding in your hand this very minute."

Pruitt felt a chill creeping over him. It might be true— no, it couldn't be true! How did Davitt know about Lawton? The gun he held . . . ? He was not sure, and, not being sure, his supreme confidence deserted him.

"Drop it!"

Pruitt's fingers relaxed, and the weapon clattered on the floor. The sound seemed to bring him back into the world.

"Take out your gun from that drawer and cover this man, Graham."

Out of the corner of his eye, Davitt saw Graham obey in a business-like way.

"Now step on that alarm of yours and, when help gets here in a jiffy, turn him over to the sheriff. Maybe the sheriff will show him the hat he stole from Harley's store. If he makes a move, plug him. Don't take a chance. I'm not in on this, except this far. Step on that button!"

The very next moment the street rang with the clanging of the bank alarm.

Davitt stepped out the door just as two shots rang out above the clamor. He turned back to see Pruitt sinking to the floor. A wisp of smoke curled from the gun Graham held.

"He went for it," Graham creaked, his voice trembling with terror that also shone in his eyes. "Tried to get the gun!"

"And you protected your bank!" rang Davitt's voice. "Remember that!"

He was out the rear door and into the shadows, making

for the Graham house, while an uproar from the street sounded above the urgent ringing of the gong, giving its alarm for the first time in Milton.

The banker entered his home, accompanied by Sheriff Hal Drew, twenty-five minutes after Davitt had allayed Virginia's tears and soothed her nerves, following the alarm. Sylvester Graham's face was white and stern, but there was a starry look in his eyes. Virginia ran to him and threw her arms about him.

"Wait, Virginia," he said in a low voice. "Something has happened. I . . . I. . . ."

"Let's go into the study," Davitt spoke up, with a quick look at the sheriff.

They went into the study, leaving Jay and Georgia in the living room.

Davitt spoke in an aside to the sheriff while Virginia was getting her father settled in a chair. "Buxton . . . what about him?"

"He's at the hotel," the sheriff answered. "It'll be all right. He told me a little. He was supposed to see the door was unlocked so Pruitt could get in. Funny part is he didn't touch the door."

Graham looked at Davitt. "You know how it . . . ?"

"Miss Virginia," Sheriff Drew interrupted, "your dad is something of a hero. The rear door of the bank was left unlocked by mistake, and a desperado entered while Syl, here, and Buxton were talking business. Your dad pressed the alarm button, and the gong startled the outlaw out of his wits. He tried to shoot your dad, but stepped into a couple of bullets, instead. And that's all there need be to it for tonight."

The girl read the truth in her father's eyes and hugged him.

"It's a terrible thing," Graham muttered. He was still looking at Davitt.

"Before I quit the business I used to be in," Davitt drawled significantly, "I never felt very bad for putting a dangerous bandit and killer out of the running. I congratulate you, Mister Graham."

"It was the same man who robbed the store last night and shot Harley," Drew told the girl. "They tell me now that Harley's going to make the grade. But I've got to be getting back on the job."

When Drew had gone, Virginia, her father, and Davitt were alone in the study.

"I wanted Drew to get Pruitt alive and get the credit," Davitt told the banker.

"That's pretty fair of you," Graham reflected. "Since it's got around town that you're going to buy in here and settle, I suppose you know you're already being hinted of as a future sheriff."

"The very thing I don't want!" Davitt declared vehemently.

Graham looked at Virginia, whose eyes were sparkling.

"Humph," he said. "I suppose you think this . . . er . . . matter puts me in much the same position as yourself, eh?"

"Not a bit of it. I stopped outlaws for money," Davitt said.

"We've got a ranch up north a ways I was going to give my girl for a wedding present," said Graham, putting his arm about Virginia and scowling with mock severity at Davitt. "I'm still going to do that . . . when she picks her man."

"But, Daddy, I've already picked him," said Virginia, catching Mel Davitt's eye.

"It's a good ranch and well-stocked," Graham went on.

"I wouldn't object if she chose somebody who knew how to run a stock ranch profitably. I wouldn't object to a son-in-law holding public office, either. And I sure want one who knows how to keep his mouth shut when occasion requires."

"Well, this isn't one of those times," said Davitt cheerfully, his eyes dancing. "Virginia and I don't want that ranch as a gift. I'll buy it. We'd rather start off on our own, wouldn't we, sweetheart?"

Virginia laughed deliciously and went to his arms.

"What do you say, Daddy?" she asked over Davitt's shoulder.

"I say it's a danged outrage!" Sylvester Graham declared, with a genuine smile. "But"—he raised his brows—"I'll accept an offer for the property."

The Texas Hellion

Walt Coburn

Walt Coburn was born in White Sulphur Springs, Montana Territory, on October 23, 1889. He was the son of cattleman Robert Coburn, then owner of the Circle C ranch on Beaver Creek within sight of the Little Rockies. Coburn's family eventually moved to San Diego. While still operating the Circle C, Robert Coburn used to commute between California and Montana by train, and he would take his youngest son with him. When Walt got drunk one night, he had an argument with his father that led to his leaving the family. In the course of his wanderings he entered Mexico and for a brief period actually became an enlisted man in the so-called "Gringo Battalion" of Pancho Villa's army.

Following his enlistment in the U.S. Army during the Great War, Coburn thought he would try writing Western short stories. It was at this time that he came across the Western story by Robert J. Horton in *Adventure* and wrote to him. "The following week I received a lengthy letter from Bob, now living in New York, encouraging me to start writing without delay," Coburn recalled in his autobiography. "When Bob Horton was enthusiastic about anything, he was like a prairie fire backed by a forty mile wind. He said the only way to start was to get at it, borrow or steal a typewriter, buy a ream of good bond paper, a ream of second sheets, and a box of carbon paper. He enclosed the carbon copy of one of his stories he had just sold, to give me a working example. I was instructed to send him a copy of my manuscript for his criticism and blue-penciling, informing me in no uncertain terms that I was his protégé from then on, that it was the interesting letters I wrote him from the Circle C Ranch which gave him the idea of writing Western stories, and it was because of those letters and our talks in the Mint Saloon that he was now sitting on top of the world. He told me that I was a natural storyteller, and that I had a way with words, predicting in his outgoing exuberance that someday, if I could weather the storm of rejection slips, I would climb the rungs to the top of the ladder of success. It was this first letter from Robert J. Horton which launched me on the rough and rocky road as a writer of Western fiction for the pulp magazines. Something of his absolute confidence in my unproven ability as a writer, along with his buoyant enthusiasm, must have rubbed off on me because it has lasted through many years."

Coburn sold his first Western story to Bob Davis at *All-Story Magazine*, the editor who had once befriended and published the young Frederick Faust whose most familiar pseudonym, Max Brand, was born in this magazine. Coburn married and moved to Tucson because his wife suffered from a respiratory condition. In a little adobe hut behind the main house Coburn practiced his art, and for almost four decades he wrote approximately 600,000 words a year. Coburn's early fiction from his Golden Age— 1924–1940—is his best, including his novels, MAVERICKS (Century, 1929) and BARB WIRE (Century, 1931), as well as many short novels published only in magazines that now are being collected for the first time. COFFIN RANCH: A WESTERN TRIO (Five Star Westerns, 1998) and THE SECRET OF CRUTCHER'S CABIN: A WESTERN TRIO (Five Star Westerns, 1999) are the first of these collections. Many of Coburn's short novels served as the basis for motion pictures, especially in the series Tim McCoy made for Columbia Pictures in the early 1930s, but I think the best film derived from his work is THE DESERT OF THE LOST (Pathé, 1927) [based on "The Survival of Slim" in *Western Story Magazine* (5/3/24)]. There is a good deal more about Coburn's life to be found in my Foreword to COFFIN RANCH, and so I shall not repeat it here. In his best Western stories, as Charles M. Russell and Eugene Manlove Rhodes, two men Coburn had known and admired in life, he captured the cow country and recreated it just as it was already passing from sight. He died on May 24, 1971, survived by his beloved wife, "Pat," as he called her, who had been the model for so many of his heroines, including Nadia La Motte in the short novel that follows. It is a story from the period of his Golden Age, first appearing in *Action Stories* in the issue dated July, 1931. It was later reprinted under the title "Two-Gun Lobo" in *Action Stories* (2/39).

I

"Shotgun Sam"

Four men sat at a card table near the end of the bar in Shotgun Sam's place. All four of these men bore the indelible stamp of cowmen. All four of them were armed. A bottle of whisky stood on the table, and there was a single glass in front of each man. A deck of cards lay scattered on the floor, unheeded—because it was a bigger game than poker that brought these four men together at Shotgun Sam's place. They had been talking nearly all night. They still talked in low tones.

Now and then Shotgun Sam, big of frame with the neck and shoulders and chest of a wrestler, stood over them, sharing their talk. But mostly he stood in the doorway of his log saloon on the bank of the Missouri, his pale, bloodshot eyes peering into the moonlit night, his ears alert for any sound that might betray the presence of eavesdroppers. His shotgun, a sawed-off ten-gauge weapon, was never far from his hairy paw.

Under the twenty-foot bank the muddy river whispered and muttered its secrets. Sometimes the big saloonman seemed to listen to the sound of the river, as if he understood its voice. Perhaps he did, for he had lived here, winter and summer, for many years, and during those years many things had happened at the log saloon just below the gravel crossing. Many sinister things were chalked up by decent men against the name of Shotgun Sam. Unproven things, for the big saloonman bore the name of being wise in the ways of covering crime. His log walls never talked. The muttering of the muddy river could not be translated. The man himself was as tight-mouthed as a wooden image.

The four men inside were cowmen from the head of the badlands. Pete La Motte, owner of the Lazy-K iron, sat nearest the door—a short, swarthy, wiry man with restless little black eyes and hands that never remained still. Pete La Motte had done time in prison for being mixed up with horse thieves, but had somehow been pardoned. A bad enemy, Pete La Motte, and not so trustworthy as a friend. Tricky, dangerous, merciless.

The tall man with the drooping gray mustache was Ed Roper, Pete's neighbor on the east side of Snake Creek. Roper branded Bench-T, and was rated as one of the best cowmen in the badlands. He rode top horses and wasted few loops. A slow-tempered, deliberate man with cold blue eyes. He had killed two men here at Shotgun Sam's and had come off clear at his trial.

The heavy 'puncher, a red-faced man who seldom spoke, was Fat McKee. He ran cattle down on the river between Snake Creek and The Narrows. Fat McKee, for all his surplus weight, was a fast man with a rope or gun and had once ridden the Outlaw Trail, so it was claimed.

On McKee's left sat his partner, Tom Sellers. Sellers was a raw-boned man with a freckled, sun-reddened hide and a wide grin that showed enormous teeth stained yellow from tobacco. Sellers talked a lot but seldom said anything of value. He laughed too often with his mouth. But never once did his gray eyes smile. By far the most dangerous man of the four, Tom Sellers. He had been known to shoot a man in the belly and laugh while the man died there on the floor of Shotgun Sam's saloon. He was rated as the best rough and tumble fighter along the river, was a slick hand with a wet sack and hot branding iron, and spent his odd moments figuring out new methods of changing brands on other cow-men's stock.

Sellers and Fat McKee owned half a dozen brands. While their outfit was not a large one and they were not big land owners, yet they ran cattle in each of these half-dozen irons. Tom Sellers had been arrested some years ago in Utah as being a member of a gang of outlaws who rode through the Southwest like a whirlwind, robbing trains and banks. But the law had lacked proof, and Tom Sellers had been turned loose.

Such was the nature of the four men who had spent nearly all night drinking raw whisky and talking at Shotgun Sam's place, while the big saloonman stood guard, his shotgun ready, his ears listening to the endless muttering and chuckling of the muddy water that hid so many black secrets.

Now the big saloonkeeper stiffened. He stepped outside and into the black shadow of the log wall, his shotgun ready. As he quit the lighted doorway, he called something over his shoulder to the four cowmen. Sellers kicked the door shut. There was no window in the place. As if by some prear-ranged signal, each of the four men stood at a different part of the room. Thus, anyone entering could not possibly cover all four at one time. Pete La Motte turned the lamp low.

From outside came the thud of a horse's hoofs. A rider dismounted and boldly opened the heavy plank door. As he stepped inside, blinking in the dim lamplight, the saloonman's shotgun prodded him in the small of the back. Each of the four occupants of the saloon held a six-shooter in his hand. Pete La Motte turned up the light with his left hand. All of them eyed the newcomer with narrowed gaze.

When Sam's shotgun poked him in the back, the man in the doorway raised his hands. The four saw a tall, well-made cowboy in faded overalls and jumper. His hat was old, his boots rusty, and his square-cut, blunt-featured face needed a shave. Despite the menacing guns, the newcomer managed a crooked grin. He did not flinch under their ugly scrutiny.

"What's your brand, stranger?" grinned Tom Sellers. "Who might yuh be and what kind uh business fetches yuh here at this time uh night?"

"I bin ridin' out some broncs for the Long-X. Finished up with 'em and headed this way to buy me a bottle and hunt me a new job on the south side uh the river. My name is Bob Lake, if I need a name here."

"How come yuh ride at night?" growled the lanky Ed Roper.

"I reckon I must've got tuh smellin' likker, so I kep' on. My horse and pack horse was fresh, so I just kep' a-comin'. Stopped fer supper at a 'breed camp, and they told me which trail would fetch me here. That is about the size of 'er, I guess. I'm a stranger in a strange land. I'd be proud tuh buy yuh all a drink."

The four men exchanged glances. Their guns went back into their holsters. Shotgun Sam lowered his weapon.

Bob Lake dropped his arms, and they stepped to the bar. Shotgun Sam set out bottle and glasses.

As hoofs sounded outside, the four men and the saloonkeeper gripped their guns. Bob Lake chuckled as he filled his glass.

"That'll be Cotton, my pack horse, ketchin' up. He found some grass a ways back an' stopped tuh graze a spell."

Pete La Motte stepped to the door, peered outside, then nodded his black head. "She's right about dat. Jus' de pack horse."

They stood at the bar, two men on each side of the stranger. They eyed him coldly, suspiciously.

"We was havin' a little private powwow, mister," said the ever-grinning Tom Sellers. "We ain't invited no outsiders."

"If I'd uh knowed that," said Bob Lake, "I shore wouldn't uh horned in. But I had me a thirst, and I knowed there was a saloon here. I figgered, naturally, that it was open to one and all as had a dry tongue. I'm sorry I got you boys all kinda stirred up this-a-way. I'll buy me a bottle an' drift along."

Again the four men and the saloonkeeper traded quick glances.

'Now that yo're here, feller," said Shotgun Sam, "yuh might as well stay. Have another. Best whisky along the Missouri River. Best in this part uh Montana. It's shore enough fightin' likker. This is cowpuncher likker yo're drinkin'. Got another brand fer the Injun an' the 'breed trade. Drink hearty, gents."

They took several more drinks. Bob Lake, growing a little talkative, seemed to be the only one of them affected by the stuff, despite the fact that the four cowmen and Sam had emptied several bottles during the course of the night. The newcomer's face took on a reddish flush. His tongue became more loose, his words a trifle blurred. The others watched him covertly.

Now Bob Lake asked if he could put his horses in the barn. Shotgun Sam helped him unload his pack. He jerked the saddle from a gelding that, so far as the saloonman could tell, wore no brand. Nor did the white pack horse have a brand.

"Likely lookin' private horses yuh own, stranger."

Bob Lake chuckled and winked. "They're as good as I could locate. Listen, mister, I was told a man could talk a little here and his words never got no fu'ther. Where I got them geldin's is nobody's affair. They come from a long ways from here, I kin tell yuh that. I don't know them four gents in yore place. Don't give a damn who they might be, yuh savvy? I dropped by here fer a bottle. Mebby a jug. Anyhow, I was told by a certain feller down in New Mexico that a feller here in Montana named Shotgun Sam, a feller who had a place on the river, was a man I could trust. The gent that told me this lives in the rough hills uh New Mexico."

The eyes of the two men met.

"And what would be the name uh this feller?"

"He said you'd know the name of Reb Waller."

"What else did he say?"

"He said that you'd know the name of a creek called Sand Creek. And that you'd recollect uh place called La Paz." Bob Lake threw another forkful of hay to his saddle horse.

"What else would I be knowin' besides La Paz an' Sand Creek?"

"You'd know where there's a pile uh boulders. The name uh the man whose bones is under them boulders was Jess Stroud."

"Correct as hell," admitted Shotgun Sam. "What's Reb a-doin'?"

"Reb," said Bob Lake, "is a-kickin' hot clods now. He was shot about a month ago by a gover'ment detective. I bin aimin' to git here before this, but I bin afraid I was watched. I done made Bob a promise a long time back that, if he was tuh run into bad luck, I'd fetch yuh this. He said he was owin' it to yuh."

In the light of a smoky lantern Bob Lake handed Shotgun Sam a budging wallet. The big saloonman opened it. The banknotes inside were all of large denomination. One corner of the wallet was mutilated, the corner gone. The banknotes were likewise marred. The wallet itself was darkly stained.

"The bullet that took Reb Waller," said Bob Lake, "hit the wallet which he packed pinned to his undershirt."

"How did you git a-holt of it?"

"I was with Reb Waller," said Bob Lake simply, "when he died."

II

"The scarlet warning"

Back inside the saloon, Shotgun Sam's manner was changed toward Bob Lake to a marked degree. The saloonman called the four cowmen aside and conversed with them in low tones. He showed them the wallet and the money inside it. The four men looked from Sam to the now tipsy cowpuncher who leaned heavily against the crude pine bar, a slight grin on his bronzed face. The four nodded—came up and shook hands with the stranger from New Mexico. The saloonman introduced them.

"Yore money is wooden from now on," Shotgun Sam told Bob Lake. "Yo're all right. So is these boys. Whatever yuh say never gits repeated."

"Tell us how ol' Reb got 'em," said big Ed Roper.

"Me and Reb was camped in the Burro Mountains," said Bob Lake, lowering his voice. "We was butcherin' a fat yearlin' when a shot sounds acrost the cañon. I got my horse saddled, so I leaves Reb there an' takes a *pasear* aroun' the head uh the cañon to see who's shootin'. Mebbyso, thinks I, it's some dude hunter in there after deer. I'm about a quarter of a mile from camp when I hears shootin'. I high-tails 'er back as fast as my pony kin kick gravel. Finds pore ol' Reb layin' in behind the half-skinned carcass uh the yearlin', swappin' shots with a feller up under a rimrock. I comes an Apache on this gent and takes the deal. When I'm done shootin', I lopes on down tuh see how Reb is feelin'. He's dyin' hard. I takes the wallet an' pulls out fer Montana like he wants me to do. But they foller me some, and it takes a long time tuh git here. That's how come I git here at night. Figgerin' I'll find Sam alone, I rides in. That about tells the tale. There's what Reb Waller told me tuh fetch up here. It's there . . . to the last yallerbacked bill. And I reckon yuh know from where the yallerbacks come. How about another drink, gents? I bin dry a long time."

"I'll tell a man we'll heist another," chuckled Shotgun Sam. "All you kin hold, Bob."

Bob Lake got drunk before sunrise. They led him, staggering, half asleep, to his tarp-covered bedroll, and before they got his boots off he was snoring heavily. Deftly, expertly, Pete La Motte went through the pockets of the unconscious man. Together the four cowmen and the saloonkeeper examined what they found there.

There was a check from the Long-X outfit, cards of saloons and hotels patronized by men of uncertain identity, some loose banknotes crumpled in a wad and bearing serial numbers that corresponded with a list kept by Shotgun Sam. A jackknife, odds and ends of trivial importance. The five men again lined the bar inside the log saloon. They drank in silence.

"He's the man we need," said the lanky Ed Roper. "He's all right."

"Fits the bill," nodded Fat McKee. "He ain't used tuh drinkin' Sam's pizen. Or, mebbyso, Sam put a drop or two uh somethin' in his glass."

"She's de man," agreed Pete La Motte. "Me, I'm look hindside de shirt. In de shoulder in de fresh scar from de bullet. She'll do, hall right."

"We need him," grinned Tom Sellers. "But if he's what we think he is, he'll want top wages. Which we kin shore pay if he kin deliver the goods. We don't want no more mistakes like that Texas gent."

At the mention of the Texas gent, the eyes of all the men looked instinctively toward a dark stain on the floor near the table. The plank floor there had been covered with dirt and the dirt rubbed into the wood by boot soles. But there still remained the sign of where a man had lain, bleeding profusely.

"We should've got 'im outside," complained Shotgun Sam. "That'll show there for a week. You didn't need to shoot him in here, Tom."

"Aw, hell. A man can't pick his spots, always. The play come up in here. That ends it."

"I seen the Bob Lake gent lookin' at it," muttered Fat McKee.

"I reckon it didn't turn his stomach none. It looks like we'd spilled somethin' there, that's all. Sam poured a quart uh Injun whisky over the place. What the hell! Give us another shot uh the red-eye, Sam. I always git thirsty after I pull a gun trigger." Tom Sellers laughed harshly as he reached for the bottle.

"Texas is a long ways down in the muddy ol' river," said Shotgun Sam. "Ner he ain't the first sneakin' detective tuh be fattenin' the catfish, neither. I was leery uh him from the start. I had him all sized up. Didn't I tell yuh as much six months ago?"

"What he learned," growled Ed Roper, "he never got a chance tuh tell. We never let him git outta sight."

"But just the same," said Tom Sellers, "he wasn't workin' alone. He has a pardner somewheres. He might've had some way uh passin' news. Them gover'ment dicks is slick articles."

"Texas might've bin slick," grunted Fat McKee, "but not slick enough tuh keep his ticket tuh hell from bein' punched. Gittin' daylight. We better be hittin' the trail. Who's gonna proposition this Bob Lake feller?"

"Sam kin handle that," said Ed Roper. "Us boys better be slidin' along. Sound him out, Sam."

"We'll pay him what he's worth," grinned Tom Sellers. "In money or in hot bullets."

As they passed the tarp-covered bed, Bob Lake lay on his back, his mouth open, snoring heavily. But his right hand stubbornly gripped the butt of a Colt .45.

"He's all right," chuckled Shotgun Sam. "Hangs onto his ol' equalizer like he was brung up with it. With the slug I slipped him in his likker, he'll sleep for some time. So long, boys. I'll proposition Bob Lake, and I bet he makes a top hand."

"He'd better," grinned Tom Sellers. "Otherwise them catfish git a heap fatter. There wasn't a hell of a lot uh meat on Texas."

III

"Killer's wages"

A crimson dawn was streaking the sky above the badlands behind the river. A little breeze rustled the green leaves of the giant cottonwoods along the bank. Bob Lake opened his eyes, blinked hard in a futile effort to rid himself of a headache, then lay there motionless. About thirty feet away, sitting on the high bank above the river, was Shotgun Sam, a thick-necked, hulking figure that stared unblinkingly down at the swirling muddy water, the water that hid the body of a man they had called Texas. Texas was a government detective whose game had been discovered and whose life had been taken as forfeit for his carelessness.

Bob Lake slid his gun into its holster and reached for his boots. The big saloonman turned his head at his visitor's first movement, as if some animal instinct warned him. The shotgun across the big man's knees seemed to cover the cowboy. A wide grin spread across the face of Shotgun Sam.

"How yuh feel, stranger?"

Bob Lake made a wry face. "Feel like hell. Must've bin dynamite in that bottle."

"She's potent," admitted the whisky peddler. "Takes a real man tuh stand up under 'er. Git yore boots on an' we'll heist an eye opener. Some uh the hair uh the dawg that chawed yuh. I was just goin' out in the skiff tuh have a look at my trot-lines. Like catfish?"

A queer smile twitched at one corner of Bob Lake's straight mouth. "I ain't much of a hand for fish. Beef or sow-belly is good enough for me."

"Same with me. Fish is all right fer Swedes." The big saloonkeeper chuckled. Shotgun Sam's catfish jokes were a river tradition. No man who knew the man by reputation ever ate catfish at his place, and he enjoyed his own grisly jokes.

Bob Lake had slept fully clothed save for his hat and boots. As he accompanied Shotgun Sam to the log saloon, the cowpuncher made a quiet discovery concerning which he spoke no word to his host. A man forms the habit of carrying certain articles in certain pockets. His jackknife in a right hip pocket, perhaps, or a shirt pocket, loose change and currency in another pocket, and so on. In frisking him, Pete La Motte had been a little careless in replacing things in their proper pockets. Bob Lake knew that they had searched him, but he said nothing.

Shotgun Sam set out a bottle and two glasses. Bob Lake rubbed his hand across an aching forehead, the gesture bringing a deep chuckle from the other.

"Yuh ain't in trainin', that's all, young feller. I bin drinkin' a quart a day fer forty years, and I ain't bin sick a day. If you kin hold down two, three good slugs uh this, yuh'll feel like a daisy in bloom."

Bob Lake acted upon his advice. After the third drink he felt a lot better.

Although he lived on the riverbank, the saloonman got his water from a well behind the cabin where he lived. Bob Lake soused his head and face in the cold water, while Shotgun Sam was getting breakfast in the cabin behind the saloon. Then Bob Lake went to the barn to care for his horses.

There was one other horse in the barn—a big bay gelding branded Bench-T. From the saddle marks Bob Lake judged that the horse had been ridden hard yesterday. He watered and grained the bay horse and his own two. In a space used to put saddles, Bob Lake paused briefly to examine a saddle, a double-rigged kak bearing the trademark of the Arizona Sadlery Company at Prescott, a fully stamped job, service-worn. Across the cantle was an old scar, deep into the leather, about six inches long.

As footsteps sounded outside, Bob Lake dropped the Navajo saddle blanket over the hull, but not before the bloodshot eyes of Shotgun Sam had seen the movement. For an instant the big saloonman's face wore an ugly expression. Then it was gone again, and the man was grinning amiably.

Bob Lake touched the saddle with his boot toe. "I'm always lookin' for a trade. That hull uh mine is a three-quarter rig I swapped for just tuh try one out. I'm used to a double rig, and I can't never git set right on a single-rigged kak. Yuh wouldn't care about snakin' some kind of a swap, would yuh, Sam?"

"Mebby. Mebby not. The hull ain't what yuh might call mine. A feller owed me some money an' left the saddle here in hock. He ain't never showed up tuh claim it. If he don't claim 'er in a week or two, we might make a dicker uh some kind. Grub's ready."

They walked together back to the saloon where they took a drink, then went on to the cabin where they ate a breakfast of flapjacks and steak and fried spuds and strong black coffee. The cabin was neither clean nor dirty, a one-room abode that served as kitchen and sleeping quarters. On one wall was a gun rack that held half a dozen carbines and rifles. Several six-shooters hung in holsters, filled cartridge belts looped over a wooden peg driven in the wall.

"Fellers leave 'em in hock," explained Shotgun Sam, noticing Bob Lake's glance. "A drinkin' man will swap almost anything he owns when he needs whisky. The trappers pay in cordwood an' do my hayin' and pay up my ice in winter. Now an' then a good yearlin' colt gits into my hoss pasture or I find a heifer among my cattle. Not much cash trade, excep' when boys like Reb Waller sends me a little present or comes past in a hurry needin' a fresh hoss and a lift acrost the river. That dinky ferry uh mine makes me two bits now an' then. High water when no man or hoss livin' kin cross, I git mebby a leetle trade. Some gents in a rush, mebby, with the law close behind. . . ."

He looked at Bob Lake with that crooked grin on his face. "Funny thing about that ferry boat," he went on. "Seems like by the time the law gits here, there'll be a busted cable or somethin' that'll take two, three days tuh fix. Take the time Reb Waller an' two more boys crossed after somebody . . . I never knowed who . . . had stuck up the Chinook Bank. They had me ferry 'em acrost. I no sooner git back than the pulley busted. River runnin' bank high. Had tuh send plumb to Chinook fer a new pulley wheel. It took a week, while that posse set here on their hocks madder'n hell. But cussin' me out never fixed things. Nope. That pulley didn't git here for a week. By that time Reb Waller was plumb outta the country.

"That fool sheriff was so ringy he tried tuh accuse me uh feedin' 'em stolen beef. Wanted tuh see the hide. I took him on foot about two, three miles to some old weanin' sheds I don't use no more. He was wearin' new boots that was too tight for him . . . an' I showed him strips uh fresh rawhide I used tuh wrap the corral poles an' fasten the stringers to the shed posts. More strips laid acrost the willers I'd laid on fer a roof. Rawhide bein' plumb cheap and there bein' no barb wire tuh fasten things with, I'd used that beef hide. 'There's yore hide, Sheriff,' says I, pleasant as hell. 'The whole blessed hide, cut in strips. If yo're handy at puzzles, you might patch 'er together while we're waitin' fer that new pulley wheel. But what yuh take off that shed yuh gotta put back, accordin' tuh law.' "

Shotgun Sam laughed heartily. He went on, chuckling to himself: "Was that law man mad? His feet all swole up raw with blisters. An' nary a thing he could do about it. The hide was there. Then, on top of that, the whisky didn't agree with any uh the posse. They laid aroun' sick fer two, three days. We run outta beef, an' they wouldn't eat catfish because uh some reason or other. I made 'em pay top price fer the steer they butchered. They had their own chuck wagon but hadn't fetched enough grub. I let 'em have a sack of flour fer twenty-five dollars cash. Beans fifty cents a pound, sugar a dollar a pound. Nothin' but cash money. Well, sir, that dude-dressin' sheriff got so's he'd hardly speak to me. They finally pulled out when the new pulley wheel busted after I had taken half of 'em acrost. That sheriff never comes here no more. He must be mad at me fer some reason."

Bob Lake and Shotgun Sam pitched horseshoes and shot at a mark and sat around in the shade and whittled. Now and then they went inside and lifted a drink. The saloonman had sprinkled the saloon floor with water and swept up. He used a shovel for a dust pan and dumped the litter of dirt and cards, some of them bloodstained, into the big sheet-iron stove. And then he shoved in some old papers and set a match to the rubbish. The plank floor still wore an ugly stain, but neither man commented on it.

Shotgun Sam was an entertaining host with a fund of anecdotes that invariably poked fun at the law and the men paid to enforce it. Several times he had Bob Lake re-tell the shooting of Reb Waller. And gradually, subtly, the big saloonman broached his subject.

"Yuh seen them fellers that was here last night, Bob? Well, they own most uh the country around here. Run a pool outfit and he'p one another out. Neighborly as hell, them gents. They pay top wages and stand behind their men. If a young, close-mouthed feller like you was tuh be lucky enough tuh th'ow in with them, he'd be makin' real money."

And some time later: "Bob, I heard Ed Roper sayin' not more'n a week ago that they needed a good man. Sorta general manager. I bet you could hold down the job. A man that's trailed with Reb Waller has tuh have the stuff in him."

"I was aimin' tuh drift on south, Sam, before winter. I don't know the range here good enough tuh be much good to 'em."

"The range ain't hard tuh learn. She's rough, but yo're used to a rough country. The cattle ain't as wild, I don't reckon, as them yuh follered in New Mexico and Arizona. Then, when yuh got better acquainted with them fellers, there might be other leetle ways uh pickin' up a few dollars uh real money. Think 'er over. Hang aroun' here a week or so. When one uh them fellers shows up, which they does every few days, I'll put in a good word fer yuh. A friend uh ol' Reb's is a friend uh mine."

"I'll think 'er over, Sam. But I'd hate tuh tackle a job I can't hold down."

Toward evening of that same day they had some visitors, several unshaved, cold-eyed cowpunchers who stopped for an hour or so, had several drinks, then rode on. They were men who worked for Fat McKee and Tom Sellers. Bob Lake made no effort to get acquainted. Beyond including him in their drinks, they paid him little attention, although they looked him over whenever they thought he was not watching. Later, when they pulling out, Shotgun Sam went outside with them. Bob Lake stayed behind in the saloon.

The saloonman and the cowpunchers walked together to the corral where they had left their horses. Bob Lake watched them until they were at the corral. Then he stepped to the stove, opened the door, and with his bare hand dug into the cold ashes inside the stove. For some minutes he pawed the ashes. Then his hand came out. In his fingers was a fire-scorched metal badge. Bob Lake wiped it off and examined it. Then he put it in his pocket, closed the stove door, wiped his hands clean, and poured himself a drink, just as the saloonman reëntered. He filled the glass Shotgun Sam had been using.

"I was about tuh take me a shot. A few drinks uh this booze shore calls fer more." His tone was casual, his grin easy, but his eyes held a steely glitter.

Shotgun Sam said nothing, just nodded and reached for his drink. They drank, then the big man went in behind the bar and began washing the glasses left by the recent customers. Bob Lake strolled idly to the door, then stepped outside, whistling. He reached for tobacco and papers and was rolling his cigarette when he made an uncomfortable discovery. Along his shirt sleeve was a sooty, black smudge. Had Shotgun Sam noticed?

IV

"High stakes"

Shotgun Sam, if he had noticed the telltale smudge on Bob Lake's shirt sleeve, gave the cowpuncher no hint by word or gesture. Yet Bob Lake felt that the big saloonman had seen and that he was under suspicion. Bob Lake was playing a dangerous game, as dangerous and bold a game as a man could ask for. A single blunder and his fate would be that of Texas whose blood stained the floor under the poker table. Texas had blundered, even as other government men had blundered; and, like those others, Texas had paid the extreme penalty. Texas had been working under Bob Lake's orders. Now Texas was dead. Bob Lake might be in that same watery grave before another sunrise.

Bob Lake had not lied when he told Shotgun Sam that he had been with Reb Waller when that quick-triggered gentleman had died with his boots on. A bullet from Bob Lake's gun had ended the career of that cold-blooded killer who rode the Outlaw Trail. Bob Lake's left breast bore the freshly healed scar that had nearly ended his career as a government detective. He and Reb Weller had shot it out in the rough mountains of New Mexico. Reb Waller had died there, and by the same blue-barreled gun Reb's partner had died.

Bob Lake was not the name of the government man now enjoying the dangerous hospitality of Shotgun Sam. Bob Lake was the name of Reb Waller's partner who had died in New Mexico. The government man, taking a dangerous chance thrown his way by the hand of fate, had assumed the identity of Reb Waller's dead partner. Gambling on the chance that Bob Lake was not known north of New Mexico, this government man, a man of many aliases, had changed identities with the dead outlaw. By certain clever maneuvering on the part of his chief and the law, the public was given the news that Reb Waller was dead. That a certain government detective had sacrificed his life in an effort to capture Reb Waller and Bob Lake, that Bob Lake, although wounded, had made his escape. There was now a thousand dollars reward offered for Bob Lake, dead or alive. Because fate had further served the scheme of the government detective—inasmuch as the same general description fitted both the dead Bob Lake and the man now using the identity of the dead outlaw—this pseudo-Bob Lake had so far passed the scrutiny of the renegade riders of the Outlaw Trail. So far, so good. But in this game, played for high stakes against tremendous odds, to lose meant death. To win meant something greater than even the chief of the government service suspected. For behind his dangerous game lay a reason, a reason that no one save this gritty government man knew about. Glory, money, praise, all were insignificant compared to the secret reason that had fetched this man who called himself Bob Lake up the Outlaw Trail to the log saloon on the bank of the Missouri River in Montana.

Bob Lake regretted the passing of Texas. Texas had been a good man—game, fearless, but not quite smart enough. A man needed much courage and a keen brain when he pitted his gun against the guns of those four cowmen and the big saloonman who was their real chief.

That sooty mark was still on Bob Lake's shirt sleeve when he came back into the saloon. Now, as he again stood at the bar, he openly rubbed the black mark to some semblance of obliteration. He swore softly at the soiled cloth.

"Put 'er on clean this mornin'. Dunno how come I . . . shucks, I recollect now. Got 'er off the stove when I started tuh burn this, then changed my mind. Them fellers here kinda got me uneasy. And with this damned thing in my pocket . . . !"

He handed over a folded square of paper, a little charred along the edges. Shotgun Sam unfolded it and read the printed words that offered a thousand dollars, dead or alive, for Bob Lake. Below it was the description of the man. Six feet tall, weight one hundred and eighty pounds, gray eyes, clean-shaven, quiet of manner. Weakness for whisky and gambling. A fast cowboy in any country and quick to use a gun. Bore the reputation of being a hard fighter and had killed several men. Officers were warned to take no chances with him. Was wanted for the killing of a United States government peace officer.

Shotgun Sam looked from the reward notice and into

Bob Lake's steady gray eyes.

"I was startin' tuh burn the thing when I seen 'em ride off," explained the cold-nerved detective. "They hadn't acted none too friendly, and I was scared they might be framin' me tuh git the thousand bucks reward on me. A man in my fix has got to be careful." He took the notice from the saloonman, touched a match to it, and, opening the stove door, shoved it inside. Then he walked to the bar. Shotgun Sam was grinning widely.

"Yuh'll have tuh wash that shirt yet, feller. Got 'er shore smeared black."

Bob Lake looked at the fresh smudge. "Don't that beat hell!"

Shotgun Sam nodded. "Don't it, though?"

Bob Lake, looking into the bloodshot eyes of the saloonman, found them cold, questioning, a trifle suspicious. Or was it that the nerves of the detective were pulled a little taut and his imagination was playing him tricks?

There was still time for Bob Lake to pull out of the game he was playing. He could shoot it out with this saloonman, kill this big murderer who surely needed killing, and ride away. But that was not the way of the man who went under the name of Bob Lake, although Shotgun Sam's next words sent a cold shiver along the detective's spine.

"Fat McKee an' Tom Sellers is due back here tonight, so the boys was a-telling me. Mebbyso Pete La Motte an' Ed Roper will be with 'em. Likewise an old friend uh yourn. Leastwise, when the boys told him there was a gent named Bob Lake here, he said he knowed yuh from down along the border."

"What's his name?" Bob Lake made his voice sound casual.

"Joe Robbins."

"Joe Robbins," repeated Bob Lake, his eyes narrowing. "I know him. Let's tilt that bottle once more, Sam."

The name of Joe Robbins, gunman and outlaw, was like pronouncing the detective's death warrant. Joe Robbins, former member of the Reb Waller gang, had once worn a pair of handcuffs belonging to this government man. Robbins was a man who had done most of his killing from the brush, a loud-mouthed, tobacco-spitting bushwhacker who had, on two occasions, saved his own unclean hide by squealing on better men. A double-dealing, treacherous snake, this Joe Robbins. Along the Outlaw Trail were a few real men who would be glad to kill this squealer.

"Friend uh yourn, Bob?"

The detective smiled thinly. His eyes met Shotgun Sam's questioning stare. He lifted his glass. "Here's lookin' at yuh, Sam."

"Happy days, Bob."

The two men ate supper and washed the dishes. Shotgun Sam asked Bob Lake no further questions. Bob Lake gave him no kind of information regarding Joe Robbins. But the saloonman, after Bob Lake's second refusal to drink, did not again invite him to the bottle. Shotgun Sam drew his own conclusion.

The two men were sitting in the saloon when Fat McKee and Tom Sellers, followed by two more men, came in the door. One of these men, a loud-voiced, swaggering fellow in greasy overalls and jumper, quit talking at the sight of the detective who sprang to his feet.

Bob Lake kicked his chair backward. "Yuh double-crossin', split-tongued snake!" he spat at Joe Robbins. "Fill yore hand!"

They drew at the same time. Fat McKee and Tom Sellers

and the other man sprang aside. Now the two guns roared. Bob Lake's gun spat flame with the rapidity of a machine gun. Joe Robbins, his jaw sagging, his rat-like eyes slitted, sagged heavily to the floor. Bob Lake leaped across toward him, smoking gun in his hand.

Joe Robbins lay on his face, and the man who had killed him knelt quickly on one knee, turning the limp, bullet-torn frame over on its back. The detective's hand tore away the bloody shirt. There was a ripping sound, and Bob Lake faced the drawn guns of the other men. Shoving his own gun back in its holster, he walked to the bar and tossed a bloody bit of metal toward Shotgun Sam.

"Look at that, Sam. That's the kind of a snake yore Joe Robbins was. If I killed a friend uh yourn, I'm regretful. But Joe Robbins is the dirty skunk that turned in two, three good men to the law. I kin name yuh half a dozen boys that has swore tuh kill him on sight. Yuh asked me was Joe Robbins a friend uh mine. There's yore answer, Sam."

Shotgun Sam looked at the bloody badge on the bar. He grinned crookedly at Fat McKee and Tom Sellers.

"Looks like Bob Lake done called the Robbins feller's hand, boys. Didn't he know you was wise to him, Bob?"

"I reckon not. Or else he aimed tuh lie out of it some way." He grinned at the saloonman. "I'll lap up a big 'un with yuh now, Sam. Call the boys up." Sam smiled his approval.

"You shore work fast," said Tom Sellers, his big teeth showing. "Never give Robbins time tuh say good evenin'."

"I give him an even break fer his gun," said the detective. "That is a damned sight better chance than he give three, four men I kin name."

"It was as clean an' neat a play as a man could ask fer," said the saloonman. "Bob shot three times to his one that went wild. It was shore purty."

"I hope," said Bob Lake, his glass in his left hand, "that none of you boys won't be takin' up his fight where he left off."

"Not me, podner," chuckled Tom Sellers.

"Ner me," grunted Fat McKee, visibly impressed by Bob Lake's skill with a six-shooter.

"And how about you?" Bob Lake asked the cowpuncher with them.

"I got troubles enough without takin' up another man's fight," said the cowboy quickly.

"Then we down our drinks and git rid uh that skunk's carcass," suggested Shotgun Sam. "He's gittin' my clean floor all messed up."

V

"Marked to die"

Before midnight that night Bob Lake hired out to Fat McKee and Tom Sellers.

"Yo're a-workin' fer Pete La Motte an' Ed Roper, to boot," the grinning Tom Sellers told him. "We're what's called the Hell Crick Pool. Play the game right and yuh'll wear diamonds. Play 'er wrong and yuh'll have some awful bad luck."

There, near the door, was the ugly stain where Joe Robbins had bled. A close call, that, for the man who called himself Bob Lake. In another second Robbins would have denounced him as a government man. The badge he had supposedly ripped from the dead man's undershirt was his own badge. It lay on the back-bar, where Sam had put it.

Now he was hired by the sinister Hell Creek Pool. He was now one of this dangerous, law-breaking gang who rode the badlands on both sides of the Missouri River. Upholding the reputation of the dead man he was impersonating, Bob Lake got drunk again that night. But this night there were no knockout drops in his glass. Just Shotgun Sam's barrel whisky that was powerful enough for any hard-drinking man. Bob Lake's stomach revolted at the stuff. A mild drinker, he was suffering with nausea, but he kept on drinking, when the others drank, until his head was spinning like a top and his tongue was thick. Several times he stepped outside the smoke-filled saloon for fresh air. It required all his will power to keep any sort of control over his faculties.

Yet, save for that slight thickness of speech, he showed no outward sign of being intoxicated. His eyes were clear, his legs steady, his hands did not fumble when they picked up his glass. Nor did he become talkative or quarrelsome or maudlin. He felt that they were putting him to a sort of test. Men who babble in their cups cannot be trusted with secrets. And a man who worked for the Hell Creek Pool must keep a silent tongue behind his teeth.

About midnight Fat McKee suggested that it was time they got going. Bob Lake made as if to go with them.

"Fer the present," said Fat McKee, "you stay here, Lake. Sam will kinda put yuh onto things a little."

When they had gone, Shotgun Sam grinned crookedly at Bob Lake.

"Well, yo're hired, feller. That gun play clinched 'er. I never did trust that Robbins cuss. Well, he's gone now. Hope no more fool detectives git killed here. Gives my place a hard name. But them things can't be he'ped.

There's another gover'ment man somewheres in the country. The news come up last night, so Tom Sellers told me. This feller is supposed tuh be shore enough slick and a tough 'un tuh kill. Goes by any name he might think sounded good. He lived all one winter in Wyoming under the name of Les Lawler. Ever hear tell uh him?"

Bob Lake nodded. "I've heard uh him, Sam. Few men I talked to ever met him to know him. They tell a lot uh yarns about how bad he is, but I dunno how true they are. How'd the news git around that this Les Lawler was in the country?"

Shotgun Sam shrugged his hulking shoulders. "Hard tuh say. Them things travels with the rustlin' uh the leaves. Yuh wouldn't know this Les Lawler feller if you was tuh meet him, would yuh?"

"I dunno, Sam. I never knowed him to talk to. Never met him tuh git a look at him. Why?"

"Well, yore first job with the Hell Crick Pool is tuh locate this Les Lawler and kill him where yuh find him."

Bob Lake smiled twistedly. "They shore put a man tuh work right smart, don't they? How do they figger I'll know this feller, anyhow?"

Shotgun Sam winked. "Yuh might as well know 'er now, mister. I'm the head uh the Hell Crick Pool. They take their orders from me. It is me that put yuh on tonight. It's me that is tellin' you to hunt down this Les Lawler detective. Tomorrow you pull out. I'll take yuh across the river on the ferry. Back in the badlands along Hell Crick yuh'll find two fellers camped. They're holdin' a bunch uh cattle in there. One uh these gents claims he knows this Les Lawler plenty well because he was arrested once in Oklahoma by this dick. You stay with them two boys tomorrow night. This one gent will give yuh a good description uh the man yo're after.

Then you come back here an' we'll see how's the best way tuh hunt him. Better turn in now an' git some shut-eye."

They had a last drink together. With a grisly chuckle the saloonkeeper tossed the bloodstained badge on the pine board bar.

"Little souvenir. Fetch back this Les Lawler's badge and there will be a thousand dollars green money paid yuh. Yuh might pack this badge along fer luck. Like some feller says, a man had orter have a hobby. Some collects old coins, some stamps. Injuns used to collect scalps. Why don't yuh commence gittin' a collection uh badges?"

"Not a bad idee." Bob Lake smiled and boldly pinned the blood-marked badge to his undershirt.

This brought a rough laugh from Shotgun Sam. Then the saloonman leaned across the bar, his bloodshot eyes boring into Bob Lake's. The big man's face took on an expression of sinister cunning. For a second the detective tensed, every nerve in his body taut, his hand ready to jerk his gun.

"I got a idee, Bob Lake." Shotgun Sam's voice dropped to a husky whisper. "That damned badge. Wear it, savvy? Wear the thing hid like that. I'll pass the word to the boys, so's, if they see it, they won't commence killin' yuh. Then, yuh understand, if yuh meet up with this Les Lawler feller, you kin kinda ease him on. Make him think yo're a dick. Git what information yuh kin from him before yuh kill him. And if the information is worth money, you'll git paid handsome. Wear that badge!"

Bob Lake nodded. "I will, Sam."

The detective, his brain whirling from the whisky he had been forced to drink, crawled between his blankets, his gun in his hand. He grinned to himself in the darkness.

Luck certainly was playing a lot of pranks. They were

sending him after a detective who once had lived in Wyoming under the name of Les Lawler. That was a good joke. He himself was the man who had been in Wyoming that winter under the name of Les Lawler. Shotgun Sam had given him his own badge and told him to go hunt down himself. That sure was a good joke. But not so funny, either. How had they known that the man who had once used the name of Les Lawler was now in Montana? Who, back there in New Mexico, had let the cat out of the bag? Nothing very comical about that.

Bob Lake had always tried in every way he could to avoid killing. Yet a man working at this sort of a job was forced into it—in the name of the law. The law said such killings were justified. But what about God? Was Bob Lake any more fit to live than those men he hunted? Some of those who rode the dim trails were men who had, by some ugly humor of fate, been thrown into the life of outlawry. The detective knew of men like that. Under various names he had ridden the Outlaw Trail with men he liked and trusted and pitied. Yet the law he served classed them as enemies, and hunted them down as such. But what did God Almighty whose stars shone above tonight—what did He think?

Tired as he was, his brain blurred by whisky that should have brought on sleep, Bob Lake found little sleep that night. He lay there under his blankets and tarp, watching the stars, thinking, remembering elusive snatches of prayers. Thinking . . . wondering. . . .

Tonight the man who called himself Bob Lake had taken the life of a fellowman. Why? Because that man could, with a few words, send Bob Lake into eternity. Self-defense. But that did not wipe out the indelible fact that the soul of the dead man had left his body. In the eyes of the Almighty, was that killing justified?

There was that commandment—*Thou Shalt Not Kill*. A law of God. A law broken by those who made the laws. A law broken thousands of times in the name of justice. In the name of war. Nations at war, throwing thousands of men into the belching maw of cannon mouth, each nation claiming that God was on their side—what commandment of God has been more flagrantly violated?

There was the blood of murder on the badge pinned to the breast of Bob Lake. Perhaps, by moonrise tomorrow night, Bob Lake must take the life of another man. Self-preservation. To save himself that he might ride on with his guns to take more lives in the name of the law he served. It was all bewildering. Bob Lake wondered if it was the whisky that was so upsetting his mental equilibrium. Or was it that the souls of dead men were accusing him tonight? He lay there, his mind tortured, his body bathed in nervous sweat.

Thirty feet away, crouched on the bank of the river, was Shotgun Sam, a motionless, hulking form. Except for the glow of his cigarette the saloonman might have been asleep. Shotgun Sam, boss of the Hell Creek Pool, killer, squatted there on the high bank, listening to the whisper of the muddy water below, the muddy water that shared its hidden secrets with him for many years. There was something subtly terrifying about that hulking, crouching figure—that giant of a man who never seemed to sleep, who spent his isolated hours sitting on the high bank above the whirling, muttering current that washed the high clay bank. He seemed unreal, like some heathen image carved from black, sinful material and set there to chill the blood of brave men.

The detective gripped his gun. Why not call out to that big devil, tell him that he was about to die, kill him, and push the ugly bulk of meat and bone into the river that held the bodies of better men? Why not kill this acknowledged leader of the Hell Creek Pool? But the man who called himself Bob Lake did not shoot. Instead, he lay there, watching—wondering what black thoughts filled the mind of the big saloonman.

A cloud drifted across the white moon. An owl boomed its mournful call. Back in the badlands a wolf howled. Dawn was not far off when Bob Lake dropped asleep. His slumber was ridden by ugly, distorted dreams. He twisted and tossed and turned between his blankets, but never once let go of the gun in his hand.

The sunrise brought him awake. Pulling on his overalls and boots, he walked to the saloon. There was no sign of Shotgun Sam.

Acting on yesterday morning's advice, Bob Lake helped himself to the whisky. He went around to the pump and washed. Still no sign of the big saloonman. The door of the cabin was shut, however, and the detective thought perhaps Sam was still asleep. Better not disturb him.

The detective went to the barn to care for the horses. His own two stood in their stalls, but the big bay gelding was gone. Gone also was the double-rigged Arizona saddle.

Bob Lake went back to the cabin. He shoved open the door and stepped inside. The cabin was empty. The bunk had not been slept in.

VI

"Double-cross law"

Bob Lake cooked himself some breakfast and ate alone. An uneasy feeling gnawed at his nerves. He knew that, sometime during the hours before dawn, something had happened to change the saloonkeeper's plans. Shotgun Sam had told him that they would cross over on the ferry in the morning and that Bob Lake was to ride up into the badlands along Hell Creek. Also, the big saloonman must have been very quiet about leaving. He must have used a lot of caution in making such a silent getaway. What had been the reason for that night ride?

For a while a feeling of panic gripped the detective. He wanted to saddle up, load his bed on the white pack horse, and drift yonderly. But perhaps that was exactly what Shotgun Sam wanted him to do. Maybe this was just another test. Something was wrong here, that was certain. And the only thing Bob Lake could do was sit tight, keep his guns handy, and expect the worst.

So it was that the detective was sitting with his back to the wall outside the saloon, his hand near his gun, when two men rode up. Bob Lake nodded indifferently. Both men dismounted. Bob Lake caught the glint of a nickeled badge pinned to the flannel shirt of one of the men.

"Where's Sam?" asked the bigger of the two.

"I don't know, mister. He'd pulled out before I got up this morning."

"Who are you, anyhow?" growled the law officer.

"I'm a stranger here. Bin breakin' out horses for the Long-X outfit. Got done there an' drifted here tuh wet my tongue. Will you two gents join me in a snort uh Sam's trant'lar juice?"

The big man nodded to the other. They followed Bob Lake inside the saloon. The detective stepped behind the bar.

"There's beer, Sheriff, if yuh'd ruther have it."

"Whisky will do. What's yore name, stranger?"

"Bill Jones," lied the detective glibly, for he had no intention of revealing his identity or his business to these two, even if they were officers of the same law he was serving at such a great risk. It was his policy to work alone as much as possible.

"How'd yuh like to go to town with us, Bill Jones?" The sheriff's smile was not pleasant. "Wearin' a pair uh handcuffs, mebby?"

Bob Lake shrugged his muscular shoulders. "What have I done?"

"Plenty, I reckon, if we was to run down yore record. I'm thinkin' we'll just take yuh along on general. . . ."

"Up with 'em!" the detective's voice was brittle, commanding. In each hand he held a .45. Slowly the two law officers raised their hands.

It made Bob Lake a little peeved for these two law men to think they could run him in so easily. Whatever their reasons for this play, he wasn't revealing his identity—yet.

"The next time yuh want me, talk with yore guns in yore hands, gents. Keep them paws plenty high. This is my deal."

Bob Lake stepped around the end of the bar. Shoving one of his guns in its holster, he relieved the two officers of their weapons. Next he handcuffed them together. Then he marched them out to the hitch rack, and with the second pair of handcuffs he anchored them safely by making them put their free arms around one of the upright posts and handcuffing them.

Thus they sat, growling, cursing, threatening, facing one another, their arms embracing the stout post. The cross pole of the hitch rack prevented them from escaping. Bob Lake grinned at the pair good-humoredly. Then he searched their pockets. In the vest pocket of the sheriff was the reward notice for Bob Lake, outlaw. Also several John Doe warrants. The pseudo-outlaw took the reward notice and, with the sheriff's pocket knife, tacked it to the post in front of that fuming gentleman.

Now the swift pounding of hoofs. Bob Lake whirled and jumped inside the saloon, his guns ready. He had no wish to kill anyone, certainly not any member of a sheriff's posse. But it was no posse man who rode up through the cottonwoods. The lone rider was none other than Shotgun Sam. The big saloonman stared comically at the helpless sheriff and his deputy, as Bob Lake stepped from the saloon, a gun in his hand. Lake winked broadly at the saloonman as he covered him with his gun.

"I'll be needin' yore he'p, Mister Saloonman. Do like I tell yuh and no harm will come to yore health. Try any funny business and I'll make yuh feel awful sorry. Ride on to the barn . . . I'll foller."

At the barn, out of sight of the two law officers, Bob Lake shoved his gun in its holster. He smiled thinly at the big saloonman. "I hope, Sam, that you didn't have no hand in them two gents tryin' to take me."

"You know better'n that," said Shotgun Sam earnestly. "Just before daybreak I spots a campfire back up in the hills. I saddles up an' rides that way tuh see who's camped there. I find the camp, but no men, so I high-tails 'er back plenty quick. Me turn a man in to the law? What the hell kind of a man do yuh think I am, anyhow? I got no love fer that new sheriff an' his deputy, bet on that. They're after yuh?"

"Looks that-a-way. The sheriff had a reward notice in his pocket. Likewise some John Doe warrants. Time I was movin' outta my tracks here. Here's the keys to their handcuffs. Turn 'em loose sometime this evenin'. Think I better cross the river."

Shotgun Sam nodded. "These two will haul freight fer

town directly they git loose. They're new in office or they'd have better sense than tuh come here hopin' fer luck. Time I git done dealin' 'em misery, they'll be willin' tuh drift fer home. You kin mosey on up into the Hell Creek badlands like we figgered. I bet this is some uh that Les Lawler's doin's, Bob. Man, don't them two things look plumb silly, settin' yonder in the dust with their arms aroun' that post. I'll make out you throwed the keys in the river, savvy? It'll be late this evenin' by the time I find them keys in the mud. Meanwhile, they'll be a-settin' there, lookin' foolish. The customers that drop in will git a laugh. How'd yuh snag 'em, feller?"

"Just beat 'em to it, was all. They must be green hands."

"Elected by the scissorbill farmers that's swarmin' over the country. Just two farmers weaned away from a hayfork an' plow. Man, wait till the Pool boys hears about this. Pete La Motte is due past here this mornin'. He'll spread the news. Like as not Fat and Tom will ride on down the river tuh git a look at what we got tied up to the hitch rack. Feller, this shore puts you in solid."

Shotgun Sam insisted on giving Bob Lake a couple of quarts to wrap up in his slicker. Then they went down to the ferry. The big saloonman kept chuckling to himself and slapping the detective on the back. His rough mirth was genuine. Plainly Bob Lake stood solid with the chief of the Hell Creek Pool.

They crossed on the ferry. A laborious process. On the south bank they parted, and Bob Lake rode away alone.

Luck had favored the detective. The wrath of those two blundering greenhorn law officers had helped his game a lot. But it also made his position more precarious than ever. The law was after him now. He was caught between two fires. Of course, he could tip his hand to the law officers in this part of the country, but with such clumsy men holding office it was risking a lot. They might, by some careless word or sign, betray his real identity and purpose. And that would seal his fate. Better to play a lone hand. Better to have the law hounding him. For these men whom he hoped eventually to put in prison were far more dangerous than the law officers. So Bob Lake rode along the trail that led to the Hell Creek badlands. He rode on a dangerous mission and one that held the promise of gun play.

VII

"Hell Creek"

Hell Creek is as rough a country as ever was stood on end and spotted with soap holes and ripped with cut coulées. There are shale banks that a horse must slide down on his rump—white-crusted soap holes with boiling black mud underneath that would suck down a native four-year-old steer—patches of scrub pines—blind gulches that led nowhere—grass that touched a man's stirrups, there in the coulée—bald ridges that, in rainy season, would bog a snipe. Bob Lake had no easy time of it, for often there was no sign of a trail, and he had to guess at it. Twice within an hour he had followed a blind gulch that brought him up against a cliff that turned him back. He had bogged down once, and both he and his horse were spotted with black mud.

It was mid-afternoon when the bawling of a cow halted him. There is nothing especially alarming about a cow bawling for a lost calf. Perhaps the calf had been pulled down by wolves or coyotes or a lion. But Shotgun Sam had told him that the two men in the Hell Creek badlands were holding a bunch of cattle there. Caution bade the detective pull up and listen. Now, farther off in the distance, was the answering bawl of a small calf. Then, still farther away, the indistinct sounds told him that up yonder in some park among the scrub pines cowboys were working a bunch of cattle. Cutting back what they did not want, holding stuff they were gathering. That cow near here was one that had been dropped for some reason. Probably, in making the morning drive, bunching the wild cattle, she had become separated from her calf. Missing her offspring, she had begun bawling and hunting for the youngster. The cowboys, thinking that she had probably left the calf bushed up somewhere, had cut her back to get rid of her bawling presence in the drive.

The cow had back-trailed to where she had left her calf. No calf there. Then the cowboys had located the calf in the bunch of cattle, had cut the little fellow out, and left him standing there, bawling for his mammy who was now losing no time getting to her calf. The drive had been worked on into the rough hills to the spot where they could be held and the unwanted stuff thrown back.

All this was told to Bob Lake, cowpuncher, by the bawling of cattle. To the pilgrim such sounds mean nothing. The tenderfoot cannot learn the little details that go into the making of a real cowboy. For the business of cowpunching is not learned in a few months or a few years. The real cowboy is born and raised in the business. From the time he can talk, he is taught the thousand and one little things that a man must know to be a top hand. And even after a man has spent a lifetime in the cattle business he can still learn.

Bob Lake had followed cattle trails since he was big

enough to sit a horse. He had been taught by experience the many things that a cowman must learn in order to stay in the game. He savvied the rough country and the open plains country. Brands and earmarks were his ABCs. He had gained the ability to ride into a herd and cut cows and calves without making a mistake. To judge and grade beef cattle. Where and how to bed down a herd of restless steers. To train his memory for cattle markings, so that without the aid of book or pencil he could remember a critter branded three or four years ago, by mistake, at a certain spot on a range as big as some of our smaller States. These, and the thousand other things that only a real cowman learns, Bob Lake knew by heart.

The bawling of those cattle awakened something inside this man who had quit punching cows to hunt down men. The big gelding he rode shared that thrill of cattle work. Ears twitching, feet lifting as if on steel springs, the big black horse tossed his head impatiently, as if to show his ability to cut out cattle, to do his part when a rope snared a calf by both hind legs.

"Bonehead," said the man softly, running his hand down the sleek black neck. The hard light in Bob Lake's eyes softened as he talked in a soft drawl to the horse.

They caught up with a white-faced cow who was traveling at a trot toward the calf that was howling for its mammy. For almost half a mile Bob Lake followed the cow to where she found her calf. He grinned as he watched the re-union of mother and the unbranded calf. Then he rode on.

Once more his eyes were cold, alert. He rode with his hand near his gun, up a wide gulch where the pines grew thick, following the stream of running water toward the bawling of cattle beyond. Soon he located a trail that rimmed out of the gulch and toward a hogbacked ridge above. He was about to take this trail when, from not more than three hundred yards up the gulch, came the sharp-noted cry of a woman, followed by the crack of a small-caliber gun and a man's coarse voice, snarling in anger.

"Help! Help! He . . . !"

The cry was silenced with startling abruptness. Now a man's harsh laugh. Then silence.

Bob Lake jerked his six-shooter. Giving the big black gelding his head, he raced up the cañon, into a little park. Two horses stood there in the clearing, saddles empty. A girl in blue flannel blouse and buckskin riding skirt was struggling in the arms of a tall man whose hand was across her mouth.

The big black gelding jumped across the clearing. The tall man threw the girl from him and jerked his gun. Bob Lake quit his horse even before the animal had slacked its headlong pace. A bullet nicked the detective's hat crown. Quitting his running horse threw Bob Lake from his balance. Rolling, he thumbed the hammer of his six-shooter, shooting at the tall man who was firing at him.

Now the detective was on his feet again, somersaulting to an erect position with the agility of an acrobat. He was about to jerk the trigger of his gun once more when the tall man's knees buckled and he pitched headlong on his face, his sandy hair reddening with blood from the bullet hole in his skull.

Bob Lake bent over the man who, with painful effort, was trying to cock his gun as he pulled himself up on hands and knees. Bob Lake's face was close to the unshaven, pain-twisted face that would, in a few minutes, be calm in death. The man's lips snarled away from set teeth.

"You, eh? Les Lawler? Damn yore dirty. . . ."

He dropped forward limply, his blood-smeared face in the dirt. The man who had known the detective as Les Lawler, back in Wyoming, would never speak again.

Bob Lake straightened up. The girl, her dark eyes wide with horror, stood back near the horses. Her jet black hair was tumbled in a thick curtain down to her waist, making a striking background for the finely chiseled, oval face that was the shade of old ivory. Bob Lake gasped at the sheer beauty of the girl in flannel and buckskin and high-heeled boots.

She stared back at him as if stricken dumb. "You . . . you killed him!" she gasped.

Bob Lake removed his hat. "Sorry, lady, but he was shootin' at me. There was nothin' else I could do."

The girl nodded. "I know . . . you came just in time. He . . . that man has always tried to make love to me . . . when my father was not around. He worked for my father. I don't know who you are, but you saved me from something terrible."

She was swaying a little as she stood there. Bob Lake stepped quickly toward her, but was halted by the abrupt arrival of two men on horseback. One of the men Bob Lake had never laid eyes on before. The other was Pete La Motte.

Pete La Motte's dark face was almost white, and his eyes were reddish slits. His gun slid down from its holster.

Bob Lake had sheathed his gun. Now he heard the click of Pete La Motte's .45 coming to full cock.

With a sharp cry the girl flung herself in front of the grim-lipped detective. *"Non, non, non!"* She spoke rapidly in French. Pete La Motte's face changed expression. He looked toward the spot where the dead man lay on the ground. Then he stepped off his horse and came toward Bob Lake.

"Sacre, to theenk I almos' shoot! My daughter she prevent dat mistake. She tell me 'bout dat man. *M'sieu,* Pete La

Motte nevair forget what you do today. Nevair."

Bob Lake's hand was gripped in that of Pete La Motte. The 'puncher with La Motte had dismounted and was standing over the dead man, looking down at the evil face that lost nothing of its ugliness in death.

The girl, her father's arm across her shoulders, extended a slim, tanned hand toward the detective. The color was coming back into her face.

"You have put us both forever in your debt," she said in a low, vibrant voice. "We shall not forget, my father and I."

Bob Lake's ears felt hot. Unused to words of thanks, bewildered by the beauty of this girl, he groped in vain for something to say. He dropped the girl's hand and faced Pete La Motte. The dark-skinned little cowman was scowling at the dead man. Now his restless black eyes came back to the detective's. Shrugging his shoulders, he showed his teeth in a mirthless smile.

"Too bad. That cowboy was one good hand. He was de one who know 'bout dat man call' Les Lawler."

A quick gasp from the girl. Bob Lake's face watched Pete La Motte who turned to his daughter. He saw the girl smile a little.

"What's the matter, Nadia?"

"*Rien, mon père*. Only . . . I wish to be away from that . . . that dead man."

"*Oui*," nodded Pete La Motte. "My frien', you will ride my daughter to the camp, please? I, myself, look after de dead one."

Bob Lake nodded. A few minutes later he was riding with Nadia La Motte.

They had gone some distance when the girl looked squarely at the detective. Now she spoke: "Before he died . . . that man called you . . . Les Lawler?"

VIII

"Prison brand"

Bob Lake had been waiting for that accusation. He grinned at her and nodded. "What do you know about Les Lawler?" he countered.

"I know that he is a dangerous man. He is hired by the government to hunt down other men for what bounty he can get. He is like the wolfer collecting money on wolf pelts. Les Lawler is an enemy to my father."

"And what if I happened to be Les Lawler?" he grinned.

"Then, because we are in your debt, I would tell you to go away quick before you die. I would not like to see you die."

"You heard that fella call me Les Lawler. You'd take the word of a snake like him?"

Nadia La Motte looked at him with steady eyes. When she spoke, she held his gaze. "If you told me that man lied, then I would believe you."

Never in his life had Bob Lake been faced with such a problem. Either he must deliberately lie or he must tell her a truth that meant death for him. "If I was Les Lawler, and if I was the kind of a snake you say this Les Lawler is, then I'd be lyin' to yuh now, wouldn't I? Would a bounty hunter like Les Lawler tell the truth when it would mean that he'd be killed for tellin' the truth?"

He was laughing at her now, his gray eyes mocking the serious brown eyes of the girl.

"You make fun of me," she said, the hint of a scowl showing in a little line between her black brows.

148

Bob Lake laughed softly. He had slipped out of a tight situation. He had been almost on the verge of telling this girl the truth. Why? He could not give himself an answer to that question. He only knew that it was next to impossible to look into this girl's eyes and lie.

"I was sent out this morning to hunt down this Les Lawler," he told her. "I was to git this Lawler feller's description from that snake I killed."

"You are this man they call Bob Lake?" she asked.

He nodded. "I just hired out to work for the Hell Creek Pool."

"Why?" she asked bluntly.

"Why does any man hire out on a job?"

"You are another of these killers, then? You are no better than that man you killed? You are no better than Shotgun Sam or Fat McKee or Tom Sellers or Ed Roper . . . ?"

"Or Pete La Motte?" he finished, his eyes mocking her. "I claim to be no better than anybody."

"Pete La Motte is no killer!" Crimson spots showed on her cheeks. Her dark eyes blazed like sparks.

"No?"

"No! They call him bad names, yes. They even put him in prison and that disgrace killed my mother. I was a little girl then, but I remember how she cried all day and all night for many weeks, until she died. We had no money. Not even food in the house to eat. What horses and cattle we had, my mother sold to fight for my father's freedom. Then Ed Roper came to my mother with a letter and some money. But she was already dying. The law that threw my father in prison had killed her.

"When she died, I was sent away to a reform school. They made me wear a dress like the other girls. A uniform of disgrace. Those in charge of that school would tell me my father was a badman and a thief and a convict. When I fought back, they locked me up and fed me bread and water. Almost every day I was whipped with a rawhide whip until my back was raw. I learned many bad things from the older girls. I learned to lie and steal and sneak. I lied to those teachers. I stole food. I sneaked a knife from the kitchen and planned to run away. We were not allowed to laugh at that place. That is what the law did to the daughter of Pete La Motte who had gone to prison for another man's crime."

She was staring away from him, but her eyes were bright with the passion of the tale she had told. Her body trembled with repressed emotion. Her words ran on and on, as if she could not stop, as if some inner power made her tell her story.

"When I was twelve . . . six years after I had been sent there . . . I saw my chance to run away. I traveled on foot, hiding in the daytime, stealing what I could find to eat, living on berries mostly, until they quit looking for me. I had traveled many miles, for I was strong and healthy and had made up my mind that I would kill myself before they caught me. And one night I came to an Indian camp. Those Indians were Assiniboine Sioux. They took me with them on a hunting trip. They fed me and gave me moccasins and squaw leggin's and a blanket. The sun had tanned my skin. I learned to talk their language. I was more Indian than I was white.

"And when the law officers came one day looking for a man who had come past our camp, those law officers took me for an Indian. That pleased me. I hated white men and their laws. Then came an order that all children on the reservation must go to school. There was one school at the agency. There was another school at the Saint Peter's Mission. My adopted father, Eyes-in-the-Water, had told me about both schools. When the sub-agent and the Indian policemen came after the children, Eyes-in-the-Water had already taken me to the priest at the mission and put me in school there.

"There I went to school as the daughter of Eyes-in-the-Water. Not even the good priest knew that I was not a full-blood Assiniboine until I had been there many months. Then I told him. I had learned many good things at the mission. They gave us good food and good clothes. We played games and laughed. Their teaching drove the badness out of my heart, and I knew that I could not keep on living that lie. So I told the father and he promised that nobody would know my secret. He was a real man, that jolly, white-haired, red-cheeked Irish priest.

"I learned many things there. Books, music, cooking, sewing, everything. I was happier than I had ever hoped to be. I thought that, when I was well enough trained, I would teach there. But that was not to be. News came that my father was out of prison and had taken up a ranch on the Missouri River. He was sick and needed someone to look after him. So when summer vacation came, I had Eyes-in-the-Water take me to him.

"I did not know my father. He did not know me until I told him who I was. He was very sick from those years in prison. Eyes-in-the-Water left me there. I never went back to the mission to finish school. Now and then I go there to visit. Sometimes I go and live with the Indians. They are my friends. But mostly I stay with my father who needs me."

Bob Lake had listened intently to the story of Nadia La Motte. He had watched the ever-changing expression of her face—now smiling, now wistful, now sad, at times fierce and a little bitter. Her thoughts were mirrored in her dark eyes.

Now she looked at the detective. "Why am I telling you, a stranger, these things? I do not know unless it is because you class my father with those others. Pete La Motte is no murderer, no thief. He hates the law, yes. Why not? Would not any man hate the law that had put him in prison for a crime committed by another man? Why does he travel in bad company? Because he is squaring his account with that same law that took away fifteen years of his life, a law that killed his wife who had done no wrong to anyone in the world . . . a law that sent a six-year-old daughter of his into a place that was no better than a prison.

"That is why Pete La Motte hates the law. That is why he hates the men who are paid to hunt down other men no better than themselves. That is why he has attached himself to such men as Ed Roper, Fat McKee, Tom Sellers, and Shotgun Sam. He has sworn to get revenge. He will get it. And I, his daughter, will stay with him."

She tossed her head proudly. She reined up her horse. Bob Lake did likewise. Once more he looked into a pair of eyes that questioned him. This time the girl voiced no question. Only her eyes—eyes that he had seen smile, eyes that had misted with tears—asked him the question he could not meet with a lie.

"I am the man who once used the name of Les Lawler," he said slowly.

IX

"The back track"

"What is your game?"

Bob Lake and Nadia La Motte were at the camp on Hell Creek. For the past half hour, since the detective had made his impulsive declaration, they had ridden in silence. The man felt that the girl had known his secret from the start.

"My game?" The smile left his lips. The sunlight was gone from his gray eyes, leaving them clouded with some bitter memory. He rolled and lit a cigarette before he went on talking. "Perhaps I have a story that might equal yours." Gone was the vernacular of the range, the careless drawl of the Southwestern cowboy.

"I have told mine," she reminded him.

He nodded. "Yes. You've told yours. And, perhaps, some day . . . some night, more likely . . . I will tell you mine. It is not a pleasant yarn. Not pleasant to recall. Call me what hard names you wish . . . think of me what you will . . . but remember this, please . . . I am not collecting any bounty on any man. I am in the service of the United States government, that is true. But here, in Montana, the work I am doing is not purely government work. Behind it lies a personal feud. A blood feud. Your story is not unlike my own, in a certain sense. And I have had my life gutted of happiness, even as yours was. I am talking to you now as I have never talked to any man or woman. Nobody knows my real name. Nobody knows my real purpose. I hope that there will come a time when I can tell you why I am here."

"You are here to smash the Hell Creek Pool. You are here to kill, to send men to prison. You are the enemy of my father. You are the law."

Bob Lake looked squarely into the accusing eyes of the girl. He was smiling a little. His eyes had lost their hardness. He shook his head slowly.

"I have put myself at your mercy. If your father is what you say he is, then I will fight *with* him, not against him. I am going to ask you to give me an even break. One word from you to the Hell Creek Pool and I am as good as dead.

You must know that. You must know that there has to be law. There must be men who are strong enough, cold-blooded enough, if you will, to enforce those laws. You understand that?"

"Of course."

"Such killers as Tom Sellers, Fat McKee, Ed Roper, and Shotgun Sam must not be allowed to keep on murdering and plundering. You can't help but admit that. You can't help but know that those men are not the kind of men to make their own laws. Am I wrong?"

"Of course, you're not wrong. I am not upholding them. I hate them and for good reasons. Father does not know, does not see the things that go on. He does not know about the ugly, loathsome advances they have made because I am his daughter and they think I am bad. Today, when that vile beast of a man was killed, I think Father was shocked into some sort of reality. You killed that man. I tried to shoot him, but he knocked my gun aside. Those men of the Hell Creek Pool think that I am common property, bad, immoral. They lie."

"I know that. And you must know this. I'll fight any of them to keep you from any of their dirty insults. I may be a despised detective, but I'm not like they are. Down in Arizona I have a kid sister who thinks that I'm about the greatest man that ever lived. I'm putting her through school down there, at a convent in Prescott. When I get the chance, I go to see the youngster. But if I ever did anything dishonorable, I don't reckon I could ever face that kid again. And she's all that I have in the world. The only person that ever worries about me. The only one who ever says a prayer at night for me. I'd a heap rather die than not be able to see that little gray-eyed girl who thinks that I am a real man."

They sat there in silence for a long time. From the distance came the bawling of cattle—stolen cattle. Pete La Motte was helping steal those cattle. This girl who sat there beside Bob Lake was Pete La Motte's daughter. The daughter of an ex-convict, the daughter of a cow thief. The daughter of a man who was one of the notorious Hell Creek Pool. And yet, to Bob Lake, she seemed the most decent, most honest woman he had ever known. He wondered if it could be possible that he was falling in love with Nadia La Motte. He had known her for less than an hour. Yet it seemed that he had known her always.

He felt the touch of her slim, tanned hand on his. He looked away from the sunset and into her eyes. Dark brown eyes that were misted with unshed tears.

"I . . . I think that I understand," she said.

"I wonder." His hand held hers now. Together they watched the sun drop behind the ragged skyline of the badlands. So they sat for some time. Now he looked at her again.

"You will keep my secret?" he asked. "You'll give me a chance to do what I must do, if I promise you that you and your father will not suffer? A word from you signs my death warrant at any time. If ever you feel that I am not living up to my promise, then tell those men who and what I am, and I'll stand the verdict."

"Your secret is safe with me. When I say that, I mean it. God in heaven knows that I would give anything to get my father away from those men. I would go out and work my fingers to the bone for him. I'd devote my whole life to him, if only he would break away from the Hell Creek Pool. They are badmen. Wicked men. Men who steal and kill. I know them better than my father knows them. They do not insult me when he is there. But every one of them, and nearly every man who works for them, has tried to paw me and make love to me. And I dare not tell my father for fear they will kill him. Father is not quite sane. Those terrible years in prison changed him. He is not responsible for what he says and does. Every night I pray to God that we will go away somewhere and find a little happiness. But until today I have met no one except the father at the mission, and Eyes-in-the-Water, to whom I could talk. They can't help me, can't help him. But you can. Today you have proven that you are a man. You saved me from that ugly brute. But you also were man enough not to lie to me, even though it meant that I might call those men and they'd kill you. I'll keep your secret. I'll even help you all I can to break up the Hell Creek Pool."

"And I'll help you, Nadia. I'll play the game square with you. Pete La Motte is not the man I'm after. But one or more of the gang who call themselves the Hell Creek Pool are men whom I've sworn to hunt down and kill or send to the gallows. We've made our bargain. We'll keep it. There will come times when you may doubt me. I'm playing a dangerous game, and at times I have to use all the tricks I know to save my own hide. So, until some time that I hope will come when I can tell you what I will tell you, I'm just Bob Lake, outlaw, with a price on my head.

"My present job is to hunt down Les Lawler and kill him. Remember that. Don't even think of me as anything but an outlaw. And if luck is kind to us, I'll blaze out a trail for you to some sort of happiness. And perhaps you'll think I'm getting fresh when I say that I'm going to do some hoping that I'll be sharing that happiness with you."

"Perhaps," she told him gravely, "I will want you to share that happiness of which you speak, my friend."

X

"Seeds of murder"

A woman's good name. Life can give a man no finer thing to fight for. There in the rough badlands of Montana the man who called himself Bob Lake had found fate had certainly dealt him some queer cards. The man who had known him in Wyoming as Les Lawler was now dead. His death had come about in such a way that no man suspected Bob Lake. The one person who shared his secret, who held the life of the detective in her two small hands, was Nadia La Motte.

They camped there that night. Pete La Motte and Nadia, two rough-looking cowboys, and Bob Lake. There was now a fresh grave on Hell Creek.

Bob Lake never turned his back to the two cowpunchers. Their attitude toward him was none too cordial. He had killed a man who had been their friend.

Pete La Motte, however, was friendly. The girl sat beside the detective at the edge of the firelight.

"You go back to Shotgun Sam's tomorrow?" asked Pete La Motte.

Bob Lake nodded. "No need of me stayin' here. I got a job to do."

The cowman agreed silently. The two cowpunchers eyed Bob Lake from under slanted hatbrims.

Pete La Motte treated the detective with respect. Within a week he had seen Bob Lake give two men fair chance and kill those two men. Bob Lake was the type of man he liked. Quiet of tongue, quick to move, sober.

Bob Lake had brought forth the whisky Shotgun Sam had given him. Now he was purposely plying the two cowpunchers with the stuff. He and Pete La Motte drank sparingly.

Whisky usually brings out the good and the bad in a man. Bob Lake figured that, if these two men intended killing him, that intention might as well be hastened along by applying the whisky theory. He watched them carefully. When either of them moved back from the firelight, Bob Lake also moved back into the shadow, his back to a tree. Pete La Motte, if he noticed the tension, gave no sign.

"I'll be driftin' about daybreak," said the detective.

"We'll be riding with you then," said the girl quickly. "Dad and I are crossing the river and going to town for some stuff. We'll ride with you as far as Shotgun Sam's."

Her father gave her a sharp, sidelong look, then smiled and nodded. "*Oui*. We go dat far."

Pete La Motte had been raised in the Cree country across the Canadian line. Although pure French, he talked the vernacular of the Cree 'breeds. Many people thought Pete was a half-breed, with his dark eyes, his black hair, his broken talk, his gay-colored Hudson Bay sash. Even as Nadia had passed for an Indian girl.

The shadows played across the girl's face, making her more beautiful than ever. Those same shadows were on the face of Pete La Motte, shifting against the black and silver background of his thick hair. A sort of fierce brooding expression dominated his features. His eyes seemed to see ugly things beyond the firelight, things that haunted him, tortured him, drove him into black moods. Prison had done that to Pete La Motte who had loved life and laughter and the music of a fiddle. In punishment for another man's crime the law had sent Pete La Motte to prison. That unjust

sentence had murdered the man's wife, robbed him of the
best years of his life, had treated his baby girl in a shameful
and degrading manner. So Pete La Motte, who had once
laughed and sang and danced the Red River jig, came from
behind the stone walls and steel bars of a prison cell a
broken man. A man whose hand was against society, against
law. Robbed of all that a man holds sacred, his health im-
paired, his heart twisted and shriveled, the law freed him.
But that man-made law could not give him back his lost
years, his health, his wife. Not even God could undo the
wrong man had done to Pete La Motte and his family.

Bob Lake could not find blame against Pete La Motte
for being so bitter. Who, under the circumstances, would
not feel bitter and resentful? Bob Lake knew what prison
meant to men like Pete La Motte. He had seen big, husky
men from the plains and mountains shut in prison cells. He
had seen those men die because they could not be out in the
open. The routine, the discipline, the food, the confinement, the punishment of black solitary. The old-time
guards whose brutality was horrible. And those men from
the open country came in for their share of punishment
when they flared up in anger against some undeserved punishment. He could not blame this little cowman with his
restless eyes and his hands that were never idle. He had seen
men like Pete La Motte go stark mad in prison. No man can
spend many years in prison and come out unmarked.

Bob Lake knew, because Bob Lake had served a term in
the same kind of a prison. Bob Lake had known what it
feels like to be stripped of name and citizenship, put into a
prison uniform, and made to pound rock with a sledge. Bob
Lake had done time. He had spent five years behind the
sun-baked walls of the State's Prison of Arizona when the
prison was located at Yuma where the thermometer regis-

ters a hundred and twenty in the shade, where men could not live long in those cells that had lacked sanitary conditions. He had seen men go crazy. He had heard others beg God for death.

Now, as he looked at the expression on the face of Pete La Motte, the memory of those five years of living hell came back. Five years ripped out of his youth. Five years at Yuma was equal to twenty-five years in the northern prisons like Deer Lodge. Few men knew that the man who called himself Bob Lake had ever done time in the pen, but the law he now served knew it. The law knew why Bob Lake had turned detective, knew what made him one of the most able operatives in the game. Bob Lake, detective, cowpuncher, sometimes outlaw, was a law unto himself. He rode alone, worked alone. A story ran that he was from Texas—some men called him the Texas Hellion—but that story was a lie. Or at least its truth was never proven.

A few of the outlaws knew him for what he really was. Those few would never wear a pair of handcuffs belonging to the detective. They were men who trusted him, who knew why he wore a badge pinned to his undershirt. They knew why he had killed Reb Waller and Reb's partner. They knew why he had now come to Montana, even as those select few knew why he had lived in Wyoming all one winter under the name of Les Lawler.

Now, as Bob Lake sat beside Nadia La Motte, her father across the fire, he remembered things that he had spent many years trying to forget. He felt the restless eyes of Pete La Motte studying him, watching him, asking him silent questions. And so Bob Lake made a certain sign with his hands—a sign known to few living men. It was a gesture that served as mute password between men who have worn a number instead of a name, men who have lived on stale bread and bad water in the black hole of solitary. A sign that brands a man as one of the lost. Lifers, men booked for death on the gallows, know it. Men who foresee an unmarked grave know that sign. They are the elect, these few who make that gesture outside a prison cell.

Pete La Motte caught the sign. The two men with him saw nothing, nor would have understood even had they seen.

"Where?" Pete La Motte's lips moved imperceptibly. No sound came from behind those lips.

"Yuma." Bob Lake spoke aloud. "Yuma, Pete, is shore hot in the summer." Bob Lake rolled a cigarette and lit it. "Passed through there once."

The hands that cupped the flame of the match that lit Bob Lake's cigarette were so held that five fingers stood apart from the others. That was all. Yet a story had been told. Bob Lake had told Pete La Motte, and had not lied when he told him, that he had spent five years of a life sentence in the State's Prison at Yuma, that he had spent time in solitary, that he was a member of that nameless fraternity the membership of which is mostly made up of dead men. Few men alive belong to that silent-lipped lodge to which only men doomed to death belong. Therefore, Bob Lake had been booked to hang, or else he had been marked for death by some turnkey, some inner mob in prison, or some enemy who held a measure of authority inside the prison, because only the dead or those marked for death know the sign that the detective gave Pete La Motte.

That secret sign that Bob Lake had given, had been recognized. It meant that, from now on, Pete La Motte and the man who traveled under the name of Bob Lake must be bound together by a silent oath of fidelity that could be broken only by death. Deliberately Bob Lake unbuttoned the top buttons of his flannel shirt. A queer smile on his lips, he unpinned the badge pinned to his undershirt and tossed it across to Pete La Motte.

The astounded cowman looked at it as a man might stare at a snake.

"It's the real thing, Pete. I don't need it now. I don't ever expect to wear it again. I give you that for a present. I've worn it a long time."

"What kind of a game yuh pullin', feller?" snarled one of the two cowpunchers.

Bob Lake grinned across the fire at the pair. Their hands were on their guns. The detective mocked them.

"Unless you both want to eat breakfast in hell," said Bob Lake, "keep yore hands off them guns. Pete and I talk in a language you never would be able to savvy. You saw me kill a snake today. My special fun is killin' off just such sidewinders. If either one uh you two hot sports care for a demonstration, commence somethin'."

XI

" 'To kill a man' "

The light of the campfire glittered on the barrel of Bob Lake's gun. On his feet now, he backed away from the firelight. Pete La Motte sat there, turning the badge over and over in his hand. He looked up at the detective, and Bob Lake grinned twistedly.

"For you, Pete La Motte, and for yore daughter, I'll do anything and everything that any man kin do. I'm here in Montana to kill a man. That man is one uh the Hell Creek

Pool. To accomplish that one killin', I may have to put away a few such skunks as cross my trail. I gave you a sign. I'm layin' out my cards on the table. String yore bets with me or play with such men as Shotgun Sam, Ed Roper, Fat McKee, or Tom Sellers. I didn't aim to turn up my hole card tonight. I thought, all along, that I'd play my game as I should play it. But I can't cut 'er. I had to come clean. I've done time. I've done harder time than you ever took at Deer Lodge. I've sweated where the sun cooked a man's brains to a crisp. I've fed on bread that a decent hog would pass up. Drank water out of the old Colorado when it was so damned muddy you couldn't see through a glassful of it.

"I've bin throwed into a black cell and kept there till my eyes forgot the look of daylight. I've bunked with men that died coughing red slugs out of lungs that had bin withered there by the foul air. I've helped carry 'em to their graves down by that river. I've busted rock under a sun that would kill most men in twenty-four hours. I've had my hands tied to high iron rings and stretched till I stood on my toes and passed out and hung there till they remembered to cut me loose. I've had the water cure. I've had the whole hellish works.

"When you were in stir, in the place where they put you, that was heaven compared to what we got at the old Yuma pesthouse. Negroes, Mexicans, white men. Men with every disease known and not a doctor to look after 'em. The well with the sick. The fit with the unfit. Sane men with men driven crazy. What in hell do you or these two fools sittin' here know about the pen?

"Pete La Motte, they took some years off yore life. You blame the law. They took five years outta mine. Five years when I fought the sun in the summer, the cold in the winter, when I fought every disease that kin be carried into a prison, when I was locked up with men that went crazy and died. Doin' a month in the black hole with never a sight of the sunlight. What do you or any other man know about the hell that a cowboy finds at the old pen at Yuma?

"Why did I go there? What put me there? I can tell you in few words, but I won't. You, Pete La Motte, you know. You understand things. These other two never will or never can savvy.

"The man that put me in Yuma lives near here. He's one of the Hell Creek Pool. When I find him and know that I've found the right man, I'll kill him like I'd kill a snake. Where or how I get him won't matter. But I'll get him. And I won't be hidin' behind the law when I pull the trigger."

The two cowpunchers stared at the speaker from slitted eyes. Pete La Motte's face was a study in bewilderment. The girl sat there, stunned, speechless.

Bob Lake had talked too much. He had spoiled his own game by his frank confession. He himself wondered why he had so spoken. But when Nadia La Motte laid a hand on his forearm, he knew why he had made a clean breast of his business here. Utterly sick of lying, of living a life filled with deception, weary of dodging and playing a part he hated, the detective wanted this girl beside him to know him for what he really was, to judge him accordingly.

"You have mak' de strong talk, *m'sieu*," said Pete La Motte. "By gar, dem fellers who mak' de Hell Creek Pool, dey keel you now for certain. You have talk too moch, my frien'. At daylight you ride from here alone."

"There's enough of a moon to show me the trail," said Bob Lake. "I don't want your hospitality. When you see your friends of the Hell Creek Pool, give 'em my best regards. But if my luck holds out, I'll see that nest of snakes before you see 'em."

He faced the two cowpunchers who waited some sign from Pete La Motte.

"If either of you try any tricks, I'll kill you both. Pete La Motte, if you change your mind and decide to ride with me against the Hell Creek Pool, send me word and I'll be glad to help you. *Adiós*."

He backed away into the dark shadows to where his horse was staked. Nadia, who had followed, looked at him with fear in her eyes.

"I am afraid for you. You should not have talked. Father will never quit those men. Now they'll know that you have been working as a detective, and they'll murder you as they've murdered other men. Why did you give away your game?"

"I wanted you to know what I'd been. I was sent to Yuma because I rode with the old Wild Bunch one time. I'd punched cows with one of that gang, and they needed mounts. To help them out, I brought 'em horses. I was alone at their camp waitin' for them to come in to dinner, when some law officers opened up on me. I was shot a dozen times. The man who led the officers there, the man who did most of the shootin', the man responsible for my bein' captured there and sent to Yuma is one of the men who call themselves the Hell Creek Pool. When I was pardoned by the governor, I swore to run down that man. I'd never seen him, and he changed his name. By living with outlaws, by working for the government, I picked up his trail, time after time. Now I've got nearly to the end of that trail. They may get me, Nadia, but I'll get that man before they kill me."

"Those men are murderers, killers, trained gunmen, all of them."

The man who called himself Bob Lake smiled thinly. "So am I."

165

"When and where will you meet me again?" she asked.

"If I am alive, I'll be in Chinook a week from tonight. Now I'd better be goin'."

He took her two hands in his and pulled her to him. His arms went around her and their lips met. Her cheeks were moist with tears. He let her go.

"Where do you ride to tonight?"

"I'm goin' to Shotgun Sam's. I left my pack horse there."

"But listen! Those other men will be there, perhaps!"

"I hope so," he said quietly. "*Adiós,* honey."

XII

"The road to Hell"

To ride the Hell Creek trail after nightfall was no easy problem. Steep cutbacks of loose shale were apt to slide man and horse into pitch darkness below. Treacherous soap holes were hidden in the night's deep shadows. There was constant danger of being bushwhacked. It took courage of the stoutest kind. It took a horse with a game heart and a wise head. On and on through the night Bob Lake rode, from ridges patched with moonlight into dark cañons and cut coulées as black as sin, and the memory of Nadia—the thrill of her lips—rode with him.

Hour after hour of this difficult going, it was well past midnight when the lone horseman came to where the trail broadened and followed an easy course down the bottomlands along the Missouri.

The odor of wild roses. Giant cottonwoods against a moonlit sky. A prowling bobcat. The river lapping at the clay banks, whispering across long sandbars. The man who has made his home on the bank of that old Missouri in the Montana badlands never forgets its wild beauty.

Bob Lake halted at the gravel crossing below Shotgun Sam's saloon. The ferryboat was tied up on the north bank, which meant fifty feet of swimming water, for the river was high at this time of the year. The rider loosened his saddle cinch and slipped the bridle off his horse, using the hackamore only. A water horse, this big gelding that had carried the detective through so many dangers. Between horse and rider a perfect understanding. He did not have to fight the big gelding to make him take the water. The horse waded in, lunged into the swimming current, and with a free head started across.

The strong current pulled them downstream. They avoided a big snag by a matter of less than ten feet, and veered back on their slanting course, never fighting the current that pulled at them ceaselessly. Now and then a treacherous undercurrent sucked and swirled, and Bob Lake left the saddle to hang to the animal's tail. They hit a long sandbar and lunged ashore.

Bob Lake spent some time drying his guns. He had taken off his undershirt before they crossed and stuffed it into the high crown of his hat. Now, with that dry piece of clothing, the only dry thing left him, he wiped off his guns. He put on his boots and overalls that, although wrapped in his slicker and tied behind the saddle, had gotten somewhat wet. The night air was chilly, and he shivered from his bath as he stood there in his sodden clothing. Then he mounted and rode toward the log saloon that was about a quarter mile distant.

He was fairly certain that neither Pete La Motte nor his two cowpunchers had beaten him across the river. Therefore Shotgun Sam and the others of the sinister Hell Creek

Pool would still be ignorant of his real purpose here, and his real identity. He saw the light that came from the saloon. As he rode nearer, he caught the sound of voices. The music of a fiddle. Coarse laughter. The stamping of spurred and booted feet. He went on.

A man stepped out of the saloon. No mistaking that big hulking form. Shotgun Sam's voice hailed him.

"It's me, Bob Lake," the detective called.

"Thought I told yuh tuh stop over night at Hell Creek?" The saloonman's voice sounded ugly and menacing.

"I finished up there and come back here. Any harm in that?"

"Not fer anybody but yoreself, mister. Put up yore hoss. Then git back here to the saloon. And when yuh come, come a-whistlin' . . . *Mister Bob Lake*."

A cold chill of apprehension went along the detective's spine. Shotgun Sam's voice held a veiled threat of some kind. The way he had said those last three words promised trouble. The saloonman was drunk, too. Drunk and ugly and as dangerous as a grizzly.

Inside the saloon Bob Lake caught a glimpse of Ed Roper, Fat McKee, and a stranger whose California pants were tucked in the tops of fancy boots. They were doing clumsy dance steps to the squeaking music of a fiddle that the grinning Tom Sellers was playing after a fashion. All were hilarious, even the taciturn Fat McKee. Their mood was one of rough hilarity that might, at a second's notice, turn into bloodshed and powder smoke. But just now they seemed to be celebrating some sort of holiday.

Outside, Shotgun Sam waited in the shadow. As usual, he guarded the place with vigilant ear and eye and the inseparable sawed-off shotgun.

Bob Lake stabled his horse, shifting his saddle to the

white pack horse. All this in the dark, without the aid of the lantern that he knew the saloonman kept there.

Bob Lake swiftly, but carefully, examined the two six-shooters he carried. He smelled trouble. Something had gone wrong with his illicit contract with the Hell Creek Pool. He wondered if Pete La Motte had, by some means, gotten the information to the others that the man who used the name of Bob Lake was, in reality, Les Lawler. That didn't seem probable.

Something had gone wrong. Something was going to happen before sunrise. Bob Lake smiled grimly to himself in the darkness as he stepped out of the barn and walked unhurriedly to the saloon.

The fiddle still squalled its resined notes. The tramp of booted feet was as loud as ever on the pine plank floor. Shotgun Sam stood behind the bar, his red face spread in a meaningless, sinister grin. Now the others, at Bob Lake's entrance, swarmed to the bar. Bob Lake found himself flanked by the men who were his enemies.

"We had a shore swell time, with them two law fellers yuh hawg-tied fer us," grinned Tom Sellers, laying his fiddle on the bar. "Eh, Sam?"

"I'll tell a man."

"The bank at Havre got stuck up. The bold an' darin' bank robbers got off with a nice fat stake. Got clean away. Three of 'em, so we was told. Only fer them two law officers bein' here after Bob Lake, they might've bin on the job."

"Yeh?" Bob Lake smiled crookedly. "I thought they was from Chinook?"

"Yuh thought wrong, feller. They come from Havre. Special officers, seems like. Sam had 'em figgered wrong. They'd got word that Bob Lake was here at Sam's, high-tailed it here, and was outta town when the bank got stuck up. Now it couldn't uh bin that anybody told them gents they'd find Bob Lake here, could it?"

"Meanin' just what?" asked Bob Lake, feeling the sharp scrutiny of every pair of cold eyes in the saloon.

"Meanin' they might've had a hunch that bank robbery was comin' off an' 'lowed they'd be here tuh meet a feller called Les Lawler, and that, when the bank robbers got here, they'd run into a ambush. Yuh see, mister, there's somethin' odd about them two law officers comin' here after a gent called Bob Lake."

"I don't know what yo're drivin' at."

"Word has come up the trail," said Shotgun Sam, "that when Reb Waller got killed, his pardner Bob Lake was killed with him. And that a dirty, sneakin' coyote of a detective was passin' hisself off as Bob Lake. This damned detective is the skunk that killed Reb Waller an' Bob Lake. Talk yorese'f outta that 'un, mister!"

XIII

"The last white chip"

The shock of the accusation was like a kick in the face. The erstwhile detective looked into the bloodshot eyes of the saloonman, and read his verdict there. Now he looked at the tall Ed Roper, at the pig-eyed Fat McKee, at the grinning, deadly Tom Sellers. No man ever stood closer to the shadow of death than this man who had used the identity of the dead Bob Lake. But if fear of sudden death gripped him, he did not show it. Instead, he grinned wryly and nodded at Shotgun Sam.

"You boys seem tuh hold all the big hands in this game.

Looks like I'm about tuh shove in my last white chip, push back my chair, and quit the game. Which, if it's in the cards like that, I'll do. But before I go out, I reckon I'm 'titled to a dog's chance. You boys got me where I can't do no harm. That swim across the river left me kinda chilled. And if the game goes ag'in' me, that ol' river ain't goin' tuh be no warm grave. Is it ag'in' the rules tuh lift a drink here?"

"He might be a damned dick," grunted Fat McKee, "but he's got guts. Take a drink, feller. I'll buy it. And we'll heist one with yuh."

The trapped man grinned. "Thanks, Fat. But it looks like the likker is on me. I'm buyin'. And when I git warmed up some, I might tell yuh why I killed Reb Waller an' a feller named Bob Lake an' why I used the name uh this Bob Lake. If this is my last night, we just as well make 'er a good 'un."

"That's the right speerit," grinned the deadly Tom Sellers. "I shore like tuh see a man that knows how tuh swaller his medicine. Sam, uncork a fresh 'un. The law feller is buyin'."

When they had put down their empty glasses, the man booked for death rolled and lit a cigarette with steady hands. When he had pulled some smoke into his lungs and let it drift slowly from his mouth and nostrils, he faced the men there in the saloon.

"Gents," he said slowly, and his eyes met theirs without shifting, "what would you do to a man that turned you in to the law and put yuh in the pen?"

"You know the answer to yore own question," said Tom Sellers.

The detective nodded, his lips twisted into a thin, bitter smile. "And when you was servin' time, if a low-bellied snake robbed you of what little yuh had, would yuh feel like gittin' that snake?"

171

"I'll tell a man," said Fat McKee vigorously.

"That's what I had done to me. I was framed and rail-roaded to the pen. Reb Waller stole what cattle and horses I had while I was doin' time. That's why I killed Reb Waller. When his pardner took cards in the game, I paid him off the same as I paid Reb Waller."

"That's a damned lie!" rasped Shotgun Sam, his red face now livid. "Reb never double-crossed any man."

"Reb Waller double-crossed me. He double-crossed others. And if yuh'll take a look inside that wallet I fetched here to yuh, you'll find a name inside it that ain't Reb Waller's name. This Bob Lake that was his pardner was another snake in the makin'. A man don't lie on a night like this. I'm not lyin' now. And what's more, I ain't tellin' a lie when I say I give my badge to Pete La Motte at supper time. I killed the man that had knowed me as Les Lawler. Just as I killed a man in this place. Yore Joe Robbins was another snake that died quick because he rattled before he struck."

"Are you tryin' tuh say you ain't a detective?" leered Shotgun Sam.

"I worked for the government as a detective, yes. But before I ever wore a badge, I was somethin' else."

"Mebby a sheepherder," grinned Tom Sellers.

The detective grinned amiably. "Nope. But I'd a heap rather herd sheep an' be called a sheepherder than to be the kind of a snake that Reb Waller was."

"Prove some uh these things yo're sayin'," suggested Fat McKee.

"I'll prove 'em," promised the detective, "when I git around to it."

Shotgun Sam's huge paw banged down on the crude bar. "Prove 'em now, damn yuh."

"I aim to prove a lot more than that," came the quiet reply.

"Fer instance?" grinned Tom Sellers.

"For instance," resumed the detective, "I'll prove that somebody besides me sent for them two law officers. I'll prove to yuh that one of yore Hell Creek Pool is a double-crossin' snake. What if I tell you that this same gent is the man that put me in the pen when I was just a big ol' kid with fuzz on my face instead uh whiskers?"

"Name him," said Ed Roper, speaking for the first time.

"I will, when I git around to it. But as this is what the poet calls the last night on this plane, let's kinda prolong that answer. Sam, I'm buyin' another. And yuh needn't put any uh them knockout drops in that yuh slipped me the first night. If I'm goin' tuh wake up in hell in the mornin', I don't want tuh wake up with one uh them headaches. So keep them drops for your special customers."

Fat McKee grinned a little, his round face looking purple in the smoke-dimmed light.

"Why ain't Pete La Motte here?" asked Ed Roper abruptly.

The detective shrugged his shoulders. "Pete might be along later on."

"We don't want Pete here tonight," growled Shotgun Sam. "I told yuh that before, Ed."

"Pete's got an interest in the Pool," persisted the big Ed Roper.

"A piker's interest. Pete's not the man he was. Gittin' kinda batty."

"Mebbyso," said Tom Sellers, his grinning, cold-eyed face close to that of the detective, "it was Pete that sent fer them law officers to meet a dick called Les Lawler here at Sam's place."

"You make a bum guesser, Tom," said the detective.

"Cut out this monkey work," snarled Shotgun Sam. "Spit out what yuh know, Mister Law Feller."

"Before this sun rises," said the detective, "I'll tell plenty. Like I said, one uh the Hell Creek Pool is a double-crossin' snake. Mebbyso he's here. Mebbyso he ain't. Pete La Motte is missin' from the family circle. Now if he was here, we'd be gittin' somewhere, and I kinda think Pete La Motte will show up before sunrise."

As if it were the fulfillment of a prophecy, a gun barked twice, then a third time, on the south bank of the river. The ferry signal.

The eyes of the men who made up the Hell Creek Pool met in a swift passing of glances. Shotgun Sam moved from behind the bar.

"That'll be Pete La Motte," he said grimly.

"When he gits here," promised the detective, "we'll have our full membership. I reckon he'll have news."

"What kind uh news, Mister Law Gent?" asked Fat McKee.

"Good news, mebby. Mebbyso the news will be bad." Bob Lake was smiling.

"Talk plain, yuh damned dick!" Ed Roper's face had an ugly look.

"That's as plain as is needed right now. This is my party. My last night. No use in openin' the package till all is present."

174

XIV

"The snake strikes"

Shotgun Sam quit the saloon, his short-barreled shotgun in the crook of his arm, a six-shooter near his right hand. A tense silence followed his departure. The detective faced the three grim men who were the rest of the lawless Hell Creek Pool.

"It's none of my put-in," he said carelessly, "but Sam seems purty drunk. Might git into a mess with Pete La Motte here when I spin yuh all a yarn. Better if some gent went along with Sam, no?"

"Sam's sure ugly tonight," nodded Fat McKee.

"And he don't like Pete none too good," agreed Tom Sellers.

"I'll trail Sam. Make out I want tuh he'p him with the boat," volunteered Ed Roper.

"Us boys will look out after the Jawn Law," grinned Tom Sellers.

"One funny move," added Fat McKee in his flat, throaty voice, "and there'll be a dead cop."

Tom Sellers picked up his fiddle. He grinned widely at the detective.

"Yuh may be a cop, but yo're game. I'll give yuh a tune. Fat, watch the law man."

"With both eyes," grunted that fat-paunched renegade, "and a gun that has a hair trigger."

"Sure certain, Fat, that yore gun's loaded?" grinned the detective.

"Move a thumb, feller, and I'll be shore proud tuh demonstrate."

"Both hands on the bar," chuckled the trapped detective.

The grinning Tom Sellers played two or three tunes. Then after about half an hour, the saloonman returned with big Ed Roper and Pete La Motte. The latter eyed the detective who smiled at the cowman.

"I figgered you'd follow me, Pete La Motte. But Shotgun Sam will tell you that you took yore night ride in vain. These gents know I have bin wearin' a U.S. badge. The same badge I give you, La Motte. Now that we're all here, we might as well git down tuh business. Pete La Motte, I talked plenty plain to you. I told you why I was here in this country. Tell 'em I lied, then, when I said I wasn't hidin' behind a law badge when I called for a showdown with the Hell Creek Pool."

Pete La Motte shrugged his shoulders. "You did not mak' de lie."

"There's one man amongst you five," the detective went on, his eyes hard, his mouth pulled taut, "who would double-cross his best friend. One out of the Hell Creek Pool needs killin', and I'm here tuh do the job. You all claim to be tough men. Yuh stand five against me. Kill me and yuh'll mebbyso never learn the name uh the man that is a lowdown snake. Kill me and yuh won't find out the man that sent for them two officers. The two that I handcuffed to the hitch rack. Let me handle this crooked-dealin' snake and I'll be willin' tuh take whatever you boys kin give out."

"Yuh do a lot uh talkin'," said Ed Roper, "but yuh ain't tellin' anything. Which of us here is the snake?"

"Keep yore shirt on, Roper. I'm comin' to it in my own way. I'm askin' yuh all a question. Where did them two law officers go?"

"Back tuh town," growled Shotgun Sam. "We put the skids under 'em."

"Then who are the men that's hidin' between here an' the crossin' right now? Not two, but a dozen men? Are they workin' for the Hell Creek Pool? Or have they bin planted there tuh git the gents that held up the Havre bank?"

The faces of the men there in the saloon were a study. Tom Sellers grinned, his eyes glittering with deadly lights.

"Kin yuh prove there's men there?" he asked huskily.

"Take a walk down there through the brush and see for yourself. They was scatterin' when I swum the river. They rode past a patch uh clearin' where the moon was shinin' white. I counted twelve men."

"Then somebody's squealed," grunted Fat McKee. "Law man, did you pull this fast trick?"

"Not me, Fat. I'm here to git the man that did it. Figger it all out for yorese'ves, gents. The dirty son that gathered them lawmen that's now surroundin' this place is the same snake that was the cause uh me bein' sent to Yuma for life. I done five years and was pardoned. The same skunk was the good friend uh Reb Waller, another rat. I killed Reb Waller. You seen me kill another uh the dirty gang here in this place. Pete La Motte saw me kill a third skunk. How many more of 'em there is, I don't know. But the big boss uh the dirty gang is here in this saloon. If he has the guts of a louse, let him call my bluff. Let the man that down in Arizona and Texas called hisse'f by the name uh Pecos pull his gun. He'll die in his tracks when he does. The gent that made a tough rep as a killer under the name uh Pecos is the man I'm here tuh kill."

There was a deadly hush in the place. Tom Sellers's grin looked ghastly. Fat McKee's bloated face was mottled, purple. Pete La Motte's restless eyes shifted from one face to another, and stole furtive looks toward the darkness outside where a posse was closing in.

Ed Roper had backed into a corner, his slitted eyes watching the men inside the saloon and the door that led outside. Behind the bar, Shotgun Sam was braced on widespread legs, his right hand on his six-shooter, his shotgun handy, his face an ugly smear.

No man spoke. Every man in the place eyed the others furtively. From outside came the sound of a dry twig snapped.

"They're comin'!" croaked Tom Sellers. "We bin trapped. Who done it?"

"Ask Pecos!" cried the detective. "Ask him!"

"Who the hell's Pecos!" growled Fat McKee.

"He knows who I mean when I'm callin' him," came the brittle reply. "He's the one yuh trusted. He's the man yuh call. . . ."

A noise outside. Tom Sellers's gun cracked, smashing the swinging lamp above the bar. Now the room was pitch black. Men running. Now the thudding of two bodies. The brief flash of a gun. A short, brittle laugh. Curses—the tramp of booted feet on the plank floor as the men inside broke for the open.

Outside the saloon, rifles and six-shooters spat. Men shouted orders. The outlaws fought desperately to reach the corral where their horses were. And from the black doorway of the saloon, two men locked in death grips careened across the ground. They went down in a tangle, striking, kicking, twisting, gouging. Over and over they rolled.

Now, from the saloon, another figure. A short, wiry man who staggered as if drunk. He stumbled out into the open. The white moonlight showed him plainly—Pete La Motte, a crimson smear across his white shirt. He dropped to his

178

knees, knelt there as if he prayed. Perhaps he did pray to his *le Bon Dieu* in those last moments of agony there in the patch of moonlight. Then he slid forward on his face. Pete La Motte was dead.

The two men who fought with bare hands at each others' throats had gained their feet. Toe to toe they stood in the shadows, smashing terrible blows at one another. Sledge-hammer blows that broke skin and smashed bone.

One of these men was a hulking giant. Thick-necked, burly, heavy-shouldered Shotgun Sam, boss of the Hell Creek Pool. His antagonist was more slight of build. Wide of shoulder, slim-flanked, steel-muscled, quick and deadly as a panther. A panther pitted against a grizzly. The detective had spotted his man. Now he was killing him, if he could, with his bare hands.

The thud of their rolling bodies. The short, vicious blows smashing and tearing like pistons. Shotgun Sam, once known as Pecos, tore at the smaller man, roaring and bellowing as he fought. Trying to smother his enemy in his huge arms, trying to crack his ribs, snap his spine, then pitch him into the muddy water below.

None of the possemen dared shoot. None of them interfered. The big saloonkeeper and the little panther-like detective were fighting to the death. No compromise here. No begging for mercy.

"Fight, yuh snake, fight! I'll kill you as sure as God made yuh." The smaller man slid away from those groping, huge muscled arms. Now he ripped terrific blows into Shotgun's bloody face.

Then the saloonman lowered his head, charging like a bull. His arms were around the detective's waist. His bellowing, blood-frothed laugh roared in the other man's face. Slowly those gorilla arms tightened, crushing the breath from the smaller man's lungs. And in that python grip the ex-Bob Lake learned new pangs of agony. The blood-smeared face of Shotgun Sam bellowed wild laughter. The vise-like pressure of those huge arms increased. Then, as a twig snaps, came the crackling of a broken rib.

That stab of pain burned into the detective's brain like a red-hot needle. He jerked an arm free, smashed a maniac fist against the flesh of the saloonman's face. His thumb gouged at an eye. With a howling bellow, the big man relaxed his grip for an instant. The detective slipped free.

His body racked with terrific pain, the smaller man fought on without really feeling the pain of the punishment he had taken. He hit at the big man, timing his punches, hitting at spots where a blow took toll. One of Sam's eyes was out of its socket, a gruesome, horrible blob against the bloody face. Both men were half naked now. Both were bleeding like stuck pigs. Both badly winded, both taking and giving terrific punishment. The detective's left ear was bitten half in two. His face a red mass of flesh, his eyes all but closed. Still they fought there on the high bank above the river.

The shooting around them had died out, although neither of them knew. Some men ran toward the two who fought with their hands and feet and teeth. The detective saw them coming. He saw Shotgun Sam brace himself for one of those bull charges. Now the saloonman was at him. Once more those big arms wrapped around the smaller man, but this time the detective was inviting that rush. He had stepped a little backward. He was ready.

Thudding bodies met in terrific impact, and the smaller man gave way, upsetting them both. A horrified bellow boomed from Shotgun Sam as he and his enemy pitched from the high bank into the muddy water below.

Out of sight beneath the water they plunged, still locked in death grips. Forty feet below the spot where they had hit, their heads came to the surface. The big man was gasping, sputtering, choking. The detective, more refreshed than harmed by the ducking, for he was a good swimmer, grinned at the man he wanted to kill.

"Can't swim, can yuh?" he gritted. I knowed that . . . yuh snake . . . that's why . . . I let yuh . . . come in the water with me . . . the same muddy water that's bin the grave of better men than you . . . Pecos . . . I'm holdin' yuh now. I'm shovin' yuh under in a second . . . into the river yuh used tuh hide yore dirty crimes. I win, you dirty black-hearted snake. I'm givin your carcass to yore damned . . . catfish!"

A frenzied thrash of limbs and a choked bellow answered him. For a moment Shotgun Sam held tightly, dragging them both under in a last gasping burst of strength. Then the detective broke free. The cold water was reviving him. He floated and swam with the swift current. Behind him a horrible, bubbling, choking cry. Then silence.

Soon the surface of the river, silvered by the moonlight, was unbroken.

The detective's feet found bottom at the sandbar below the crossing. He staggered ashore and lay on the sand, panting, eyes closed, like a dead man.

There, at sunrise, the sheriff's posse found him, sleeping the sleep of exhaustion.

XV

"Rivers tell no tales"

Sunrise. The Hell Creek Pool was no more. No man of the five who made up its sinister company was alive. Fat McKee, Tom Sellers, and Ed Roper had made their last stand. They died with their boots on, with their guns smoking, in the way an outlaw dies. Hating, hated, they had asked no quarter, gave none. And so those three found graves on the bank of the Missouri River where it twists its way through the Montana badlands.

Shotgun Sam had met his fate. His treacherous soul had gone across the Big Divide to be judged and condemned. So had died that most deadly one of them all. An outlaw who had been traitor to his kind.

Of all those who made up the Hell Creek Pool, one man alone had cleaned his slate before he left. Pete Le Motte, who had served time at Deer Lodge, had been on his last night a man who gave up his life for a cause. He had listened to the talk of the detective who had served time at Yuma. By certain signs, certain words, he knew that the same man who had sent him to Montana's State Prison had also sent this detective into five years of hell at Yuma. And, knowing this, knowing what he learned from his daughter about the detective, Pete La Motte had ridden from Hell Creek to help the man whom his daughter had promised to marry.

It was Pete La Motte's signal, seen only by the detective and the saloonman, that had marked Shotgun Sam for death. And even as the quick-triggered Tom Sellers had shot out the light, Shotgun Sam's six-shooter had sent its leaden slug into the body of Pete La Motte. Pete La Motte, who had once known Shotgun Sam when that gun-toting man of parts was called by the name of Pecos. Pete La Motte had cast his die—had given up his life. He had cleaned his slate by the manner of his passing.

And there in the badlands a man who had followed many dangerous trails, a man who had used so many names that he had almost forgotten his own, found happiness and love. Under his real name, which really does not matter, he lives quietly on a ranch in Texas.

In Montana, the same muddy river still whispers dark riddles to the high clay bank where the ruins of Shotgun Sam's log saloon stand as a landmark. But no longer do men see that hulking, silent figure who once listened and seemed to understand. Yet those who dwell along the river like to tell strange tales about the old cabin. They say that when the moon is white, a light shows there. That there is a blurred muttering of voices. Sometimes the squeak of a fiddle. And that, under the black shadow of the cotton-woods, a blacker shape takes form. A black shadow that seems to hark to the eternal muttering of muddy water, telling in whispers its secrets to the shore.

The Cayuse

Cherry Wilson

Cherry Wilson was born Cherry Rose Burdick on July 12, 1893, in rural Pennsylvania. When she was sixteen, she moved with her family to the Pacific Northwest and was to live there for most of her life, although, after she married Robert Wilson, she led rather a nomadic existence for a time. When her husband fell ill in 1923, the couple took up a homestead near Republic, Washington. To supplement the family income, Cherry Wilson had earlier turned to writing Western fiction, and she had the good fortune to have one of her first stories, "Valley of Sinister Blossoms," published in Street & Smith's *Western Story Magazine* (8/27/21). Now she wrote in order to make a living. While for her professional life as a writer Street & Smith would remain her principal publisher, in the mid-1920s she also began contributing stories to Fiction House's *Action Stories*, a magazine that regularly featured a Walt Coburn short novel in just about every issue. "Guns of Painted Buttes" by Cherry Wilson in *Action Stories* (10/25) was accorded Third Prize Winner in the Authors' Popularity Contest sponsored by the magazine the year it appeared.

Cherry Wilson's early stories for *Western Story Magazine* were thematically similar to Western stories written by B. M. Bower, author of CHIP OF THE FLYING U (Dillingham, 1906), a story originally serialized in Street & Smith's *The Popular Magazine*. Bower, too, was a writer frequently published by Street & Smith. However, Wilson seems also to have been influenced by the Western fiction of Frederick

Faust, and often readers of *Western Story Magazine* would write letters to the editor declaring that Cherry Wilson was as fine a writer as Max Brand or George Owen Baxter, both Faust pseudonyms in the magazine. Certainly Wilson's literary sensibility was ultimately more mature than Bower's, and stylistically her Western stories are less episodic than Bower's, while in her fondness for horses in many of her stories she certainly rivaled Faust at his very best.

"Wilson stressed human relationships in preference to gun play and action which generally occur *en camera*," Vicki Piekarski wrote in her Foreword to Cherry Wilson's OUT-CASTS OF PAINTED ROCKS (Five Star Westerns, 1999). "In fact, some of her best work can be found in those stories where the focus is on relationships between children and men, as in her novel, STORMY (Chelsea House, 1929), and short stories like 'Ghost Town Trail' in *Western Story Magazine* (10/25/30)—a fascinating tale with an eerie setting and a storyline filled with mystery which can be found in THE MORROW ANTHOLOGY OF GREAT WESTERN SHORT STORIES (Morrow, 1997), edited by Jon Tuska and Vicki Piekarski—and 'The Swing Man's Trail' in *Western Story Magazine* (12/13/30) in which a boy doggedly pursues a herd of rustled cattle that has swept up his family's only cow."

One of the most popular and fondly remembered movie cowboys from the 1920s and 1930s was Buck Jones. He was starring in his own series of Western films at Fox Film Corporation when he made THE BRANDED SOMBRERO (Fox, 1928) [based on Cherry Wilson's short novel, "The Branded Sombrero," in *Western Story Magazine* (5/14/27)]. In the mid-1930s, when Buck Jones had his own production unit at Universal Pictures and could pick and choose the literary properties he wanted to bring to the screen, he chose several of Cherry Wilson's stories. Her short novel, "Montana Rides" in *Western Story Magazine* (12/17/27), had been filmed earlier in the sound era as THE SADDLE BUSTER (RKO, 1932), but it was Buck Jones who made the most commercially successful screen versions of her work in THE THROWBACK (Universal, 1935) [based on "The Throwback," a three-part serial in *Western Story Magazine* (4/20-29-5/4/29)], EMPTY SADDLES (Universal, 1936) [based on EMPTY SADDLES (Chelsea House, 1929)], and SANDFLOW (Universal, 1937) [based on "Starr of the Southwest," a three-part serial in *Western Story Magazine* (7/25/36-8/8/36)]. Jones was also responsible for bringing to the attention of Henry MacRae, a producer at Universal, Cherry Wilson's STORMY which was filmed under this title in 1936 starring Noah Beery, Jr., and Jean Rogers. It was about this time that Cherry Wilson was widowed. She gave up the homestead in 1936 and moved to Hollywood, California, where she lived until early in 1938 when she moved to Spokane, Washington. She was still living in Spokane when she died on November 18, 1976 at the age of eighty-three.

Both "Montana Rides" and "The Throwback" will be published for the first time in book form in the forthcoming THE THROWBACK: A WESTERN DUO (Five Star Westerns, 2002). The short novel that follows is one of Cherry Wilson's finest stories about a young man and his love for a horse, set in the Pacific Northwest, a region she knew so well.

I

"A thoroughbred"

"Two bits, I'm bid!" chanted the old leather-lunged auctioneer, elevated to a table beneath the great spreading cottonwood trees, holding a glass tumbler over the heads of the crowd. "Remember, there's seven more like it, folks! Pure glass . . . an' all intact. None of your cut stuff! Waal, not to hold up the procession . . . going . . . thirty cents? Thank you, ma'am! Thirty cents I have. Eight elegant tumblers! Everybody needs 'em. Everybody drinks . . . something. Name your poison! They'll hold it . . . lemonade, water . . . whoa! I won't guarantee that. They might crack, bein' tempered to something stronger. . . ." He was howled down by shouts of laughter. "Who'll raise the ante? I see . . . nobody likes to bid against the lady. Sold to Missus Pierce for thirty cents! Hand up that bedstead, Slim!"

The Jingle Bob auction was in full swing. Blue Buttes range folks had turned out strong. Not that there was anything especially desirable in the estate left by Cultus Kress, when he had eventually succeeded in drinking himself to death. But any auction was a diversion. And this one was devoid of the distressing circumstances that frequently dampen such occasions. For no Kress remained to bemoan the break-up of home, except an only son, Jase. And Blue Buttes couldn't feature Jase Kress caring about anything but that sorrel filly of his.

With spirits unconfined, they had taken possession of the ranch—curiously snooping through barns and house, lounging on chairs, sofas, bureaus, and other furnishings, shamefully spread to the public gaze under the trees before the dead ranch house, actively bidding, convulsed by the auctioneer's witticisms, or just gossiping among themselves. The women said it was God's mercy that Nancy Kress hadn't lived to see this day. Men greedily informed other men that everything was going for what it would bring. Nothing was reserved—oh, barring the ranch, of course! Old Cultus hadn't been able to drink that up. For the Jingle Bob had belonged to his wife, and she had left it in trust for Jase when she died. Lucky she had, or Sam Vortz would have had it before this. Vortz, huh? Yeah, he was crazy to get hold of the place. And Cultus had been crazy to sell. He'd had all the lawyers in Santo hunting some loopholes in the will. But Nancy had sewed it up too tight. Jase would be twenty-one next June, and then the Jingle Bob would go to him. And he had sworn uphill and down that he would never sell it to Vortz. The kid sure had it in for him—oh, just some cayuse notion!

One man absent-mindedly wondered what Jase would do with the ranch—stripped like this—and laughed as uproariously as the rest at the idea of Jase doing anything with it—or anything else! For, as they observed, all Jase had ever done, or shown any disposition to do, was "loaf like a Siwash," or tear over the range on his red mare, or "mess around with the Chinks" placering down on the river. Jase was too lazy to draw a long breath. Plumb cultus, like his father. A shiftless, worthless, young hound, who would certainly come to no good end!

Most of these left-handed compliments reached Jase's ear. But he didn't care. Since nine that morning, he had seen home things passing into strange hands, with no emotion save fear, as each transaction neared the moment when this mob of hungry bargain-hunters would descend to the holding pens for the sale of the livestock!

Already, men were drifting corralward. He could see them as thick as crows about the fences down there. And, half frantic, he waylaid Wes Storrs, the administrator.

"Wes," he said, not pleadingly, as he had many times, but with desperate defiance, "you can't take Firefly!"

A tone that the honest old rancher—on whom had fallen the responsibility of untangling the mess Cultus Kress left of his affairs at his death—hotly resented. Indignantly he surveyed the boy, his indignation rapidly cooling at what he saw.

He saw nothing, however, in Jase's face—so strangely still and deeply tanned by sun and wind. For it had been schooled too long to give away anything. But his fine hazel eyes—with lashes and brows so heavy and dark that they were invariably mistaken for black—burned with a fire that gave Storrs pause. And his slight, straight figure—poorly dressed in shirt, chaps, and sombrero, bleached by sun and beaten by weather out of all shape and color—had lost its lazy indolence, and was as tight as a coiled spring. Altogether, Jase Kress gave the administrator the curious impression of quicksilver.

"Now, see here, Jase," he nervously blustered, "I ain't takin' anything, savvy? I'm just administratin' this estate because the court appointed me. Firefly's part of the personal property. I can't exempt her . . . any more'n I could the cattle. I shouldn't think you'd want me to, when you know it will take every cent to square your dad's debts. Great guns, kid, I'm doin' it for your own good. So you can start square, when I turn the ranch over to you next year. For the last time, I'm tellin' you, boy . . . the filly will have to go!"

For one tense instant Jase looked at him with that

189

burning glance. Then he silently swung toward the corral, where Firefly—still saddled from a last ride with him—was waiting to go under the hammer. And Wes Storrs turned a troubled face on the nearest man.

"See that look he give me, Sherm? Mark my word, they'd better watch that lad. He's up to something desperate."

"Shucks!" Sherm's snort expressed all of Blue Buttes' contempt. "Jase Kress will never git up enough steam to blow off."

But they little dreamed the fires that burned in Jase, that had been burning since he had learned that his mare would be included in the sale. Only Storrs noticed the change in his bearing. No one else noticed him at all. He stood in one corner of the horse corral, an arm thrown over Firefly's neck, alone in the crowd, aloof from the hubbub that steadily grew, as more men pressed up to judge and appraise the Jingle Bob stock, until—over the hubbub of men and cattle, struck a blatant voice: "You're wrong, Pierce."

It sent a tremor through Jase. And his eyes, hot with dislike, flashed to the speaker—a big, burly, white-eyed man, conspicuous in a beaded buckskin vest, pearl-gray Stetson, and khaki riding breeches thrust into the high tops of costly, handmade boots. Sam Vortz. The man who wanted the Jingle Bob. Who wanted the earth!

Sam Vortz was the big toad in the Blue Buttes puddle. But he wasn't a cattleman. Instead, he bred race horses on his White Rocks Ranch, and ran them on every track west of Cheyenne. A horse breeder, he styled himself, but he was more frequently termed a horse killer by those who knew him. Since he had money to loan on ranch property, everyone had to kowtow to him. For Blue Buttes' ranchers were a hard-up lot, and those who didn't owe him at present feared they might next season.

"You're plumb wrong," declared Vortz in his overbearing tone. "Blood does lie sometimes. Not often. But it happens Take my Prairie Lass. . . ." Every nerve in Jase's sinewy form suddenly tightened. "You know, that four-year-old filly of mine, foaled by Sacajawea an' sired by Sachem? Color's about the only thing she took. Blamed if she don't look more like a cayuse than the mangiest fuzz-tail the boys bring in. But the books show her bloodline pure . . . clean back to Hobgoblin! On the other hand, take this sorrel filly of the Kress kid's. . . ."

Terror whipped white the boy's tanned face.

"This filly is straight cayuse . . . or so you tell me. But she's got more Thoroughbred markin's than my Prairie Lass. A throwback, I reckon. But, well. . . ."

"Jase." Gently a hand fell on his arm.

With a start, the boy looked around, his face relaxing at sight of the girl beside him—a slim, winsome girl of about eighteen, in riding costume. Her short, bright hair, with which the July breeze was taking such liberties, was the same tawny gold of the range in autumn, and her wide, honest eyes, the same rich blue of the mist on the buttes an hour after the sun's setting. Her mouth was beautiful, and strangely revealing of her character—loving and loyal. Kelly Shane, of the Bar Bell Ranch. Jase's one friend in all that gathering.

"Jase," she said with quiet sympathy, "this must be awful for you. Don't stay! Come over to the Bar Bell until they're through."

Utterly disregarding this, speaking the one tragic thought of his heart, the boy said tensely: "They're sellin' Firefly!"

She cried out in pity and dismay. "But . . . how can they, Jase? She's your horse!"

A bitter smile flicked his lips. "They say not! They say I'm a minor . . . so I got no legal property!"

"Oh, I'm so sorry."

He shrugged hopelessly. "It's nothin' new in my young life. That's how it's always been. A thing was mine till it got some value . . . then it was Dad's! Like that blaze-faced calf that broke its leg . . . remember? Dad was goin' to shoot it. But I made him give it to me, an' I cured it. It was mine, till it got grown . . . then he sold it to go on a drunk. An' them yearlin' steers he give me for ridin' herd all that summer you was in Spokane . . . I was goin' to sell 'em to go to school on, but . . . they went the same way." With a fierce gesture he dismissed all this. "I don't care about them!" he cried wildly. "But Firefly's different! Even Dad wouldn't have took her, Kelly!"

The girl said nothing. There was nothing to say. Just so had she seen Cultus Kress crush all his son's initiative, kill his every spark of ambition. Now, if they took Firefly from him . . . ?

"Kelly," he vowed, with a ring of purpose new to his tone, "if Sam Vortz buys her, I swear to heaven I'll shoot her right in this corral!"

And suddenly Kelly Shane, too, was aware of the change in him. And, suddenly afraid for him, her eyes sought Vortz. He stood at the fence, not far off, a boot up on the bottom rail, a half-smoked cigar in his lips, his Stetson shot over his chalky eyes at a determined angle—but not so far as to conceal the singular interest with which he was studying Firefly.

She thought of Vortz as horse crazy in the least admirable way—caring only for horses as a means to fame and fortune, of his reputed brutality, of tales spread by White Rocks stablemen, of many a helpless, high-strung animal ruined by his vicious temper. She thought of Jase, who loved only Firefly—in a way that was the talk of the country. Of Jase, in bad standing already—and with some cause, she felt, although she was loyal to him for the sake of the childhood playmates they had been. And she cared for him in spite of himself, against the advice of everyone, even of her own common sense, because—she could not do otherwise.

"Jase," she pleaded, firm in that regard, "don't talk so wild! It isn't likely he'll want Firefly. But if he does . . . Jase, you can't afford to make an enemy of Vortz. Don't spoil your life for a cayuse."

Her heart leaped at the strange quality in his gaze.

"Cayuse?" he echoed with a queer laugh. And again, as his eye ran proudly over the red glory that was Firefly: "Cayuse, Kelly?" And then—because she was his friend, and his heart was too full for caution—the secret he had kept for four long years, and until now almost forgotten, suddenly burst from him. "Kelly," he whispered, glancing swiftly around to make sure no one overheard. "Firefly ain't a cayuse. She's a Thoroughbred."

Was he crazy? Hadn't she known Firefly since the day she was born? Why, her mother had been . . . ?

"Lissen!" Jase begged, drawing the amazed girl farther into the corner of the corral, with Firefly following like a dog, thrusting her sleek head under his arm, trying jealously in every way to win his attention. "You remember, Kelly, when we found ol' Molly's foal, an' Dad give it to me?"

"Of course . . . Firefly!" cried Kelly, recalling as vividly as though it were yesterday that long-ago morning when she and Jase, picking wild strawberries on the benches below the Jingle Bob, had found the tiny, red foal in the grass.

"Not this Firefly!" the excited boy insisted. "Kelly, when that Firefly was just a few days old, I was usin' the trail through Vortz's pasture, an' I come upon his Sacajawea racer, with a foal the dead image of mine . . . but everything mine wasn't. Lively, I mean . . . like a cricket. An' with something that made it different . . . blood, I reckon. Anyhow, I . . . I went plumb loco about her. Every day I sneaked up there an' visited her. An' one day. . . ."

He paused to look around again. And breathlessly she watched him, shocked by what she divined was coming.

"One day . . . just before weanin' time . . . I . . . I swapped foals with Vortz! Nobody ever guessed. He's away racin', most of the time, an' I kept her out of sight when he was home. He's never had a good look at her till today. He can't suspect. But she's struck his fancy. He'll try to buy her." Again his dark face was raked by fire. "I swear I'll shoot her, before I let that horse killer git her!"

He saw, then, the pain in her face, and it brought pain to his own. Wildly he implored her understanding.

"Oh, I know it was stealin'. But I . . . couldn't help myself, Kelly. Something just . . . come over me. I was plumb sick of makeshifts. I wanted something real . . . just once in my life. An' after I got her, I couldn't give her up. I can't give her up now . . . to Vortz. Kelly, say you savvy? Say you won't be down on me like the rest is . . . now you know I'm a horse thief?"

Never could Kelly Shane apply such a name to him. Nor could she bear to hear Jase do it himself. He had been so young then—only sixteen. He'd had no upbringing. Nothing better was expected of him. The wonder was not that he had done this, but that he had not done worse. And, sick with pity at how dearly he must pay for his crime, she said, like the loyal friend she had always been: "Of course, Jase . . . I understand."

She saw the auctioneer coming toward the horses. She

saw Vortz still hypnotically staring at the kidnapped foal of his own prize racer. She saw Jase's face drawn with suffering. And saw—shuddering to see—the polished grip of the six-gun at his hip.

II

" 'Going, going—gone!' "

Then the crowd surged into the corral, and the auction of the horses began. There were not many to go, and they were going for a song. One by one, they were knocked down to the highest bidder. Soon must come Firefly's turn.

Yet, to Kelly Shane the moments before it came were longer than her whole experience of time. Long enough to sear that scene in every detail forever upon her mind. The blue arch of the sky above; the savage grandeur of the broken buttes around; the far gleam of the mighty Columbia River winding below them; the immediate background of the Jingle Bob with its dead, looted buildings; and here, with the corralled stock, the crowd of men, all neighbors, friends, but all strange with that sharp, inquisitive look, as if not caring so much about getting a bargain as selfishly fearing that someone else would. And so would she remember, forever, the auctioneer's drone; the excited stir of cattle and people; even the sigh of the wind in the Jim Hill mustard that had taken the ranch—such dry, ugly skeletons of plants after flowering, rattling their dead bones in the faintest breeze, but now in delicate, golden flower, and beautiful.

As for Jase—she saw that he had forgotten her very existence. He stood at Firefly's head, his dark face set, his white lips tight, waiting. And she could have sobbed with relief when her father came over to them and stood beside her. Instinctively, as a frightened child, she slipped her hand into his, clinging to it as to an anchorage, when, like a great swarm of locusts destroying all before it, the throng swept down on their corner.

Taking up his position at Firefly's head, opposite Jase, the auctioneer began his harangue: "Now, gents, here's your chance to buy real class. A four-year-old saddle horse, sound of wind and limb, without a blemish. A cayuse, but . . . cast your optics over her! Ain't she a humdinger! Red as a harvest sunset. Proud as a sultana. Slim an' trim as the light of any Arab's tent. An' trained to a fare-you-well. In fact, gents, her training represents the life work of Jase Kress."

Whoops of mirth drowned his voice. Kelly's cheeks burned with resentment for Jase. But he gave no sign of resenting—of hearing. And most likely he did not hear, she thought, with the awful dread in his heart. She saw the auctioneer stepping back to let the red filly's splendor abet his sales talk.

"Come, you young bucks who like to cut a swath. Ever see a niftier saddle horse? See this head . . . light, lean, set on like a picture. Get the fire in them eyes . . . wide set, to show she's got brains to match. An' her hair . . . feel it? Silky as your sweetheart's. See that back . . . strong an' short . . . with the length in shoulders an' quarters. Why, she might be one of Sam Vortz's racers! Can she step? You've seen her! Now, make me an offer. What am I bid, gents? Don't all speak at once!"

Nobody spoke for some time. Blue Buttes was not to be fooled by this ballyhoo. He could boost the filly all he pleased, but she'd still be a cayuse. And they were cayuse poor. Why, you could feed a cow on what it took. . . .

"Five bucks," timidly offered a young waddy, who had long envied Jase Kress his saddle horse.

Jase flinched with pain at this first step toward the end, and his eyes met the waddy's with a light in them that was remembered long after Firefly was gone!

"Obliged for the start, Handsome," the auctioneer grinned. "Five, I'm offered! Who'll make it ten?"

"Seven," another cowboy, enamored of Firefly, struck in.

He was promptly raised by the first. And here and there a scattering bid boosted the ante by halves and dollars. But yet, to the vast relief of Kelly and Jase, Sam Vortz took no part. He seemed, in fact, to have not the slightest interest in the proceedings, merely looking on with a tolerant expression.

"Seventeen, I have," came in monotonous singsong.

"An' a half!" called the first waddy.

Whereat the second, offering his whole roll in the hope of bluffing him out, recklessly fired back: "Twenty!"

The bluff worked, for the other cowboy, embarrassedly shaking his head to show that he was out of the race, stepped back.

No other bids seemed forthcoming, although the auctioneer extolled the horse with enthusiasm. Overdid it, he soon saw. For all that oratory about a cayuse struck the assemblage as hilariously funny. And forced to give up, he began the swan song: "Going, go-ing, then . . . ."

"Twenty-five!" boomed a voice, turning Jase pale as death, and jerking the crowd up with interest.

"Now we're gettin' somewhere!" yelled the auctioneer, highly gratified to see this bidder. "Here's a man who knows a good horse! Gents, it means something when Sam Vortz puts in his bid. Come on, give him a run! Twenty-five, I have. . . ."

But no one could afford to bid against the White Rocks man. No one dared to. And, as silent seconds passed, Kelly Shane, unable to endure the suspense, frantically entreated her father to bid Jase's horse in. She could not tell him Firefly's history. Could tell only: "Jase swears he'll kill her, if Sam Vortz gets her. Please . . . Dad."

Amazed by this, by her distress, big Pat Shane glanced keenly at Jase. His feeling was neutral in regard to the lad, but his warm Irish heart always went out to the underdog. And something about Jase now touched him deeply. But he smiled reassuringly down at Kelly. "Don't worry, girl. Sure he thinks far too much of that mare to kill her."

"But that's why, Dad. Can't you see?" Kelly shook him in her frenzy. "Oh, Dad, for my sake . . . hurry!"

Understanding only that he could not resist her, Shane called: "Thirty!"

Sam Vortz whirled to see the man with temerity to bid against him. He saw, with a sense of stark outrage, Pat Shane of the Bar Bell Ranch. One man who had never kowtowed to him. One man who owed him like the rest, but who seemed to think that if he paid his interest that settled the obligation. Vortz had no doubt he would get the horse, nor that, in the end—his white eyes shone with vengeful gleam—Pat Shane would pay for it. "Thirty-five!" he snapped.

"Forty," bid Shane, his quick temper up.

"Forty-five!"

"Fifty!"

"Fifty-five!"

Vortz's anger, as he made this offer, jerked Shane back to sanity. Gray with worry, he glanced at his daughter. He knew only too well that he had no money to squander on a cayuse. Kelly did not realize. The drought last year—the

198

cattle had been in no shape to sell. He'd had to mortgage the Bar Bell to feed them through the winter. This year was starting the same. July half gone—and no rain—and yet. . . .

"Sixty!" he bid, as her mute eyes begged.

"Seventy!" Vortz jumped hoarsely.

Absolute silence prevailed. This was more than the auction of a horse. Blue Buttes knew about that mortgage. Sam Vortz never forgot a grudge. Shane was cutting his own throat—he knew it, too, and was shivering inwardly. But Kelly knew the horse's value. As he looked over again, shaking his head, she sent a last, silent, frantic appeal to him.

"Seventy-two," he nervously called, instinctively responding to it.

"Seventy-five!" capped the White Rocks man.

The Bar Bell rancher went back to his daughter.

"It's no use, lass," he told her. "No matter how high I go, he'll outbid me. But don't fret yourself about Jase, he won't. . . ." He saw then that she had not heard a word.

No, for Kelly had heard the boy's tortured sigh, as the auctioneer pronounced the words that separated him from Firefly: "Sold to Sam Vortz for seventy-five!"

As Vortz swaggered up, shelling out the cash, loudly declaring to those who remarked that it was a stiff price to pay for a cayuse—"I calkilate I got my money's worth!"—Kelly awaited that shot. It did not come. As Vortz walked over to his purchase, running a hand down Firefly's satiny foreleg, she saw the boy's right hand twitch toward his gun, and looked away in quivering horror. Had her father been right? Did Jase love the horse too much?

"Here, kid," she heard Vortz's sharp arrogant voice, "come peel your saddle off."

Kelly steeled herself. It seemed to her that every breath was suspended with hers—so still was that vast assemblage.

So still was it that a horse's restless stamp rang on the hush like a cannon, bringing a scream to her lips. Yet Jase did not keep his threat. In joyful relief that he had resigned himself to the situation, she was turning to him, when there was the sound of a rushing horse, of wild scurrying, and a man, leaping for safety, crashed against her, throwing her violently back against the fence. And there struck over all, the boy's defiant yell.

"Like hell, I will!"

Between scattering forms, she saw the red mare, with Jase on her back, bowl over Sam Vortz, bound through the gate, slue into the drive, and streak down the road like a red meteor, vanishing from sight behind an intervening butte.

Slowly, then, her dazed, blue gaze came back to the race horse man. He was picking himself out of the dust. His chalky eyes were as hard and opaque as polished marble, and his face was like a storm cloud, in its reflected threat—black, terrible.

Wes Storrs was first to catch his breath. "I knew it!" he yelled to the throng. "I knew he had something like that in mind!"

But Kelly Shane knew he was wrong. Jase had not planned to do it. As on that first time when he had stolen Firefly, something must just have come over him.

Voluntarily the auctioneer offered to return Vortz's money. But he refused it curtly.

"You'd better take it," advised Storrs. "You may have trouble gettin' her back. Everyone knows how dead set Jase Kress is on that horse."

Vortz, in a voice so thick that it almost clogged in his throat, said: "Don't worry . . . I'll reclaim my property. An' when I do, that young buck goes up for horse stealin'. I'm some set on that mare myself."

200

III

" 'That horse can't be hid!' "

Set on that horse—Sam Vortz?—perhaps. But there were some who said he was far more set on using this hold on Jase Kress to win the thing on which his heart had been set so long. At any rate, almost before Jase was out of earshot, the White Rocks man had dispatched a rider to Santo with instructions to start the full machinery of the law in motion to apprehend him. And placing himself at the head of a band of riders, numbering half the men at the auction, Vortz took up the trail. It was lost in a few miles, and the band split up to search the boy's usual haunts and scour the range.

One of these small bands wound up at the Bar Bell at dusk, far from home, tired, and supperless. Although not in sympathy with the chase, Pat Shane had, perforce, to extend the hospitality of the ranch to them. Kelly was forced to wait on them and somehow hold her tongue, as they heartlessly discussed the boy's desperate act, callously asserting that it was only a question of time—and not much of that—before he was caught and sent to prison. And she heard— her blue eyes blazing, her cheeks crimson—what a good riddance that would be. Good, too, for him! He'd run wild plenty long. It was time he was "broke" and made to work. They'd have ways to curb the worthless cayuse in the pen. Like father, like son. And so on.

To keep from speaking her mind, she rushed at last out of the house, sick with worry for Jase and in sudden rebellion against range opinion. What did they know about him?

She knew him better than anyone. She knew he was kind, and gentle, and decent, and clean. She knew there wasn't a mean thing in him—even if he had traded colts with Sam Vortz, when he was too young to realize how wrong it was, because he was sick of makeshifts—wanted something real just once—and had come to love Firefly too much to give her up to a brute like Vortz.

Why couldn't folks see Jase without seeing old Cultus behind him? Jase wasn't like his father. He was like his mother. And a finer woman never lived than Nancy Kress. Jase wasn't lazy, either. He would work harder than any man at things that interested him. The trouble was they weren't the things that paid in dollars and cents. He would work for weeks curing a crippled animal on which another man wouldn't waste a minute. Why, Jase's long sensitive fingers—not blunted out of all feeling by this hard work they set so much virtue on—could set a butterfly's wing.

This far Kelly had gone in her fierce defense, when she reached the bench beneath the hedge that bordered the drive. Sinking on it, lost in the shrubbery's velvet black, she compared Jase to other men—to the disadvantage of all of them. Nine out of every ten men she knew could hardly tell a robin from a crow. But Jase knew every bird on the range, the kind of nests they built, and where to find them. He could tell you if the one you heard was a finch or a kinglet—just by his singing. And flowers, too—other men didn't know a jack-in-the-pulpit from a hollyhock. But Jase knew every wildflower that grew.

There must be some virtue in such knowledge, some use, some worth. Yet here, alone, in the dark, looking deeply into her heart, Kelly remembered with shame and remorse that she, too, had tried to cast Jase in the Blue Buttes mold. She had lectured him on his indolence, had hoped to make a good worker of him. Why, the world was full of such men, but there was only one Jase in all of it. And he was gone. Such desolation swept Kelly then that she dropped her head in her hands and cried—until someone gently lifted her face, and she saw Jase. He had just stepped out of the hedge. She saw Firefly standing back in the shadows.

"Kelly," he cried anxiously, "what's makin' you cry?"

She faltered tearfully: "You. . . ."

"Me?" He laughed shakily, suddenly excessively happy. "Why, I ain't worth wastin' a tear on, Kelly."

Then she had wasted many.

"Jase," she whispered, swiftly rising, fear wiping out all other emotion, "you shouldn't have come."

"I had to," he said in his downright way. "I couldn't go till I said good bye. An' I've got to go, Kelly. I've got to turn tail an' run . . . for Firefly."

She knew that. Yet, it was as though her heart had been looted, and she was seeing its last, beautiful, worthwhile thing going to auction.

"Yes," she said again, "you've got to go. But where?"

He didn't know. He'd never been anywhere but here. One place, he guessed, was as good as another. "Just so it's far enough to get Firefly out of that brute's reach."

Nervously she glanced toward the house. Suppose someone came out? The whispering wind in the hedge drew her nervous glances.

"Jase," she nervously warned, "Vortz has got the sheriff an' all his deputies on your trail. He's wired a description of you an' Firefly everywhere. He's having the roads watched. . . ."

"Like I'd murdered someone," was the boy's harsh comment.

"Murder," echoed the girl, bitter for him, "wouldn't be

half the crime on this range that it is to defy Sam Vortz."
Then she cried, shuddering: "Oh, I'm afraid of what he'll
do, if he finds out that Firefly is Sacajawea's colt! They say
he's mad about that racer."

"Mad . . . is right," retorted Jase. "An' I'll tell you why.
Because she's the fastest horse in the state, an' can make
him big in other folks' eyes. You can bet he don't jam her
around. He's mighty careful how he treats Sacajawea."

"But," Kelly pointed out, "he'd be just as proud of her
colt . . . more, if it proved to be faster. Jase, is Firefly as fast
as her mother?"

She saw his face grow suddenly thoughtful. "I don't
know," he admitted at length. "She's the fastest horse I've
ever ridden . . . but that don't mean much. I've never dared
to run her against a fast horse for fear someone would suspect her blood. Anyhow, Kelly, I never cared. I liked her for
herself. It makes no difference to me if she's a world beater
or not."

Said the girl strangely: "I hope you never find out."

"I won't . . . on this range," replied Jase with a wistful
catch. He did not dream how wrong he might be, nor the
difference it would make to him whether or not Firefly was
true to her heritage.

She asked him where he had been while the search was
going on, and he told her down at the placer camp. From
the hill ranch, she could see the faint gleam far down the
terracing buttes, marking the cluster of huts on the banks of
the Columbia, where, from time immemorial, a handful of
Chinamen had lived by washing gold from the river sands.
It was an industry the cattle range frowned upon. Why,
Kelly wondered? No white man would slave like that for the
few cents they earned a day. Why begrudge it to them? Why
condemn Jase for his friendship with them?

"They're real friends," said the boy gratefully. "Vortz and his men come tearin' down there first thing. But Lo Wing hid me an' Firefly in one of the tunnels they dug in the bank. Vortz done some tall quizzin', but he couldn't get a thing out of Wing. I waited there till dark, then I come. I had to tell you good bye, Kelly, an' thank you for tryin' to buy Firefly. But," he worried, thinking of that mortgage, "I'm afraid it'll make you trouble."

So was she—having seen how worried her father had been since the auction. "But," she asked Jase earnestly, "how can it? What can Vortz do, if we pay the interest? And the Bar Bell can always do that."

It was, he thought, more than the Jingle Bob could have done, if it had been mortgaged—as it would have been, if his father had had the power. But he realized, now, that the old place hadn't had half a show. He had come to realize so many things—seeing home things go, hearing what folks thought of him, and having the heart torn out of him by the realization that he must leave Kelly Shane.

Tensely he caught her hands. "Kelly"—his tongue was halting, but his dark eyes were eloquent—"I ain't ever amounted to much. But I've woke up. I'm goin' away to earn money to square myself with Vortz. I'm goin' to make something of myself, if I can."

"You can," in simple faith said Kelly Shane.

Earnestly Jase said: "I sure will, then. No man ever amounted to much, I reckon, unless somebody believed in him. But if you think I got it in me to. . . ."

Could they not hear the muffled hoofbeats of those horses in the drive?

"I'll make good!" promised Jase.

Oh, he talked bravely. He would remember in black discouragement, with stinging shame, how bravely he had

205

talked. How easy it had seemed that night at the Bar Bell Ranch, not knowing what he was up against, with Kelly encouraging him, and with that in her blue eyes—still starry with tears for him—that put hope in his heart.

"Girl"—he tried to speak of that but found it hard—for he wasn't anybody, and she—she was Kelly! "I'm goin' but . . . I'm comin' back. Next summer I'll get the Jingle Bob. I'll fix the ol' place up. I'll stock it again. Then. . . ."

Both heard now—the hoof scrape of a stumbling horse, the rider's low curse at its clumsiness. Seeing his peril, Kelly panted: "Oh . . . go! It's Vortz!"

Jase sprang toward Firefly. The White Rocks man, knowing he had been seen, plunged openly toward them. But, to Kelly's dismay, Jase turned back. He had not said what he must say to her before leaving the country.

"Kelly . . . ," he began, although men were bearing down on them.

But, in her terror for him, she would not listen. If they caught him, it might mean prison. As he still hesitated, she seemed to know all that he was trying to say, and answered it like a true woman. Throwing her arms about him, she clung to him for one tense instant, then, pressing a wild kiss to his lips, she pushed him toward Firefly.

In a bound he was in the saddle and—gone! She heard him on the road that led to the barn. Then the men swept past her, all but riding her down. More men burst out of the house, yelling to know what was up, and stood there, gaping.

But Sam Vortz—who had seen the sympathy between the Shane girl and the Kress kid and remembered the old adage about watching the woman in the case—confidently settled himself to outride that flying shape, vaguely discernible in the starlight. He had no doubt of the outcome, for he and his men were riding the best saddle horses on the range. Nor was he worried when Jase shot behind the high poplars that hid the highway and out of his sight for a time. All was open country beyond. It would not take long to run down a cayuse—even one as fast as the red which, undoubtedly, had some Thoroughbred blood—but the cayuse strain would tell in the end.

But, thundering onto the highway himself, he was astonished to see that Firefly had lengthened the distance between them by fifty paces, and was more astonished by the rapidity with which that distance increased. Sinking his spurs in his horse, he yelled to the men coming after him: "Give 'em the leather!"

They did, tearing down the dim road, drawing from their fast mounts the last ounce of speed, as madly following, with no heed to the dangerous footing, when Jase abruptly left the road and took to the sage. But for all their reckless riding, the boy steadily drew away from them, disappearing altogether behind a swelling hillock. Vortz, soon topping it, could see him nowhere. Realizing the hopelessness of finding him in the dark, he halted and sat there, his blood bounding through every pulse.

"That horse . . . ," he gasped, as his men plunged up. "Did you see her run?"

They had seen!

"Men," he swore thickly, "I don't savvy. But . . . when I bought that filly, I bought something. I'll have her, if it breaks me. Go where he will, I'll get that kid. That horse can't be hid."

IV

"Against speed"

However, it was not Firefly who betrayed their whereabouts. Down in Oregon, she rested up from the long trip in one of the Q Ranch's thousand-acre pastures. And Jase who was doing the last thing expected of him—working—rode a saddle stirrup supplied by the ranch. But often of an evening, when work was done, he took Firefly for a run over the high sage plains. Sometimes Pasco, his long, lean, lachrymose bunky, accompanied him. And it was Pasco who told the other Q waddies: "The kid's red filly sure kin leg it like a scairt rabbit." Naturally, those of the cowboys who had pride in their mounts challenged Jase to a race, and many friendly matches were staged, until it was established that Firefly was the fastest horse on the ranch.

How much faster she was, even Jase did not know. It had never been necessary for the filly to extend herself against these cow ponies. And her speed was still a mystery. It counted nothing with him that she had outrun Vortz that night since, obviously, Vortz would not have used his best horses in that chase. Not Sacajawea, for instance. And Jase knew that the percentage of horses with the outstanding speed and stamina that makes races was small, even among Thoroughbreds. So the chances were that Firefly was merely fast, and that suited Jase.

But riding her in these uneven contests, thrilling to feel the unrestrained power in her fleet, smooth pace, he wondered if, indeed, she had inherited the speed of her racing forebears. And he remembered that Kelly had hoped he would never find out. What had she meant? As often as he thought of her, he wondered that, and he thought of her continually. Not an hour of the day, at work, or play, but what his wistful eyes went north, where, hundreds of miles away, was Blue Buttes range and the blue-eyed girl who had stuck by him through thick and thin, his whole life long. Always he worked toward one end—to square himself, so he could go back, build up the Jingle Bob, and tell Kelly Shane what he had tried to tell her that last night at the Bar Bell.

Long ago seemed that night to him, and far had he journeyed since. By keeping to unfrequented roads, or forsaking any, he had escaped all the traps set for him. Penniless when he left, he had starved through, eating only when a rabbit or grouse came within range of his six-gun or he was offered a meal at some free-handed ranger's camp. After two weeks of flight, he had dropped rein before the Q bunkhouse one night—played out, pale and thin, with his old sun-bleached, weather-beaten garments all but dropping from him, and the Q foreman had taken him on.

Now, more than two months later—October in blue, hazy Indian summer—his hard, healthy young body had filled out. And, in new blue shirt, new leather chaps, new ten-gallon hat, and new everything else, he was a new Jase. A striking-looking, up-and-coming young chap, whom Blue Buttes would never have recognized. He even had a new pride. For here folks had only himself to judge him by, and, to his rather pathetic surprise, they rated him highly. The proudest moment of his life—barring, of course, that last, delirious one with Kelly—was when his first pay check was put in his hands. He had just stood and held it, as if he expected someone to take it away from him.

"Ain't it right, kid?" the foreman had brought him back

to earth. "Thirty bucks. I had to deduct twenty for togs."

"Right?" the boy had echoed, with shining eyes. "Gee, I'll say it's all right."

The foreman had almost passed out, when Jase handed it back with the request that he let it ride.

When the next pay day came, and the foreman held back his check with a grin, saying—"I reckon you want me to keep this one?"—Jase had flushed right back at him: "Not on your life! Will you write me a check for seventy-five, an' give me the rest in cash?"

The foreman did. Pocketing the five silver dollars, all he had left to show for two months' work, Jase endorsed the check and put it in an envelope addressed to Wes Storrs, along with a note asking the administrator to settle with Sam Vortz for Firefly. When the letter went out with the ranch mail, he felt better than ever—free, clean, as he really amounted to something.

"You belong to me now," he told Firefly in that twilight gallop. But he added unhappily: "Anyway, you belong to me as much as you did before the auction."

For his first theft of her—never considered as such before his awakening—now haunted him. He was pretty certain that, even yet, Firefly legally belonged to Vortz. And since he could not bear the thought of giving her back, he could see no way to make it right before he returned to Kelly Shane. Long he brooded over the problem.

One noon, lazing in the sage far out on the range, he put it up to Pasco, impulsively stating it as a hypothetical case, in which he had no personal concern.

"Suppose a man . . . ," he began, and went on to suppose the whole thing. How the man had swapped colts; how much he had come to think of it—which occasioned as much wonder here as it had at home—how it had been sold back to the very man he had taken it from; how he had fled with it again; and how he had returned the price that owner had paid.

"Now," Jase earnestly asked, "does it belong to this man . . . since he's paid for it once? If not, Pasco, how can he square himself?"

Pasco pushed back his hat to scratch his head, as he always did to think, as if the action somehow put a spur to his wits. After moments of this, he observed: "It's pretty deep for a cowpunch'. I'd sure like to put it up to Pete." Pete, his brother, was sheriff of that county and, Pasco thought, the final authority on all points of legality. "Pete could tell you quick as a wink. But jist as a everyday lay citizen, I'd say the hoss belonged to the *hombre* it was first took from. As to how the other feller could square hisself . . . that depends. If the colt substituted was worth as much as the one took, why, he could jist forget it. For there'd be no loss, an' what the other *hombre* didn't know wouldn't hurt him. It'd be even easier, if the colt was worth more. But since the swiped colt was worth the most, it's my humble opinion that he ought to make good the difference."

"Suppose," said Jase, bending to pick up a twig of dead sage and breaking it into minute bits, "suppose this man don't know what the difference is?"

"Then," Pasco thought, "he ought to find out."

"But suppose"—persisted the boy, his eyes, as Pasco saw, going far and kindling at some dark scene that was not in his own range of vision—"suppose the *hombre* who first owned the colt was plumb mean . . . the sort of varmint who takes out his hangovers on his horses. Suppose he had. . . ." And he recounted instances of cruelty that made Pasco jerk up, his cheeks red with mounting anger although he knew they were mere supposition. "Suppose," Jase went on in a low, repressed voice, "you'd seen him take a high-lifed colt that was car shy, put a spade bit on her, an' ride her through them all day, braggin' how he'd break her or kill her. An' you'd seen her come in with her flanks raked raw, her breast all red, an' her tongue . . . well, just hangin' by a thread. What would you say then?"

"Say . . . nothin'!" exploded Pasco, mighty grim. "By Christmas, I'd half murder him!"

"That's what I . . . I mean, that's what this man would have done," said Jase as grimly, "if he hadn't been just a kid at the time. But what I want to know . . . would it be right for him to give back the colt, sayin' he could bring himself to it? . . . a horse he'd made a pet of? One that was spoiled some, an' headstrong . . . high-lifed herself . . . an' apt to make that buster fly off the handle?"

It didn't take Pasco long to decide that it wouldn't. "Sometimes," he philosophized, giving Jase a straight look, "there's a law above the law . . . an' justice due the horse. Come right down to cases, it don't all belong to that he-reptile it was swiped from . . . just the shell. The real heart an' soul of it is what the second owner made it. That much is his. The other *hombre* might have plumb ruined it. So, if I was you . . . I mean this feller we're talkin' about . . . I'd develop a blind spot in my memory. I'd plumb forget how I got the colt . . . for its own sake, savvy?"

That was what Jase wanted to do—just call it quits, forget that Firefly wasn't his, and ease his conscience by telling himself that he was doing it all for Firefly's sake. But even with Pasco's moral support, he could not. And now he was wild to know Firefly's value. If she had inherited her parents' speed, she would be worth far more money than he could ever hope to save. But if she turned out to be merely a good-blooded saddle horse, he might easily make good the difference to Vortz and own her legally.

He prayed that this last was the case. Yet, the very next day when he thought it might be, he prayed with all his heart that it was not. This was on Saturday. The crew, having been given a half holiday, was going into Crater to celebrate. Jase had not been to town since he came, as Pasco aggrievedly reminded him, and what difference did it make if he was broke, when his pard—Pasco—had a full pay check that hadn't even been cashed yet? So Jase allowed himself to be persuaded and set off with the Q outfit, so happy to have removed the threat of Vortz, to have Firefly under him, that he was the gayest one in the bunch, eager for fun, ready for anything.

He found Crater different from Santo in that it was laid out on the level floor of the plains, while his own home town had hilly environs. But, otherwise, it was just the same—a lively little cow town. Anything went when the boys rode in. And everything was going—with boys riding in from all directions. Girls, too—scores of pretty, sombreroed girls, in sunset blouses and scarves. And, from a nearby reservation, picturesque Indians in gay, gaudy blankets. Ranchers and their wives were wheeling in from all sides, to exchange gossip and stock up with supplies. Altogether, they jammed the one, long, straight street of the town. With everyone out for a good time, it would be his own fault if he wasn't having it, but Jase sure was. Having tied their horses to the hitching rail before the hotel, he and Pasco left the rest, enjoying just drifting through the crowd, stopping here and there to jolly with the other 'punchers. Suddenly their attention was attracted by a group of cowboys gathered about their horses in what was, to judge by the sound of their voices, a hot, verbal contest.

Pressing up, they learned that Firefly was the cause of the argument.

"She's the best li'l hoss whatever came down the pike," boasted a waddy from Jase's own outfit. "You gotta admit that, Des Chutes."

Whereat the hard-featured, wry-mouthed buckaroo addressed flung back in a tone that made Jase see red: "Oh, she'll do . . . in a pinch."

"That bird," Pasco whispered, "is one of the Hat Creek bunch. He's mighty set up about his own hoss."

"That gray he's holdin'?" Jase was thinking that it was a good one, and he said, as Pasco nodded: "I don't blame him."

"Oh, it's a winner all right," his partner owned. "It's the fastest horse on this range. . . ." He stopped abruptly, his mind leaping back to their talk yesterday, his eyes going swiftly to Jase's red mare, and suddenly his whole being took fire. While Jase wondered at his change, Pasco swung and swaggered up to the Hat Creek man.

"She'll do, huh?" drawlingly he jeered at Des Chutes. "I guess she will! She'll fade your gray in a quarter mile!"

Loudly the Hat Creek men hooted at that. Des Chutes snapped in jealous rage: "I've got twenty that says she can't!"

Again Pasco threw Firefly a swift glance, and even more cocksure now he drawled: "Kinda dubious, though . . . ain't you? Twenty . . . shucks! I'm backin' my say with a full pay check!"

Instantly the goaded cowboy covered the bet, and the Q boys rallied around Jase, betting left and right on Firefly. Although she had beaten their horses, not one of them—Pasco, perhaps, excepted—dreamed that she was anything but a fast pony, too light for range work. But loyalty demanded that they back her with their last cent. Almost before Jase knew what was happening, the race was planned.

Firefly and the gray would run from a furrow drawn in the gravel before the sandwich stand at the far end of Crater's main street to a line drawn here before the hotel—an exact quarter mile, and evidently a favorite course. Word spread like flame in prairie grass, bringing men in hordes. And these, quickly appraising the horses, showed by the size of the bets they feverishly placed that they sensed it would be no ordinary cowboy race.

Pasco, seizing his first chance, drew Jase aside. "Pard," he confessed, "I've let you in for somethin'. That gray's a whirlwind. He's beat everything goin' in these parts. Firefly's got to do more than I've seen her. . . ."

"She can!" wildly excited, Jase cut in. "Pasco, I've always held her back when we raced at the ranch! Why, I don't even know how fast. . . ."

"That's what we're findin' out!" cried his friend, to whom all this was oil to flame. "It'll be worth a month's pay, if we lose. An' if we win, I'm splittin' fifty-fifty with you for takin' the conceit outta that Hat Creek outfit! Remember, pard, git everything out of that mare she's got!"

V

" 'Red baby!' "

Oh, but it was a thrilling moment for Jase—this, before his first real race—with Firefly pitted against a horse of recognized speed, with men risking their money on his little red mare, after just one look at her. She tingled with pride as he untied her and led her through the throng, repeatedly halted by Q boys, pressing up to give him some last word of advice or encouragement.

Already, Des Chutes was riding downstreet, grumbling at the delay. Jase broke away and was mounting to follow, when he saw a man with a star on his shirt beckon to Pasco from the curb. Rightly he guessed that it was his brother, Pete—the sheriff, whom Pasco was always talking about. He thought, as he rode in Des Chutes's wake, how fine it was to be able to look at a sheriff's star and not shake in his boots.

Past him a cowboy dashed, clearing the street by the simple expedient of galloping down it, yelling at the top of his lungs—"Race! Race!"—a proclamation that emptied the stores of patrons and clerks, and brought the populace of the town to the curb to watch. And their preparations, the air of tension, fanned Jase's excitement. He tried to control it, and it steadied him somewhat to study Des Chutes's horse as he rode along. Seeing, now, with a qualm of doubt, that it was better than he had thought. Speed was revealed in its every line, although it had not the slim, racy lines of Firefly. It was of heavier build, with the powerful quarters of a sprinter. He remembered, too, and with a sharper misgiving, that the race was only a quarter mile long, and the gray was a race veteran. But—Jase clung hard to this— Firefly was the daughter of Sacajawea and Sachem, for, suddenly, he could not bear to think of her being beaten.

At the starting place, a few yards behind Des Chutes, he turned, to see Pasco galloping toward him. He was shocked at the wild look on his partner's face, grown old and gray in the few moments since he had seen it, stunned by what Pasco was wildly saying, as he hauled up beside him.

"Beat it, pard. Cut an' run. Pete . . . my brother . . . is on your trail. He's got a warrant . . . hoss stealin'. Said you

216

was traced here by a letter."

Jase just stared at him, his color fading. That letter . . . then Vortz wouldn't take the money. Then he . . . ?

"Don't you savvy? Pete's after you, Jase. I begged him to let you run this race. Told him I had to start it, an' come to tip you off. You gotta chance from here . . . a quarter mile start. Pete don't suspect I'd warn you . . . me bein' his brother. But you're my. . . ."

"Is this a race, or a gab fest?" bellowed Des Chutes, chafing, at a distance.

Jase's stricken gaze went to the crowd upstreet. Up there, a sheriff was waiting for him. Up there were the Q boys, who had treated him fine.

Pale and resolute of face, he called to Des Chutes. "It's a race!"

"Now, don't be loco," entreated Pasco. "Pard, they're just waitin' to nab you."

The boy's misted gaze turned back to his friend who had betrayed a brother to warn him. "Pasco," he said tensely, "you're the first pal I ever had. If I had a million, you'd still be the best."

"Right back at you," flashed Pasco, so huskily that Jase could hardly go on.

"I sure appreciate this out you gave me. But I can't take it. The boys up there backed me . . . I can't let them down. An' you. . . ."

"Never mind about me!"

"So I'm goin' to run," Jase said steadily, "an' win, if I can. An' then . . . but first I want you to know. I'm the man who took her. An' the two-legged skunk I took her from is behind this warrant."

Pasco nodded. That's how he had doped it. But he begged Jase not to race. "You'll be headin' straight for jail.

That hoss beater will git the mare."

With no time to tell Pasco his plan to save her, Jase just said: "Firefly would want to pay her debt."

"Fer Pete's sake, pry loose!" roared Des Chutes, suspicious of all that low-toned talk.

Jase swung from his still protesting partner, and rode up. Pasco with a fervent—"Good luck!"—which did not apply to the race, as Des Chutes thought, pulled the gun from his belt. And Firefly, quivering in every slim, red limb, tossing her sleek, red head, swung beside her big gray opponent. There were several false starts, interspersed with Des Chutes's lurid curses. Then both horses swept down to the line in a perfect start, Pasco's gun crashed, and—they were off!

Off but with despair seizing hard on Jase's heart, as a gray flash shot past. And sickeningly his heart sank to see Des Chutes's horse full three lengths ahead in the first fifty yards. Wasn't Firefly fast, even? Was she—with the blood of racing kings in her veins—to go down in her first race before a horse bred on the range? Was he racing straight back to the thing he had run hundreds of miles to get away from—all to no end? Was he not to repay the Q boys—in the only way he could possibly pay—for having been so good to him?

Jase could not know that the gray's record was due to his ability to make that thunderbolt start, to gain such a lead in the first few jumps as few horses could overcome in a short run. He only knew that the horse he loved as if she were human was the first time in her life taking the dust of another horse, and it hurt. But he also realized that the distance between him and the gray was not increasing, and he thrilled at feeling the smooth, mechanical rhythm of the flying form beneath him. Then, as Firefly strained and drew on that reserve he had always felt, but which had always been held in check, he was swept by a delirium of joy that burned up all thought save to win.

He flattened himself on her neck, straining with her, talking to her, seeing—through eyes narrowed against the gravel thrown back by the gray's pounding hoofs—the howling spectators lined up at the curb on either side, hearing through all the far roar of the mob at the finish line and forgetting that it numbered a sheriff in his mad exultation that Firefly was creeping up. She had cut the handicap in half. Could she gain enough in the short run left?

"You can do it, girl," he encouraged her, as Kelly had encouraged him. "I know you can!"

She seemed to take wings at his voice. For, suddenly, wind was cutting his face. Faster—more blurred—rushed back the line on either curb. He saw that she had won to the hips of the gray, but less than a hundred yards were left. Des Chutes flung back a derisive grin, spurring his nobly running horse. But its best had been put in that whirlwind start, while Firefly, to whom a mile run was only exercise, was just hitting her stride. At fifty yards her red nose was stretched even with Des Chutes's stirrup, and his grin faded. People—wild at the close way they would finish—roared down the pound of their flying hoofs.

"Come on, Firefly!" screamed the Q outfit.

"Oh . . . red baby!" cried the enthusiasts.

And, over and over, the white-faced boy endearingly murmured in Firefly's ear: "You can do it, girl."

To come in first, to win, Jase prayed. On they ran, through the swelling sound, gray and red, fighting it out, inch by inch, in the few yards left, while watchers went crazy, and even a sheriff momentarily forgot his duty. Steadily those on the left curb saw the gray head draw behind the red, and the red strain out. The crowd seemed to come at Jase with a rush, and every sound in the universe seemed to be enveloped in the Q boys' victorious shout: "Firefly!"

And then—everything lay behind! Des Chutes, ugly in defeat, was sawing his reins, slowing his mount. But Jase made no move to check Firefly, now running faster then ever—straight on, out of town, out over the sage plains.

They had won, but they were outcasts again. Looking back, Jase saw a far rider—the sheriff! But though he soon shook him off, his heart did not lift. So, he thought, his eyes smarting hot, it might be always. Always the byways. Always the back trail to watch.

Whatever possessed Jase to set the course of his flight straight north, back toward the very place he had fled from, will never be known. Perhaps it was something of the same instinct that draws a wild horse back to its home range. Perhaps he felt that it was safest—since Vortz would continue the search at farther points. Or perhaps it was only that he could not bear to put more distance between himself and Kelly.

At any rate, he retraced the hundreds of weary miles he had come to reach the Q Ranch, stopping but once. The last of his money gone, he called a halt in a little mountain town near the state line and hunted work. A rancher, rounding up cattle that had been running on the forest preserves through the summer months, hired him for two weeks' riding. And then, thirty dollars to the good, Jase rode on—still going north.

One gray November day—again pale, thin, and unkempt—he sat his horse on the rim of the high plateau that formed the south wall of the great gap through which the Columbia flowed, looking with wild longing across the miles of jumbled brakes, across the silver thread of the mighty river at their feet, to the far, pine-blackened ridges of Blue Buttes range. Eagerly Firefly snorted, tossing her head for a free rein, and pranced.

But the boy said brokenly: "No, girl . . . we can't go home."

Long he sat there, feasting his starved eyes on this far glimpse of it, wondering which way to turn, seeming to realize for the first time that he could not go on. He dared not seek work here. Someone who knew him might come along at any time. But he must do something, for his money would not last forever. The chill nip of the air cut through his woolen Mackinaw, a forcible reminder that winter was coming, and work anywhere might be hard to find.

Then out of his sheer necessity to hide himself and Firefly and earn a living for them somehow, a great idea was born. One that would have seemed the natural move to another man, but to Jase so foreign, so revolutionary, that it had all the daring of an expedition to the Polar regions. He would quit the range. He would lose himself in some big city. What city? He had never been to any.

Beyond the Cascades, whose shaggy heads, already white, towered to the west of him, lay many of them—Seattle, Tacoma, Bellingham. To the east, a hundred miles or so—Spokane. Which one? The first named were coast towns, which—to a cowboy—counted against them. Spokane was the trading center of the Inland Empire, and had more of the range flavor. Besides, Kelly had gone to school there. Any place that Kelly had been was dear to Jase. So, after contemplating a bit, he headed east.

Two days later, he was urging the nervous Firefly across the high bridge over Hangman Creek, and was in the city. With the red filly skidding and slipping, desperately trying to keep her footing on the slick pavement, and so terrified by the clang of trolleys, the roar of cars, the thunder of trains over viaducts, that her flanks were foaming from her constant pitching and shying, the boy had all he could do to keep her from bolting. Scarcely less nervous, Jase wanted to bolt himself—and, afterwards, would wish to heaven he had.

He put Firefly in a feed barn and was directed by the stableman to a lodging house in the vicinity, and there—entered upon a nightmare. But soon he would look back to it as to happiness. He had had Firefly then, and Firefly had been worth everything.

VI

"No opening"

That November. Truly, those were for Jase melancholy days. He was as miserable as any caged eagle up in Manito. If there was beauty in fine architecture, well-kept parks, in the river, saddled with many bridges, that ran to its famous falls where buildings were thickest—the Place of Broken Sunbeams, as the Indians had called it generations before the white man had harnessed it to make a nightly rainbow of the city that had sprung up on their ancient camp ground—if there was beauty in such things, Jase did not see it. His eyes were trained to natural beauty only—the sun's pink rise, its gold and purple settings, wild rivers, wild God-made heights.

If there were space and freedom suggested to a degree rare in any modern city by grand mountain glimpses, Jase did not feel them—corralled in his two-by-four room, confined by the chutes that held the human herd that men call streets. If there were here pleasure, peace, and plenty, he knew them not, wearily tramping the streets for work, cutting his meals to two—to one—a day, practicing the most miserly economy. If there was companionship to be found among thousands of his kind, he did not find it—suffering from the separation from Firefly.

True, he visited her several times a day. But, heretofore, she had shared his every waking hour. It hurt to know that others were caring for her. And he had a sense of guilt when he was with her. The eager way she lifted her head at his footsteps, as if expecting him to saddle her and ride her out of there, shamed him to the soul. He felt as though he had escaped Vortz only by putting Firefly in prison. She had never been stabled before. Confinement irked her. All that this existence was to him, it was to Firefly, and more.

On the night of his arrival, Jase had stared out of his window at the dazzling lights that mocked him in steady blinks, excluding the natural light of moon and stars, his head aching from the roar that came up to him—the sound of industry's great wheels going around, music to the city man, heard by him only as a low undertone, if heard at all. But to Jase's hearing, tuned to the music of bird songs, the wind's sweet wash in trees and grass, the coyote's wild, piercing notes, it was fearful, nerve-wracking discord. He wondered if he could ever adjust himself to it, could ever stop hearing it, and other nights, standing here, he would remember this with a bitter smile that mocked himself. As if he had had any choice!

Hunt as he did, doggedly, day after day, till feet were sore and heart was sick, he could not find work. There was—how did they put it?—no opening. No opening for him, although the city was booming; and morning, noon, and night the streets ran rivers of men going to their employment. Coming, that first morning, to where a great building was under construction, and swarming like an ant hill with workers, he had sought out the foreman in all confidence, applying for work in the assurance that he had only to ask and he would receive. But the fellow had looked him over and been sorry, but—there was no opening. And Jase had lost all count of the times he had been given that answer since.

For there was no opening for a slight youth like him, with the range stamp, with a rider's smooth, well-kept hands, where men might be had—big, strapping men, skilled and work-inured. There was no place in complex city life for one whose special knowledge was of cattle, birds, and flowers. If—as Kelly surely thought—there was some worth in such things, some use for hands so deft that they could set a butterfly's wing, Jase never found it. Stores, garages, hotels were applied to by the weary range lad, and were sorry—or so they said—and there was no opening.

Firefly's feed bill was a dollar a day. Each day Jase took a dollar from his decreasing roll and put it in the inside pocket of his Mackinaw. He performed this as a religious rite, regarding the money as a sacred fund that he must touch under no circumstances. He must be prepared to take Firefly out at any time, and he planned to ride out of town before his money was quite gone and find work on some range. He had longed to do this from the first, felt that everything would right itself, if he could get back to his own element. But an unexpected streak of tenacity held him from day to day, while his money ebbed away.

So far, he had failed in everything—except those two months in Oregon. He had had to run then. But Vortz would not find him here, and, if he ran now, it would be because he had let the city lick him. So he stayed, and tried working harder hunting work than ever he had dreamed a man could, and returned at night, exhausted in body and spirit, to his cheerless room, where he would lie, too tired to sleep, and think—of Blue Buttes—home. Where there were no streets to tangle a fellow. Where a man could ride all day without opening a gate. Home—where Kelly was.

Kelly! How vividly he saw her at these times—standing against the wild mustard blossoms of the old Jingle Bob. Standing by him through the auction, as she had through everything, as she had stood by him when his mother died. He had not minded Kelly's seeing him cry. She had been with him when his father died, too. He had not cried then—outside. He had seen his dad dead to the world so many times it had kind of taken the edge off. How plainly he saw Kelly, with her tawny hair, and the true, blue eyes of her! How plainly he heard her, as on that starlit night at the Bar Bell, believing in him, and—maimed as he was, his heart sang—kissing him! Would he ever see her again? Would he ever go home?

Often, too, he wondered about Firefly's value. Nothing had been settled by that race. The distance was not right and the gray not in her class. The only real test would be to run her against Thoroughbreds.

So the days passed, until the day came when, adding a dollar bill to Firefly's fund, he had only a quarter left. And then, buckling on his chaps and spurs—doffed here, because they drew amused stares—Jase gave up his room.

Heading for the stable, he was conscious of a great relief. The fight was over. The issue had been taken from his hands. He would get Firefly and hit for the range. Yet, walking with lighter step than he had been wont to walk, crazy to get "a-horseback," his pocketed hand closed upon that lone coin, halting him. He was not broke—yet. It would buy his breakfast, and he could leave Firefly until noon tomorrow before owing the stable another dollar. There was still a chance.

Taking out the quarter, he flipped it in the air. "Tails I go now," he vowed, hoping fate would will it so. "Heads I stay for one last day."

It fell, heads up, upon the slushy sidewalk.

Well, he would go the rounds in the morning, then. He would have to sleep out tonight. But that held no terrors for him—although the nights were bitter. He was used to sleeping out in all kinds of weather.

Despite the change in his plans, he went on to see Firefly. It seemed to him that she had never been so glad to see him before. Sure that he would fail tomorrow, he promised, as he patted her: "I'm takin' you out of this, girl."

She might have understood, her nicker was so joyous. The stableman, coming up, was moved out of his impersonal calm by it.

"By jinks," he exclaimed, "she can almost talk!"

Jase pitied him for the *almost*. And, unconsciously putting a hand on that hard, comforting bulge in the pocket against his heart, he said with a lilt: "In the mornin', I'll be takin' her out."

It was after dark and sleeting hard when he went back to the street. Aimlessly, for hours, he wandered about, finding himself, near midnight, at the big railroad viaduct, chilled through and through, ready to drop in his tracks. In there, out of the storm, he saw many men sleeping, sprawled on the ground beneath blankets, coats, and sacks. Transients, like himself—tramps, misfits, outcasts. He paused near one of the great pillars, seeking a place for himself.

Suddenly a form beside him stirred, and a shaggy head

reared over a tattered blanket, its owner's weasel eyes fixed hard on Jase.

"H'lo," he growled. "Thought you was a bull, lookin' us over. Travelin', huh?"

Jase said yes, and continued to look around.

"Which way you headin'?" quizzed the weasel-eyed man.

"West," said the boy, to get rid of him.

"Seattle, huh? Ridin' the rods? There's a westbound freight goes through at daybreak. That's the one I'm. . . ." He broke off, his eyes mere pinpoints, as Jase moved out a step, and the dim street light revealed his range dress. However, the tramp made no comment but was fawningly friendly all at once. Lifting his blanket, he moved over, insisting that Jase share it.

Unwilling to offend him, too utterly weary to think of any way he could refuse without doing so, Jase, with strong distaste, stretched out beside his strange bedfellow, and was almost instantly asleep. He dreamed he was sleeping out on the home range, with Firefly grazing near him. He dreamed that she nuzzled against him, as she often did for companionship, and his sleeping lips curved in his last happy smile for weeks.

It was broad daylight when he awoke with a sense of gladness long absent from his awakenings. He tried to account for it. What was he glad about? Oh, yes, he was shaking all this. He would make one last try, then get Firefly, and line out. Automatically his hands went to his pocket, as they always did when he thought of her, and, failing somehow to feel the bulge there, went into the pocket and, failing still, dug frantically to its very seam. Then he clawed and tore at every pocket and dug at the ground he had lain upon. But the money so religiously saved to redeem Firefly was gone! And so was the friendly tramp. And so was the westbound freight that had passed at daybreak.

For the first time in his life, Jase knew stark, paralyzing terror. He could not pay for Firefly! What could they do? They would have to give him his horse, wouldn't they? He almost ran the ten long blocks to the feed barn, weaving along as drunkenly as ever old Cultus had weaved in his cups. And, staggering into the place, faint from the run, from the short rations he had been on for days, he poured out his tale of robbery. What little hope he had was crushed by the lack of interest on the face of the stableman to whom hard-luck tales had lost all novelty.

"So," Jase said desperately, trying to sound trustworthy, "I'll just have to ask you to stand me off, an' take her out. I'll get work, an' send the money back."

The stableman was unimpressed. "We'll have the money, kid, before you take the horse."

"You think I'm lyin'!" Jase flamed, not in anger, but in fear. "You think I'm tryin' to beat you?"

The stableman did not. "But," he said apathetically, "it's against the rule. We have to hold a horse for the feed bill."

It was the rule! Nothing could move him. Presently Jase ceased trying, as a new terror struck him.

"Suppose," he faltered, not daring to look at Firefly, "suppose I couldn't pay . . . no time? What's the rule . . . then?"

"Why," was the calm response, "we'd sell her to pay the feed bill."

Dazed, Jase left the place to find a job. He had tried for weeks and failed. Now he had to get one! And before the stores were open, he was down in Trent, studying the boards before an employment office. Most of the jobs offered were out of town. Standing in the icy street, slighter than when employers had first balked at his slightness, his

228

face pinched, and with a betraying pallor, he read the morning offerings, determined to take anything. A driller, he read, was wanted at a Coeur d'Alene mine. A cook in a construction camp. Loggers and scalers in the Kettle Falls country. The same old story. Work for everyone—but him.

Despairingly he was turning away, when someone touched his arm. He swung to see, with joy that made his eyes sting, an honest-to-goodness range man. A lean, leathery cowman was drawling: "Huntin' work, cowboy?"

Fervently Jase owned it. And he was so afraid he would not find it that he felt himself shrink beneath the man's appraising gaze, and thought his nerves would shake his body all to pieces. "The bright lights," his grin was piteous, "don't agree with me. I'm kinda bleached out. You know . . . livin' soft! But put me on the grass, an' I'll pick up. I'm a bear for work!"

"Then," the ranger smiled, "we ought to make connections." But he was not deceived. Hunger looked out of Jase's eyes. Also a dauntless spirit, which this man had remarked before accosting him. He had no big, strapping men to choose from. Or rather, those he had chosen would have nothing to do with his proposition, and his need was as desperate as that of Jase.

"My name's Rudge," he said, "an' I need a man to feed cattle this winter. I warn you, it's no snap. In fact, half a dozen men have tried the job an' give it up. But I pay high . . . sixty an' board. An' fare from Spokane, of course."

Fare! Leave Firefly here? The boy's face fell. He asked: "Where?"

"Where? Across the Bitter Roots . . . out of Bear Paw."

Montana! He could not go so far away from Firefly! But maybe—this man might . . . ?

"That's what I thought," said Rudge warmly. "Real waddies ain't studyin' these boards. I've tried out three this mornin', an' every mother's son of 'em hemmed an' hawed, an' allowed they didn't need work, when I told 'em it was a feed job. Two of 'em wanted to see the color of my money before they ever started."

Jase had been on the point of making a third. He had been about to ask an advance that he might take Firefly with him. It terrified him to think how near he had come to losing this first chance. Sixty a month! Firefly was safe here. He could soon pay her bill. But if he let this chance slip, he might not get another, and they would sell her.

"I'll go," he said.

"But will you stay? I tell you, this job's a stem-winder. I don't want a man who'll be quittin' on me in the dead of winter. Will you agree to stay till the Chinook comes?"

"I'll stick," Jase promised, "till the spring Chinook."

"Fine!" Heartily Rudge took his hand. "The train leaves at nine sharp. It's now . . . le's see"—he looked at his watch—"eight o'clock. I've some business to attend to. Say you meet me at the G.N. dépôt?"

So they arranged it. And the instant Rudge left, Jase made a beeline for the feed barn, arriving there so excited and out of breath that the stableman cried: "You've raised the riffle? Well," he actually grinned, "that's fine! Rules is rules, but. . . ."

"I've got a job!" cried Jase. "A good one . . . in Montana. I'm leavin' right off. Will you keep my horse?"

"Sure!" That's what he was in business for.

"I mean"—Jase could not go while any doubt remained—"you won't sell her . . . no matter how long I am?"

"Well," the man went by rule again, "that depends. We keep a horse a reasonable length of time."

"What do you call reasonable?"

"A month or so . . . not longer, as a rule. Unless we know the owner will stand good."

"Lissen!" Jase caught the man's arms, his desperate eyes burned into him. "I'll stand good for Firefly, if it's a million years! Will you keep her till spring?"

Stirred to the heart's core, ignorant of what fate had in store for them, the stableman said: "I'll keep her, kid."

VII

"For Firefly"

Worthless—Jase Kress? Too lazy to draw breath? That most damaging, all-embracing, range encomium—cultus? The cattle he cared for that winter put the lie to that. They had no tongue to do it, but their survival proved it.

He was brought to this lonely out-camp, twenty miles from the Pot Handle—Rudge's home ranch—and left with over two hundred head of hungry, bawling cows for which he must account in spring, and an inadequate supply of hay to feed them. Left to work, work, work, while winter took Montana by the throat; and the wind went by the line cabin in long, shuddering moans; and the hungry coyotes ran the white hills around; and there often struck, deep into the startling silence of the glittering moon-bright nights, the wild, sobbing song of the hunting packs.

From daybreak until dark, Jase worked. Forking endless quantities of hay from stacks to feed racks. Giving constant care to weaklings in separate corrals. Up early and late with calves unseasonably arrived. Chopping ice from the creek that the herd might drink, and chopping it out as it froze again. Doing all this—and more—cheerfully. It was for Firefly. He worked to take his mind from her, from what she must be thinking—for he gave the little mare every human attribute!—of his desertion, from his haunting dread lest something happen despite the promise of the stableman. And to forget, he worked the harder, dragging in at night to cook and eat his solitary supper, and mark off another day on the calendar above the table.

Other men had rebelled at this task, because of the loneliness. Jase was glad to be alone. He wanted no more friends. No one whom he might have to leave as he had left Pasco. He guarded against such another hurt, shrank, even, from forming a friendship with Rudge. But he found this hard.

Once a week, all through December, the rancher had bucked the drifts to bring supplies in and see how his new hand was getting on, to marvel at the slim lad's fortitude, until he would see again the spirit in his dark eyes—and understand. January brought a cold snap of such severity that Rudge could not make his weekly visit. For days he delayed, hoping the weather would moderate. At last, seeing no prospects of a change, worried by thinking of the many things that could happen to a man alone in a forty-below atmosphere—when even the most trifling accident might have a fatal result—Rudge, at considerable risk to himself, made the trip.

Riding by the corrals, he saw the cattle, humped up, shivering in the freezing wind or hobbling around on stiffened limbs for the hay that had been recently pitched to them. He heard more bawling down by the creek, and he knew Jase was down there working with the water. Easy, then, in his mind, he went on into the cabin, built up the fire, and set about getting dinner.

It was ready and waiting when the boy came in, carrying a day-old calf in his arms. The calf's hide was a solid glare of ice. Rudge knew, even before Jase told him so, that it had been crowded into the creek—a common accident, and usually a fatal one at forty below.

He asked—as Jase tenderly laid it on an old blanket some distance from the stove—"How many have you lost?"

Pride flared in the boy's sunken, deep-rimmed eyes as he said: "Not any . . . yet."

Rudge could hardly credit it. No losses here? When at the Pot Handle, better-manned, with a better-conditioned herd, he was suffering appalling loss. "Waal," he said, and his regret was all for Jase, "it's too bad you have to spoil your record by losin' this calf."

The boy glanced up. "I don't aim to lose it," he smiled. "I'll warm it up, an' give it a good start. I 'most always have one thawin' out on this blanket."

How many hired men, overworked as Jase was, would give a calf individual attention? Rudge could only look his gratitude. But when, dinner over, he was filling his pipe by the roaring fire, he said suddenly: "Boy, you shame me! I'd send help if I could. But there ain't a man to be had for love or money. Right now, I'm doin' with half a crew. I hate like sin crowdin' you this-a-way. An' I hate to ask it, but . . . I hope you'll stick."

Jase looked up in surprise. "But I said I would."

"I know," Rudge nodded solemnly. "But there's times, boy, when a man just naturally can't live up to his promises."

Jase said then, as resolutely as when Rudge had hired him: "I'll stick . . . till the spring Chinook."

But as more killing days snailed by, he realized what Rudge had meant. For it seemed as if he just could not live up to his agreement, that he had lost all the sand he ever had. He was too tired when night came to undress—even to mark off days. And work no longer brought forgetfulness. Instead, as body and spirit failed, his brain grew morbidly active, painting a thousand disasters that might overtake a stabled horse. Something seemed to tell him that this money he was so dearly earning would never go to redeem Firefly. And then he knew such frenzy that he might have given up—had he not heard from Kelly.

Since all this was a direct consequence of his writing to Wes Storrs, Jase was afraid of letters. But, no longer about to control his desire to hear from the Bar Bell girl, he had written to her, under an assumed name, posting the letter at the little town of Horizon, across the divide in the opposite direction from Bear Paw, where Rudge transacted all his business.

He let a week go by, then he struggled over the same frozen ground for his reply, hungry to get it, but fearful lest someone be waiting to apprehend him when he asked for it. But there was only the harmless, rather spinster-like post-mistress, who fluttered a sigh at how beautifully the cow-boy's tired eyes lit up, as if the letter she gave him were a passport to heaven.

And such it might have been! For, reined in the lee of a great drift just outside the little settlement, Jase was trans-ported far above fatigue and cold by this first news of home. Kelly missed him. She was so sorry about Firefly. He must be careful, for Sam Vortz was hunting him as relentlessly as ever. Why was Vortz going to all that trouble to recover what was—for all he knew—a comparatively valueless saddle horse? Kelly thought she knew. She wrote:

He wants your ranch, Jase. He has to have it, almost! For, as you know, the dry seasons have exhausted the springs on White Rocks Ranch. He wants the permanent springs and streams on the Jingle Bob. He knows you'll never willingly sell to him, but he hopes to force you into a position where you'll have to! I know it, Jase . . . I saw it in his mean, white eyes!

Almost every day I ride over to the old place, to keep it company. And twice last fall I met Vortz there! I could just see him taking possession in his mind, making repairs. But he won't get it. Things will straighten out. We'll even find some way to make right how you first got Firefly. About that . . . Jase, I'm going to take your permission for granted and tell Dad. We can trust him. And he can help us if anyone can. So be sure we'll be working for you here. Don't look back, Jase, but on . . . to coming home! Think how useful all this experience will come in when you take over the Jingle Bob in June! Soon spring will come, and you'll have Firefly again.

So Kelly wrote, putting new heart in Jase. He wore her letter out reading it, and always it gave him fresh courage. He marked off the days again, surprised to find how many were gone, exulting to see a line drawn through half of February. Eagerly he looked ahead to seeing Firefly. Looked further on—to going home. For with Pat Shane's help things might be straightened out.

He laughed at the idea of Vortz's getting the Jingle Bob. Why, he'd see him in the hot place first. He'd take over the ranch in June. And he planned—far more bravely than he had talked to Kelly—of what he would do then. He'd be a big stockman—branch out himself—maybe swallow White Rocks. If all this hadn't happened, he might never have woke up, and so lost the Jingle Bob through shiftlessness. How he loved the blue-eyed girl who kept it company. What a home he'd make for Kelly.

More weeks dragged past. Winter hung on like grim death. Faithfully the boy toiled at the dwindling stacks. Then, one early March morning, he stepped from the cabin, to hear a strange murmur in the air, to feel a strange warmth—not of the sun, for there was none!—to see the white hills overcast with a peculiar lavender mist, and banks of blackly purple clouds rolling up from the south. He threw up his hat with a wild whoop. For it was the Chinook. All day he went around, singing like a locoed Indian. He could go—almost any time. Rudge had promised to release him when the black wind came.

True to his word, Rudge turned the cattle on the range three days later, paid Jase off, and himself drove the rig to Bear Paw, where Jase would catch the Spokane train. He let him go with vast reluctance, vainly trying to induce him to stay, and a little hurt by his eagerness to get away, until, when the train whistled in, he observed the boy's singular excitement, and, remembering the direction in which a young man's fancy is said to turn in the spring, jumped to a natural conclusion.

"Waal," he teased Jase, as he wrung his hand in parting, "give her my compliments."

Thinking only of Firefly—"I sure will!"—cried Jase, almost beside himself to find he was actually on board, and the train rolling away.

"Bring her back," yelled Rudge, "an' I'll give you the best cabin on the Pot Handle, an' make you ridin' boss!"

Gaily Jase called back: "I might, at that!"

Then he was whirling west, seeing nothing of the landscape flying past, but only the way Firefly's red ears would shoot up when he walked into the barn, and how he would plunk the money down and ride her out of there in record time. His hand went to the new billfold in his hip pocket, bulky with some two hundred dollars. After paying Firefly's feed bill to date, he would have eighty left. A good stake. He'd like to see anybody take the money away from him! If the passengers thought the happy young waddy had lumbago in his hip, it was only because Jase must so often put his hand to it, to assure himself he had the money yet.

He had it when, late that bright March afternoon, he swung from the train in Spokane, wondering how he had ever found the city anything but friendly, or its roar anything but music in his ears. He still had it when he started on foot for the barn, and then, remembering there was no need to economize, caught a street car, and was swiftly borne the long blocks his weary feet had so often walked. And when he alighted at the corner, hurrying almost at a run to the stable a few doors on, he still had the money then.

He had his hand right on it when he rang the bell, barely able to restrain himself from rushing on to Firefly's stall. And he had it right in his hand, ready to plunk down, when a man appeared at the inner door. Not the stableman who had promised to keep Firefly for him, but a stranger, who inquired his wants. His heart unaccountably freezing, Jase said that he wanted to pay his bill and take out his horse—the sorrel mare.

Blankly the fellow stared. "A sorrel mare?" he parroted. Then, shaking his head: "You must be mistaken. We have no horse of that description around here."

His world slipping, Jase clutched the desk. "But you . . . you've got to!" he cried in a strangled voice. "I left him here! The stableman said he'd keep her till I came!"

Strangely the man regarded him. "When did you leave her?" he asked at length.

Jase managed to tell him last November.

"Then," the man's face cleared, "I wouldn't know a thing about her. I bought in here the first of the year. The man who used to run this place was forced into bankruptcy. Any horse held for a feed bill would have been sold sure."

Sold? Sure?

Yes, Jase seemed to have known it would be like this. But he went a little crazy, nevertheless, digging into the barn man's arms with his work-hardened hands, demanding where Firefly was, who had bought her, how he could locate her, until the other, convinced that he was dealing with a lunatic, backed off, nervously insisting: "Don't ask me! I don't know anything, I tell you! The former owner left town before I took the barn, so"—definitely shrugging Firefly from his shoulders—"I'm not responsible."

Jase still held the money when he left, but he had been robbed of everything else!

Up and down the street, far into the night, he wandered distractedly, seeking Firefly. Darting into traffic at the appearance of a horse, to see if it was a little mare, red as a harvest sunset, slim and trim as the light of an Arab's tent; and, finding that it was not, drawing dazedly back, until another *clip-clop* on the pavement sent him darting out again.

VIII

"Cabbages and a queen"

"I declare to goodness," worried the rooming-house proprietress—although it was to her sleepy spouse she made the declaration after letting a room at 2:00 a.m.—"there's something wrong with Number Seven. Why, it's that same cowboy who was here last fall. I found him in a daze before the door of his old room. Luckily, it was vacant, so I let him in. But he never offered to pay his rent. 'How long will you be with us this time?' I hinted, delicate. But he just gave me a dazed look. 'I hope you're makin' a real stay,' I put it more suggestive, 'but the rule's the same . . . rent in advance to gents without luggage.' You'd think I hit him, the way he flinched. 'The rule?' he said. 'Oh, yeah . . . the rule to sell her.' He seemed to see then how he was ramblin', for he took out his pocketbook, an' sakes alive! . . . imagine my surprise. . . ."

"It must have been terrific," sympathized her yawning escort. "Considerin' you'd practically asked for it."

"It wasn't that! But you know that lad was flat broke when . . . fiddlesticks! As if you didn't remember how upset I was about Number Seven. Him so white an' thin, like he was endurin' slow starvation. An' me, fair achin' to offer him a bite, but not able to get a word out for the pride in his burnin' eyes. Well, there he was tonight with more money than you could shake a stick at. 'My,' I said, 'you're flush. Hadn't you better put that in the safe?' An' he says, with a laugh I never expect to hear the like of . . . unless I'm face to face with ol' Beelzebub . . . so mockin' it was . . . 'Oh, it's safe enough.'

"No sooner had I left, than he crumples up on the bed, chokin' out something about a firefly. I put my ear to the door. 'Why did I ever leave her?' he was moanin' in there. 'Why didn't I let her go at the auction? *He* couldn't 'a' been meaner to her. *He* might've cut her tongue out, but I . . . I. . . .' Then he broke all up. I declare, I never had anything affect me more. What on earth do you suppose . . . ?"

"Hooch! . . . when they start to rave about fireflies, I'd say."

"You would!" declared his impatient wife, dabbing at her eyes. "Don't judge others by yourself! It ain't drink that ails the poor lad . . . or anything like that. It . . . it's a broken heart!"

Perhaps she was right. Perhaps Jase's heart did break in No. 7 that night. Certainly something happened to him, for, in the weeks that passed, he justified the worst that Blue Buttes range had ever said of him. When the stable opened its doors next morning, he was there, hoping against hope that he might find some clue. But he was convinced at last that the barn man really did know nothing of Firefly's fate. Nor could he find anyone who did. Incidentally, however, he did discover—among the miscellaneous equipment that the new owner had inherited with the place—his own old saddle. With a cowboy's instinct to possess a saddle under all circumstances, he bought it back, and bore it to his room, where he thrust it in the darkest corner of the closet, that it might not remind him of Firefly, for whom he had already lost hope utterly.

She might be in the city. She might be a hundred—a thousand—miles away. There was small chance of his finding her, less that he could buy her, if he did. And, although he continued to look his eyes out for the little filly, to start at every hoofbeat, it was not with hope. For something told him that he had lost her forever, that this was to be his penance for the way he had first acquired her—this never-to-be-done-with missing her; this blaming himself for having led her trustingly into a trap—sold her into slavery; this eternal fear that her new master was abusing her, treating her like a cayuse—his little princess, who had never had a cross word in her life.

He could not stand such thoughts. They made him loco. So he locked his mind on Firefly, on everything that brought memory. He shut away all the years since he, a boy of sixteen, had found her, a tiny foal, and gone loco about her; all the happy days when they had ranged the Blue Buttes, free as the wind; all the unhappy nights they had stayed out together, when his father was "two sheets in the wind, an' one aflutter," and it hurt him so to see his dad like that, that he wouldn't go home to the Jingle Bob. He locked in every thought of the old ranch, even, and—hardest to do, but most necessary, if he wasn't to think of Firefly—every memory of Kelly.

Now and then these thoughts would break their bonds, and he would be in torment. He had to stand guard all the time. But he had nothing else to do. For shut in with them was all the self-pride he had found in Oregon; all the high hopes he had built at the Montana out-camp; every shred of ambition. And he tramped the streets aimlessly, existing from day to day, living his money up.

That money was to Jase a constant reminder, a constant reproach, and he wanted only to be rid of it. He stayed on in Spokane, because he had shut in, also, every thought of the range. To think of the open was to think of a flying red mare, disdaining the prairie grass with dainty hoofs, tossing her proud, sleek head to the sun in the sheer joy of living. And to think of those hoofs falling in servile ways, of that proud bent head—he would not think. Too crushed was Jase to care where he was.

"It's a shame," his landlady declared—to "goodness" again—"how Number Seven's changed! He used to be such a fine-lookin' lad, full of spirit, an' so careful about his personal appearance. Yes, when he could hardly keep body and soul together, he was mighty persnickety about his dress. Now, he don't care how he looks. An' he looks bad . . . I mean, from a physical aspect . . . so bleached out an' spindlin', like he growed up under a board. Poor lad, he's goin' downhill fast."

And Jase was. March went out like a lion. April alternately rained and shone. Many dandelions gleamed like golden coins in the velvet green of the parking strips and lawns. And Jase was so far down the grade by then that, often loitering under the railroad viaduct—where he had shared a hobo's blanket to his great grief—he would contemplate the vagrants lounging there between freights, and wistfully think how theirs was the only life. They weren't trying to amount to something, when they knew they were nothing. They weren't wearing themselves out, building dreams for someone to tear down. They weren't letting anything get so tied up in their hearts that, when they lost it, it ripped whole chunks out. They weren't fools enough to work. What was the sense in working? He would ask himself that, halting before the employment offices, curiously watching the throngs scanning the boards, as he once had. And his mind would run back over his life, remembering how, in one way or another, everything he had ever worked for had been taken away from him.

One day, chancing to pass the very building where he had first applied for work, he idly stopped to watch construction. A man swung down from a ladder near him and, approaching, asked if he was looking for a job. Jase turned to see the very foreman who had first told him there was no opening. And it brought back that gray November day so vividly that he felt chilled as by the drizzle that had been falling then, and it seemed that Firefly was in the stable yet, and that he stood here in all confidence asking for work.

"Because," explained the foreman, a little disconcerted by the boy's strange glance, "I need a young, active man to help tear down scaffolding on the upper floors. If you're looking for work. . . ." He faltered at the burning intensity in the boy's eyes.

For Jase was thinking that, if this man had thus answered him that other time, he would still have Firefly. And he said, in a queer, harsh voice: "No, thanks . . . I ain't lookin' for work."

But the time inevitably came when his funds began to run low again. June found him with only three silver dollars left from his winter's work. June—the month he had looked forward to for so long. The month when he was twenty-one.

Awakening one bright dawn in No. 7, he remembered that it was his birthday. That today—but for Sam Vortz—he would have come into his inheritance. By this time Wes Storrs would have turned the ranch over to him. And he might have spent the day renting out rangeland, getting cows on shares, making some turn. . . .

"Yeah," he said, his face dark with pain, "fixin' myself to get piled again."

And he shut that heart-door with a slam. But imprisoned thoughts were beating it down. Quickly dressing, he left the room and began his inane tramping of the downtown streets. But today the city's roar was jarring discord, the asphalt painfully hot to his vagrant feet. He knew again that smothering, caged feeling. Heading toward an outlying suburb, he walked and walked until, reaching a vacant lot on the far outskirts of town, where there was grass—he did not count the barbered kind—free grass a fellow could lie upon, and a gnarled old pine, he flung himself prone, and let the door of his heart crash open.

He thought, as he had not yet, of Firefly. Of the Jingle Bob—the wild mustard would be in bud. Of Kelly wandering through it. Suppose he went back? He was not afraid of Vortz, except for Firefly. Vortz couldn't hurt her now.

Suppose he hoboed his way home? He glanced down at himself, to see how he would look returning. And he saw just what he had become. Go back . . . like this . . . ?

No, he could not go home. But he could leave here. He had to, or go to work. And he wouldn't do that. He would rather join the strays who slept under the viaduct. Why not? Tomorrow, he'd start out with them, bum his way around, see the country, be free.

So he made up his mind. But there was no enthusiasm in his decision. And when he headed back for his room, shortly after noon, he walked with a slow and hopeless step. A figure so sadly out of place, in his shapeless range dress and high-heeled boots, that a group of urchins ceased their play to stare at him, and the boldest one derisively yelled: "Hey, cowboy, where's your horse?"

Where *was* Firefly? The look Jase gave the little gamin sobered him for whole minutes, so full was it of intense agony.

Rounding a corner, he turned down a shady street, coming, midway in the block, upon an ancient vehicle drawn up at the curb. A huckster's cart, piled high with vegetables, a ludicrous and rickety affair. If he gave it a second glance, it was only because the name lettered on the side— **Wu Fong**—reminded him painfully of his Chinese friends who had hidden Firefly and him from Vortz that day at their placer camp. And if, coming opposite the cart, he looked at the dejected animal attached to it, it was only because he looked at every horse, and pitied this one more than most, put to such—for so it seemed to Jase—degrading use. And with this pitying reflection, he would have passed on. But the horse, hearing a step, raised its drooping head. And the boy started, stopped, his eyes incredulous, his heart almost bursting from his breast. For this huckster's horse—this thin, ragged, spiritless beast of burden, drooping under a heavy, patched, disfiguring harness—was, nevertheless, Firefly!

In one bound Jase had his arms around her, and was crying over and over, tears streaming down his thin cheeks: "Oh, girl! Girl! What's happened to you?"

She tried to tell him. Rubbing her rough, red cheeks on his, she seemed in her low, rapid nickers to be begging him to take her out of this. And in a burst of reasonless rage, Jase was hysterically unsnapping harness, preparatory to doing it, when someone, coming on the run, yelled: "*Haie-aie-aie!* What you do my hoss?"

Defiance blazing in his eyes, Jase whirled, to see a dried-up little Chinaman. Evidently he whose name was on the cart—Wu Fong.

"Yours . . . nothin'!" cried the boy, backing possessively up to Firefly. "She's mine!"

"You clazy!" shrilled Wu Fong. "I pay fifty dollees that mare! You take her . . . you glo jail!"

Jase had just enough sanity to realize the truth of this. This man owned her. But he need not think that he could. . . . "You get this danged contraption off her!" he stormed, waving at the wagon. "She ain't no cart horse! Dja hear? You ain't goin' to haul cabbages with her!"

His face was dead white, his eyes like live brands. And Wu Fong looked at him nervously, as had the stableman.

"Why, whatee matter cabbages?" he faltered. "No heavy. That's what I buy her fo'." Then, firing up: "What blizness to you what I haul? You talk allee same clazy!"

Jase knew he was. He tried to get a grip on himself.

"Look here," he cried, "what'll you take for her?"

Emphatically Wu Fong shook his head. "No sell."

"But I've got to have her!" Jase insisted wildly. "You

don't savvy! I raised her from a colt . . . raised her like a baby! Why, she never knew she was a horse . . . the way I raised her! She thought she was as good as anybody! It's broke her heart . . . this . . . cabbages! Oh, damn! Lissen. I come here last fall an' went broke. While I was gone to earn money to pay her feed bill, they sold her. I've been loco. Now, I can't give her up. Savvy?"

And he went on, begging abjectly, never thinking where he could get the money to buy her if the Chinese merchant consented to sell, and not needing to, for Wu Fong iterated that he would not sell. But all the while he studied Jase with a speculative gleam in his beady, oblique eyes. And when the boy gave up in despair, he suggested craftily: "You likee dlive her, mebbe? You likee work for me? Long time I think I put Melican boy on wagon. Some folks no likee China boy. Melican boy make tlade. Savvy? I give ten cents on every dollee. Velly good money."

Jase glanced at the overflowing cart. Drive that? His eyes flashed as at an insult. "You couldn't hire me," he refused hotly, "to peddle that truck for no money."

His wrinkled, yellow face imperturbable as a mask, Wu Fong climbed on the cart, enthroning himself on the high seat, with lush, bunched onions, radishes, carrots, and so forth, bristling all around him. Imperturbably he lifted the lines. Firefly tightened the tugs, and turned despairing eyes on Jase. It was too much.

"Lissen!" He threw himself over the wheel to beg. "Will you let me work her out? If I peddle this junk, till I got fifty dollars coming, would you sell her to me then?"

Wu Fong did some mental calculation. The boy would have sold, by that time, five hundred dollars' worth of produce. A big profit. Besides, he would have his fifty dollars to buy another horse.

"Any horse," cried Jase, "can pull a truck cart! She's just a horse to you, but to me. . . ." He found himself altogether unable to express what Firefly was to him.

But the Chinaman seemed to understand. For he said, his black beads of eyes aglisten with satisfaction: "Sure, yes! Velly good! Fine!"

IX

"The cowboy huckster"

It would have taken far less nerve for Jase Kress to have faced a firing squad than it did to climb into Wu Fong's ramshackle old vegetable cart. That he volunteered to do it was ultimate proof of his love for Firefly. And a weird figure he cut, perched atop the billowing green stuff! Passersby looked at him, blinked, and looked again. No—it was not an optical illusion, any trick of imagination, or daydream of a rodeo scene, but a flesh-and-blood buckaroo, in sombrero, bandanna, and boots, riding—ye gods!—a load of vegetables. The incongruity of it made everyone laugh, and every laugh stabbed Jase to the heart.

But he felt that by sharing Firefly's degradation, he was atoning somewhat. By being with her, caring for her, he could lighten her burden. He could pad up the disfiguring harness so it wouldn't leave marks; could brush her red coat until it regained its smooth, silky sheen; could rub from her trim limbs the stiffness the pavement had put into them, and thus restore some of her old pride and fire. He could— how he hoped he could!—eventually earn fifty dollars and buy her. To do that he would endure anything!

But he never forgot the first day he drove that old cart. Wu Fong, who was quite a big operator in his way—requiring two carts, besides the one pulled by Firefly, to dispose of the produce from his intensively farmed truck patch on the outskirts of town—had started him out the next morning with a full load and a prescribed route. He was to begin at a certain residential street and stop at each house, working south. But, reaching the first house, he lost his nerve, and rattled straight past. He kept going, until he found himself rolling out of the district, and realized that he hadn't commenced work, realized that he had to begin sometime. That his little filly depended on him. And if he fell down on her—kept on being yellow—she was chained to that wagon forever.

Resolutely he turned back, pulled up at the first house, and got out. But even then, weakening, he pretended the harness needed fixing, until the misery in Firefly's eyes as she looked around to see what he was doing brought a steely glint to his own. And with face set as though he were walking up into the mouth of a cannon, he made for the house and timidly rapped on the kitchen door, wildly hoping no one was home.

But it was opened by a woman, who, having glimpsed the wagon out front, had—"No."—on the end of her tongue, but was knocked dumb with astonishment to see a sombreroed cowboy. So Jase got a hearing. And the diffidence with which he mentioned his wares drew her out to the waiting cart, where, unable to resist the desperate appeal in his eyes, she purchased some lettuce.

Jase, having survived this, stopped at the next house. And while waiting for someone to come to the door, he estimated his profits from this first sale. It had amounted to fifteen cents. His commission was a tenth. So he had made—

just a cent and a half. But his hopelessness sold this house-wife two bits' worth of asparagus. And he had four cents.

So, all that horrible day, it went. Not everybody bought from him. Some were supplied. Others had scruples against buying from peddlers. Once or twice a door was shut in his face. But he kept on doggedly. And the majority of women were so intrigued by the novelty of a cowboy huckster that, late in the afternoon, he pulled into Fong's place, his wagon was empty, and he had amassed one dollar of the fifty.

Determined to save every possible penny, he rented a room in the vicinity with housekeeping privileges. There he prepared his own meals—which did not take much prepara-tion, for he lived principally on the wilted produce that came back on the wagon. And daily he grew more "bleached out an' spindlin' " than ever his old landlady had seen him. But he frequently dipped into his earnings to buy Firefly oats and bran—not content that she should subsist on the poor hay supplied by the Chinaman.

Each day found him enthroned on the high seat of the groaning old wagon, with green stuff wreathed all around him, like he was Queen of the May or something, making the same weary rounds, running the same gauntlet of grins. He was in double horror now of being seen by someone who knew him, and his disgrace published at home. What would Kelly think of him? He didn't know that she would think it the noblest thing he had ever done. He only knew that he would not be caught dead on that wagon.

But he stuck to it, and made friends along the route. Housewives, coming out to the cart, would chat with him, pet his horse, and buy garden truck, until ice boxes and husbands rebelled at holding more, and the latter were told in colorful detail all about the cowboy huckster.

"I can't say no to him," the lady of the house would explain. "He's so shy and ashamed. I'll say . . . 'What have you got today?' And he'll stammer . . . 'String beans, ma'am.' I'll ask . . . 'Are they quite fresh?' And he'll say, so apologetically . . . 'Oh . . . as good as any, I guess.' And it's simply beautiful how he treats his horse. Why, he talks to it like it was his sweetheart. And he's always feeding it a carrot."

"So I get the same fodder!" would growl her lord and master—who had not seen Jase—as he pushed back his spinach. "I'm not a horse, and I'm sick of this stuff! I want something to eat . . . a two-inch steak."

And she, with the steak in mind, would decide, when Jase came, that she could smother it in onions. And, going out to select them, would be mesmerized by him and Firefly into adding a melon.

Yet each day was as humiliating to Jase as the first. Each sale took as much courage. He could not get hardened to it, could never feel that it was legitimate. He always felt that taking money for a handful of vegetables was just plain charity. But he took it for Firefly and did so well that Wu Fong was kept busy, uprooting more, washing and bunching them, more than pleased with his bargain.

"Tlade velly good!" he would greet the return of the empty wagon at night. "Bimeby we all be lich!"

But to Jase it seemed hopeless. Each night he made an accounting. It was always satisfactory to Fong. But it did not take much money, he would reflect, to satisfy a Chinaman—remembering Lo Wing at home, washing tons of sand for a few cents. And it was rare that a day of this spiritual torture netted a dollar for him. Pinch down as he did, it cost him something to live. And at the end of a week he had only five dollars toward Firefly's freedom.

Endlessly the months before he could attain it stretched

ahead of him. He was more discouraged than ever he had been in that Montana out-camp. Maddeningly now, he longed for the open. Ever since finding Firefly, the range had called him, seemed, at times, to be pulling him right off that wagon. He was wild to hear from Kelly, to learn if Pat Shane had been able to think of some way to straighten things out so he could go home.

"But I won't go without you," he would promise the little mare huskily. "One thing at a time. I'll work you out, an' then I'll write. Someday, girl, we'll go back to the Jingle Bob."

But that day receded, if anything. June trickled out as slowly as the pennies came in. July was well begun when, one grueling day, Jase, rattling from house to house, worked out a problem. It was the same one that Fong had solved before striking a bargain—how much produce he must sell before his commission amounted to fifty dollars. He worked it out in cabbages, and found that he must dispose of five thousand of them. Five thousand cabbages! They loomed over him, a mighty mountain—crushed him. He seemed suffocated by the commingled odors of all the fruits and vegetables piled about him. He loathed the very sight of them.

Not so Wu Fong. Having filled the cart of mornings, he would stand back and survey the fruits of his labor, so glisteningly green, and his withered old face would actually beam. So Jase would remember him ever with guilty pain. Just as he had been, this last morning—standing, beaming at his vegetables.

"Nice an' clisp." Fondly he praised them to Jase. "Plitty, yes. Velly plitty."

And Jase would recollect with shame how mad that made him. "Pretty," he had muttered to Firefly, rolling out of the truck patch and into the city. "Some folks sure got a funny idea of beauty."

Although early, it was already sultry and hot. So was his heart. He let Firefly poke along, not caring whether school kept or not. He had worked three weeks for Fong, and where had it got him? He had just eleven dollars and something. He was no better than a *peon*. He was seven kinds of a fool to be working. Before he earned fifty bucks, folks would get fed up on this stuff. Or he'd die before then. Something would happen.

His spirits were at lowest ebb when he saw, on a telegraph pole ahead, a bright placard picturing a running horse. Below the horse, bold-faced type screamed **RACES!** at him. He drew up short, reading the finer print, advertising the Elk Creek Pioneer Celebration. Elk Creek! He remembered coming through the town. It was only a few hours' ride from Spokane, but out in the sage, on the edge of the range country. Longing fairly leaped from Jase's eyes. The celebration was taking place today. His heart burned more hotly at the thought that right this instant, while he was tied to this cart, some folks were going to the races.

Wistfully he scanned the program—sports of all kinds, a free barbecue, street carnival, bucking contests. Just the kind of show they put on at Santo, only it lasted a week, and they called it a stampede. He had never missed a single stampede at home. It was almost time—his eyes saw the date—July 10—and he realized with a cruel pang that the Santo stampede was going on. He could see the town jammed for the show, with bands playing, bunting flying, and everyone having a high old time. He could see Sam Vortz, strutting about, big as all get-out, showing off before the home crowd, winning every race, and raking in all the money he could not get his paws on in other ways. And he could see Kelly. The prettiest girl there. With the fellows all shining up to her. They would see to it that she wasn't missing him. One of them might make her forget to wait for him.

Through a sudden mist, with a cruel ache in his breast, Jase read down the races to take place at Elk Creek. He noticed that the prizes were liberal, insuring good horses. One, in particular, a race for Thoroughbreds, offered a prize of one thousand dollars. But his interest centered on one near the end of the list—a half-mile saddle-horse race for a hundred-dollar purse. One hundred dollars! Was there that much money in the world? Yes—and some lucky *hombre* would win it. Not in dribs by making a holy show of himself. But all in a bunch, all in a minute—by fun. For he felt again the wind in his face, his heart's wild singing at Firefly's running that day he had raced down Crater's main street and won. Today they were racing at Elk Creek. Some horse would come in first.

"An' I'll bet," loyally he told Firefly, "it won't be as good as you are. I'll bet you could win like a shot . . . cut you loose from this blamed rattletrap. You sure showed Des Chutes's horse dust."

Firefly's ears shot up. So had the sun, halfway to the meridian. It was nearly nine—the best hour of the day for Jase's business, when all the women were home and vegetable-minded. But he didn't give a hang, just sat on, his mutinous eyes glued on that placard, till all of a sudden, for the third time in his life, something just "came over" Jase. It took the sag out of his shoulders, brought him up straight. And with a strange glow on his thin, pale face, he pulled the wagon around, and—detouring by his room to pick up his saddle—drove straight out toward Elk Creek.

Coming to a side street, just before leaving the city

limits, he turned into it, stopped, and jumped down, yanking Firefly out of the fills in record time. Ripping the old harness off her back, he flung it up on the seat of the cart and cinched his old saddle on. Then he mounted and swung, leaving all those "plitty" vegetables to curl up and die in the scorching sun.

Firefly pranced off a few steps, tossing her head like a princess. But, as if missing something, she then turned astonished eyes back at the wagon.

"You don't have to drag it!" the boy's voice soared. "You're all done bein' a cart horse!"

For he meant to win that race. He meant to be back before dark with one hundred dollars in his pocket. He meant to give it all to Fong. He thought that, if Fong got double money for Firefly, he wouldn't have any kick coming.

In the delirium of being on horseback again, with the open road ahead of him and the tang of wild vegetables in his lungs, it entirely slipped his mind that Wu Fong had agreed to the sale only—if he worked out the mare.

X

"Trapped"

Elk Creek. Such a little place for such a big celebration with the race grounds—just across the railroad track from the sagebrush town—jammed with celebrants. Not all pioneers, in experience and years, but all trail blazers. Range folks. Rallied here from the free-grass country north and west. Women who never bought garden truck. Men who wouldn't stoop to raise it. So Jase rejoiced, hovering on the fringe of the throng with

Firefly, catching snatches of talk—range talk. Big plain language a man could understand.

Gee, but it was fine to be with his own kind again. To fit in—so folks didn't stare at him. Oh, if he could just smooth out the kinks in his life and go back to the range where he belonged. Just go home—that's all he asked. He wouldn't care if folks did call him a cultus. Back to Blue Buttes. He could see it so plain—the range all gold in the sun, the hills so blue in the evening, the wild forests on the highlands, the wilder cañons. And Kelly. She had seemed so far from him in the city. But here she seemed real. He seemed to know here that she was still standing by him. Still waiting. . . .

"If you just win," deliriously he kept telling Firefly, "we can square Fong . . . smooth out one kink."

But the saddle-horse race, following the headliner for Thoroughbreds, did not come off for hours yet. And seeing Firefly all aquiver, eager, charged with new life by the excitement around her, Jase had the rash wish to enter her in the Thoroughbred race—to find out if she was true to her heritage, and maybe draw down the big prize. But he couldn't for many reasons. He didn't have the money, for one thing. It cost as much to enter that race as he was hoping to win. Besides, it wouldn't do to call any more attention to Firefly than he had to. As it was, there might be someone in this gathering who would recognize him. He had better lay low until this race was called, win it, and then light right out for Spokane to make his peace with Wu Fong. But the important thing right now was to pay his fee and get Firefly's name on the entry book. Even for this he had to wait.

For it was noon, and the barbecue was the big attraction. Everyone was flocking around the big tables built back of the grandstand. Hungrily, Jase watched them. The fragrance of the barbecued beef, wedged between the great buns they were passing around, almost overcame caution and drew him across. For he was not a vegetarian by choice.

But one, he thought, swallowing hard, *would just whet my appetite. It would take a whole steer to fill me up.*

So he decided not to watch. Hunting out a secluded spot behind the paddocks, he tied Firefly and waited, until the crowd—replete with food, but thrill-hungry—returned to the grandstand, and the race officials resumed their places. Then he hurried down to the judges' stand and, before he thought, had entered Firefly under her own name, giving the clerk a fictitious one for himself. Separating the required ten dollars from the eleven so painfully earned, his first real doubt came to him. Suddenly it seemed like a whole lot of money. Why, it was a tenth of the fifty. Too much to risk. It was, he thought audibly, laying it down, "one thousand cabbages."

"What's that you say?" sharply the clerk looked up at him.

"Nothin'," Jase grinned.

But there was a do-or-die set to his lips as he went back to his horse. Suppose he lost? It meant additional weeks on that wagon. It meant—he dare not think! And he didn't, making the time spin, rubbing Firefly down, getting her into the best possible condition. The day grew intolerably hot. Heat shimmered back through the dust that never settled but hung in an ever-thickening cloud, through which the sun shone, casting a saffron glow over the scene. There wasn't enough breeze to stir the sage about Jase.

The program ticked off like clockwork. Race after race was run. Steadily he heard the announcer's call for horses, the thunder of hoofs as they ran, the roar from the grandstand. Horses were let out of the paddocks in a steady stream and back again. He could catch glimpses of them, could pick the winner every time—it stepped so high, wide, and handsome. Couldn't tell him a horse didn't know when it won. Couldn't tell him Firefly didn't know what she was going to run for. That she wasn't trying to tell him right now that she would run her legs off to free both of them from that vegetable wagon.

Keying him to the last notch, the big race was called. Catching Firefly's slim head between his trembling hands, looking straight into her fire-filled eyes—"You're next, girl!"—cried Jase, so missing the announcement that would have prepared him for what was to happen. "I did my best, but I'm slow. You're . . . fast. You can win a hundred bucks in a minnit, Firefly."

In his fierce impatience, the Thoroughbreds seemed a year getting off. But he heard them start, heard their hoofs madly volleying around the track, and around again, while the tumult in the grandstand swelled to a mighty crescendo of sound. And he knew that race had been run. The next was his own.

Too excited to wait for the call, he led Firefly around the paddocks, on to the track, and down toward the stands, his way impeded by panting, overstrung racers returning. His way, this way, was suddenly blocked by that which froze him in his tracks, draining every drop of blood from his face—by a big, burly man, conspicuous in Stetson hat and flashy vest—*Sam Vortz!*

For Vortz, who should have been in Santo, cleaning up on the home crowd, was here—in Elk Creek! So near that he had only to look up and see the boy he had hunted so relentlessly. But his mean, white eyes were bent on the groom to whom he was talking and who was leading a flaming, high-stepping sorrel—Firefly's mother—Sacajawea.

257

Acting instinctively, for he was too stunned to plan anything, Jase swung Firefly so that a curveting race horse was
between himself and Vortz, and headed back the way he had
come, expecting at each step to hear that blatant mouth
proclaim him as a horse thief. He was in such terror of
losing Firefly that, when he maneuvered her out of sight,
behind the paddocks, he fell against her, trembling, barely
able to stand, in the reaction. Overcome by the thought of
the plight this put him in, he chokingly told her: "It's . . . all
. . . off . . . girl."

He couldn't race. He couldn't pay Fong double money—
or any. He couldn't pay for the vegetables left to spoil in the
sun. He had lost every cent he had earned. He would lose
his job, sure. Lose his chance to work out the mare.
Would—after all they'd been through—lose her?

"Firefly!" came the megaphoned bawl.

They were calling her.

"Firefly!" she was called again.

He was in terror lest they hunt for him. He did not know
what they did when an entrant failed to show up. But he
found out that they didn't wait, for he heard the race start.
Hard on his heartbeat the sound of running horses—
cheers—as some lucky *hombre* won the hundred dollars.

The big attraction over, the crowd began to break up,
hurrying past the paddocks in a steady stream to be early
for the carnival uptown. As curious eyes turned on him, Jase
shrank in dread, lest they include the chalky ones of Sam
Vortz, or those of one of the White Rocks men who traveled
with him. If he could hide out here until they were gone. . . .

Just then a band of horses was led out of the paddocks
and turned toward him, reminding Jase that Vortz, too,
would be taking his horses away from the track and would
pass this very spot. Faced with the necessity of getting away

from here without drawing any attention to himself, he instinctively did again the only possible thing—swung Firefly in with the band as it passed, so naturally that anyone watching would have thought she belonged with the string. But Firefly attracted the notice of one of the handlers, making Jase nervous at the interest with which he was sizing her up.

"Didn't see her on the track," this fellow remarked, as they were leaving the grounds.

Jase told him she hadn't run.

And the man, sizing him up—thinking he had never seen a waddy quite so "beat out"—idly asked: "Makin' a long jump?"

Jase knew what he meant, for they were nearing the railroad tracks, where a train was waiting, with cars pulled up to the loading chutes, and he guessed that these men were shipping their horses to the next racing meet. But, uncertain how to answer, wishing to end this catechism, he nodded, and put a question himself: "Whose string are you handlin'?"

"Carter's from Yakima," replied the fellow. "We're runnin' next. . . ." He broke off, as a racer ahead, frightened at something, began pitching, and hurried to give its handler assistance.

Nobody else noticed Jase. He was able to hide Firefly in the band right up to the loading pen. Here he was forced to drop behind, again exposed to the curious gaze of the town-bound crowd on the road, as the other men led their horses through the gate and into one of the cars. Closely he watched for a chance to ride off unobserved. He was right on the verge of making the break when, casting a quick glance behind, he saw that he had waited too long—Vortz was coming! Behind Vortz were the White Rocks men, bringing their horses to this train. And with Vortz—talking to him—was a man who wore the star of a sheriff, or marshal.

Fighting down utter panic, Jase cast wildly about for some means of escape. But all was open both ways from the chute. If he ran, Vortz would see him. If he didn't, in a minute. . . .

The Carter men had finished loading. The last man was coming out, rolling the door of the horse car shut, but—as the boy's desperate gaze took note—failing to lock it. And as they swung from the chute, going around the car, out of sight, Jase—driven to desperation by sight of Vortz steadily nearing—seized his one, mad chance. Grasping Firefly's halter in an iron grip, he led her through the gate and up the chute, begging her not to make any fuss, just to come along quietly, so that horse killer wouldn't see them and take her away from him. Although her eyes rolled with fear, although her breath whistled through distended nostrils, the game little mare followed him up to the door of the car and in, as quietly as though she were used to trains. In a twinkling, Jase had shut the door behind them, and was searching the car for some place to hide her until Vortz was gone.

But the close-padded stalls—built side by side, lengthwise of the car, in such a fashion that the horses faced the engine—were all full. However, his swift search revealed a small space in the extreme rear of the car, railed off to prevent the racers from being jammed into the wall by the jolts of the train. A small space, but big enough for Firefly in this crisis, and she would be hidden by the other horses from view of anyone looking in the door. Hastily untying one of the racers and moving it out, Jase lowered the rail, and led Firefly through the stall, cramping her into this refuge.

Then, as quickly replacing the race horse, he crouched beside Firefly, waiting, with no thought but to get out at the first instant of safety. He heard Vortz come up. And from him—in his lordly commands to his men, loading White Rocks horses in the car behind—received a horrible suspicion as to the destination of this train, a suspicion confirmed on hearing Vortz's instructions to the officer with him. "Keep your eye peeled," instructed Vortz, not five feet from where the listening boy crouched. "Firefly's a common name, of course. But the fact that this horse failed to show up is suspicious, an' the entry clerk sure described the Kress kid. I want him bad. So, if you nail him, wire me word."

"Where can I catch you?"

"In Santo. The stampede's goin' on there now. Tomorrow's the big day. Carter an' me persuaded enough other owners to pool with us so we could hire this special train an' make a night run to Santo. Otherwise, I wouldn't have been able to make both places. I aim to clean up on the Blue Buttes Classics there tomorrow. After that, I'll be at my ranch."

Steps were coming up the chute. A Carter man opened the door, took a last look around, and, satisfied that his charges were safe, dropped the bolt in place, and returned to the caboose to join his friends in a poker game that did not break up until they reached their destination.

Jase, hearing that bolt drop, sprang up, frantic to realize that he was locked in on the same train with Sam Vortz. On a train bound for Santo—where a warrant awaited him. That he couldn't go back to Spokane. Strangely, this seemed the real tragedy. That he would be, for the third time, stealing Firefly. Not from Vortz, as he had twice—and cared no more about it than you would care about taking a mouse from a cat that would torture it!—but from Wu

Fong, who had, in his own way, been good to her. This was a real theft. It so filled him with horror that, forgetting Vortz—everything—but his determination to get out, he rushed to the door and beat on it, frantically shouting. But in the last-minute confusion, nobody heard him. The bell was ringing, the engine was panting, and—with a jolt that almost threw him off his feet—the train was at once in motion.

XI

"His pound of flesh"

Hour after hour—while day died and the car was plunged into the gloom of the longest night he had ever put in—Jase crouched by Firefly, racked by the motion of the train, racked by worry about the outcome, and by shame. *I'll make something of myself! Then I'll come back! I'll make good!* mockingly the wheels seemed to click, as they sped him home, in far worse shape than when he had made that promise to Kelly Shane. Then but one man had claimed Firefly. Now two did. Then he had had but one back trail to watch, and now . . . when the wagon failed to return, Wu Fong would notify the police, and they would be hunting him. *I meant to go back with my head up* was the cry of the boy's shamed heart. *Not like this . . . like the bum I've made of myself!* He wore himself out so completely that, toward dawn, he dropped into a sleep of utter exhaustion.

The freight, jarring to a stop, awakened him, and he rose up—train-sick and faint—to see the sun streaming in the open ventilator above him. Hurrying to it, he looked out

262

upon the most beautiful sight he had ever seen in all his life, upon dusty, crooked streets of which he knew every turn and twist. Upon false-fronted buildings, familiar to him from foundations to roof. Upon houses cuddled under the buttes, sheltering folks he knew. Upon Santos.

The trapped boy saw his home town gaily dressed for the big stampede, with a colorful throng already gathered for the climax to the week's celebration—the Blue Buttes Classic that would be run this afternoon. Why were folks so crazy to see it, when they knew Vortz always won? And he saw beyond the cowtown, and all around, the hills of home. His own home range, a blaze of gold in the sun. His dark gaze, yearningly fixed on the golden notch below which was the Jingle Bob, dimmed in despair.

Any minute the men might come to unload the horses and would find him here. The row they would kick up would bring Vortz, who would shut him up in a worse trap. *No!* the boy vowed desperately, working Firefly out of her retreat and into the clear space between the doors. He had outrun Vortz once. He could do it again. When the men came, he would make a break.

"The minute they open that door," he grimly whispered to her, "we'll bolt, girl."

He tensed, a hand on her shoulder, ready to spring to her back, as steps fell on the chute planks, and he heard someone working at the lock. The door slid back the merest crack.

"Hey, Bill!" yelled someone from down the track. "Will you lend a hand here?"

Hearing the man growl assent and walk off, a better plan came to Jase. If he took Firefly out on this—the dépôt side—he would be seen, chased, captured perhaps. But the other side of the track was a wild, brushy marsh. If he could

get around the car, unlock the other door, he might be able
to jump Firefly to the ground and get away without Vortz
ever knowing he had been near the town. He might just ride
past the old ranch, might even chance a moment with Kelly.

Willing to risk much to do this, he eased the door back
just enough to look out. Men were working down by the caboose, but they were too interested in what they were doing
to notice him. So he slipped through, noiselessly dropped to
the cinders below, and crawled under the train. Coming up
on the opposite side, he straightened and turned—face to
face with Sam Vortz! With no retreat this time. No outrun-
ning the hungry black gun that Vortz had instinctively
drawn from his hip pocket and leveled on him.

"Waal. Waal. Look at the worm this early bird lands,"
sneered the race horse man, so surprised to have seen Jase
Kress crawl from under the train that the revolver trembled
in his hand, but quick to taunt, for cruelty was natural with
him. "Right into my hands. Right where I want him."

Right where he wanted him! Jase knew that. Or—almost
there. Vortz wanted him in jail, so he could steal his ranch.
Well, Vortz had him. He would have Firefly, too. It was all
over but the shouting—and Vortz was doing that. But,
seeing him here, so merciless, so brutal in his triumph, all
the fighting blood in Jase's veins surged to the surface.
While God gave him life, he would not give Firefly up to
Vortz, nor the Jingle Bob.

As his thoughts linked his horse and ranch, something
clicked in Jase's brain. A plan so daring, so breathtaking, so
far-reaching in its potentialities that it staggered him. A
wild plan to put Firefly's speed to the ultimate test. To stake
his ranch, his every hope of amounting to anything on the
Blue Buttes range on the frail chance that his little mare had
inherited the speed of her forebears—and more. To trust

264

Firefly to save herself and him in this extremity. And if he lost, to console himself with the knowledge that—there at the point of Vortz's gun, with Firefly in that car—he could have nothing else and had, at any rate, placed the horse forever beyond Vortz's reach. Steeled to desperate calm by the necessity to play his cards exactly right, to put up the bluff of his life, he faced the race horse man.

"Put up your gun, Vortz." His eyes blazed defiance. "You wouldn't dare shoot me, if I did run. Even a Blue Buttes jury wouldn't clear you of that. Besides, I ain't runnin'. I come back to see you."

Taken aback by this stand, Vortz could only sputter: "Oh, you did, huh? An' why?"

"To pay you for Firefly."

Of all the double-distilled nerve! "So that's your story," jeered Vortz. "Waal, you seem to forget I ain't sellin'. You tried that once, an' where did it get you?"

Oh, Jase had thought of that. Swiftly, there on the hot, black track, between the red car and the wild green marsh, he thought, with his burning eyes on Vortz, of where it had got him—into trouble in Oregon; into untold hardship in Rudge's camp; into—a huckster's wagon. And the chances were that it would get him into jail here. But there was no hint of fear in his voice as he assured Vortz: "You'll take this offer."

"Is that so? An' what is it?"

Jase flashed: "The Jingle Bob!"

He saw Vortz start, saw greed glitter in his eyes of chalk. He broke out: "Oh, I knew why you been houndin' me. It ain't been for Firefly. You don't give a hoot about her. It's my ranch you've been after. You tried to worm it out of Dad till he died, then . . . you knew damned well I'd never sell. But you thought you could make me, if you put me in jail."

Killing any qualm he might have had, Vortz admitted it all in his heartless drawl: "Waal?"

"Well," Jase flamed, "you got another think comin'. I'd die before I'd sell to you."

"Then what . . . ?" Vortz was completely baffled. "You mean," he asked incredulously, "you'll give me the Jingle Bob to withdraw that charge?"

"Hardly." The boy's lips curled. "But I'm sick of bein' on the dodge, an' I'll give you a chance to beat me out of it. You can set your own price on Firefly, an' I'll borrow the money from you to buy her, an' give you a mortgage on the ranch for security."

Vortz put up the gun with alacrity. He had to have the Jingle Bob water holes or vacate White Rocks. He had schemed for years to get that ranch. And here it was—talk about luck! The kid must be scared badly. That must have been he at Elk Creek. Then how did he come to be on this train and where . . . ? Suspiciously he demanded: "Where's the mare?"

She was so near that Jase could hear her lonesome nicker, and he was in terror lest at any minute the man come back to the car, find her, and set up a howl that would upset everything. But he said, his eyes never wavering: "I left her in a feed barn in Spokane last fall, an' I lost her. She was sold for the feed bill. Last week she was pulling a huckster wagon around for a Chinaman."

This was so entirely in character with Vortz's conception of what Jase would do that it never occurred to him to doubt it. That horse-stealing charge would be a mighty weak-kneed affair in court, even with all the pressure he could bring to bear, and, as the kid guessed, he didn't care about the mare. He had been keen for her that night she had run away from him, but he had seen plenty of horses

266

run since then. It would serve his purpose better to use her to get hold of the Kress place, and he would sure work her for all she was worth. "You're wrong," he declared coldly. "I want that mare. That's why I bought her. So you've lost her? Waal, you can expect to pay a mighty high price for her."

Jase would, but tentatively he began: "You paid seventy-five for her. . . ."

"Save your breath," Vortz scoffed. "I don't dicker in cayuse terms. You'll talk my language, if you want me to listen."

Overturning a cinder with his boot, Jase thoughtfully contemplated, his memory stirred by Vortz's words to that long-ago conversation with Pasco. *Since the swiped colt was worth the most,* he seemed to hear his old partner saying, *this hombre ought to make good the difference.* It looked as though he would have a chance to do that. "Well," slowly he asked, looking up, "what would you think a fair price for one of your Thoroughbred colts? A good one . . . say, one of Sacajawea's? I mean, one that hadn't been tried, an' might be good or might be worth no more than a cayuse?"

Promptly Vortz snapped: "Five hundred bucks!"

Having appeared to consider it, Jase said: "I'll pay that."

But some hint of his eagerness thus to square himself for having stolen Firefly in the first place must have communicated itself to Vortz, for he promptly rejoined: "An' then some! It's worth something to you to get out of this scrape. I won't consider less than a thousand. One thousand bucks! That's my price, take it or leave it."

That was his price—for a horse he thought was a cayuse. Jase flushed with anger.

"For that," Vortz said, "I'll renounce all claim to her . . . an' take a thirty-day mortgage on the Jingle Bob."

Thirty days. About to flare out, Jase suddenly subsided with a weary shrug. What did it matter? He would have the money today—if ever. But quietly he stipulated: "I'll have to have twenty-five in cash."

Brutal in his triumph, Vortz laughed: "Holdin' out for the chicken feed. I see. Goin' to blow yourself at the stampede. If that ain't ol' Cultus all over. Pawn your soul to get money to spree on. Waal, you'll get it, when we execute the mortgage." And, rabid to close, he added: "Let's get it over with!"

Wild to be rid of him and get Firefly out of that car, Jase said: "I've got to round up Wes Storrs first."

"That's easy," he was told. "Storrs is manager of the stampede this year. He'll likely be at the Blue Buttes House. We'll go over. . . ."

"You go on," insisted the boy. "I'll be along in a half hour."

Oh, no, he wouldn't. He'd go right along. Vortz wasn't taking any chances this time. He wasn't letting the kid out of his sight until everything was sealed and signed. Convinced of that, realizing that he was only imperiling his chance, Jase trusted to Providence to look out for Firefly, and went with him.

Wes Storrs was in the lobby of the Blue Buttes House when they walked in, and he was as dumbfounded by Jase's return as he had been by his abrupt departure at the auction. But he recovered fast enough when he learned what was wanted, and talked himself hoarse, trying to argue Jase out of it.

"Great guns!" he exclaimed. "You've hardly had the ranch a month. Ain't even took formal possession. You're throwin' away a start that lots of men work all their lives for . . . then don't get. Boy, you owe it to your mother. . . ."

"Wes," Jase begged desperately, "will you fix up the papers for me?"

There was nothing for the administrator to do but obey, and glumly he led the way to the lawyer's office. There, while the papers were being drawn up, which took some time, Vortz swaggered about as if he owned the place already, advising the pretty stenographer to bet on him this afternoon and she'd "wear diamonds," for his Sacajawea would surely bring home the bacon. Jase, who had been straining his eyes out of the window, trying, in his anxiety, to pierce a hundred walls and see what was happening to Firefly, turned to Wes Storrs.

"Wes," he asked, "have you got that seventy-five I sent you from Oregon?"

Storrs nodded. "I'm holdin' it."

"Will you give it to me?" Jase pleaded. "I've got to have it."

And him mortgaging for a thousand! Completely disgusted, Storrs wrote him a check and mentally washed his hands of Jase Kress.

But when Vortz bawled—"Come on, kid . . . put your John Henry on this!"—there was something in the boy's face, some light of driven intensity, that touched Storrs deeply. Going up to Jase, he laid a hand on his shoulder, earnestly asking: "Boy, are they forcin' you? Are you doin' this because you want to?"

"I want to, Wes." Jase's voice was steady enough.

But Storrs was far from convinced. Only when Jase refused to sign until another paper was drawn, and the administrator learned the nature of this one, did he begin to understand. When Vortz gave Jase only the bill of sale to Firefly and a handful of silver in return for the thousand-dollar mortgage, his honest old face flamed with indignation.

"A thousand dollars for a cayuse?" he sternly protested. "That's takin' your pound of flesh. Why, its outrageous. It's . . . blackmail, Vortz."

"Mebbe so," Vortz grinned, complacent to feel the Jingle Bob and all its valuable springs crisply between his fingers. "But every man's got to look out for himself in a horse deal." As an extra taunt, or in excessive joviality at being on the way to attain his long-cherished aim, he winked at Jase: "Ain't that so, kid?"

A queer smile crossed the boy's dark face. He said: "I reckon."

"So do I." Vortz nodded emphatically. "It's plumb legitimate to beat a man in a horse trade. I always skin 'em, if I can, an' if I get skinned . . . which ain't happened often . . . why, you don't hear me squeal."

"Well," Jase said, with that same queer smile, "you don't hear me squealin'."

Suddenly Vortz had the funniest feeling—as if this Kress kid had the laugh on him, but the thought was too ridiculous for consideration. As the three men went back to the street, he said in his most overbearing tone: "Remember, kid . . . thirty days! A month from today you pay me a thousand cold cash, or I'll foreclose." And with his equanimity fully restored, he swaggered off to get his racers ready for the Classic.

Dully Jase stared after him, so terrified by what he had done, with so little faith in his plan, that when Storrs put a hand on his arm, kindly asking—"Son, what hope have you got of payin' him back?"—Jase spoke truthfully.

"I guess . . . none, Wes."

XII

"Prairie lass"

Torn with anxiety about Firefly, Jase left Storrs unceremoniously and turned toward the railroad tracks. He hurried, almost at a run, through the crowd—dense, now, at noon—thinking that, anyhow, the horse belonged to him, remembering that she did not, that Wu Fong still owned her, but not daring to worry about that, with Vortz's threat ringing in his ears: *Remember, kid . . . thirty days!*

Held up on a crowded corner, some force beyond him lifted his eyes, drew them—and then time and trouble were forgotten, all but the obliterating joy that he was looking straight into the blue eyes of Kelly Shane! For in them—as, blind to the throng, he seized her hands, his dark gaze hungrily devouring her, white sombrero, short, fringed skirt, blue-silk blouse, and all—was that which wiped out all the shame of his homecoming. The way Kelly clung to him, half laughing, half crying, put new heart in him.

"Jase! Jase! Am I dreaming? You . . . in Santo! When I thought. . . ." Then, remembering that he shouldn't be here and wildly telling him so, Kelly was stricken by the news that it didn't matter, for Jase cried: "Vortz got what he wanted, Kelly! I give him a mortgage on the Jingle Bob for Firefly."

Somehow they got out of the jam, and into a store entrance, where Jase told her everything. All his experience with Wu Fong, which led up to his being in Elk Creek, and the chain of circumstances there that had trapped him in the car and brought him home, where, at the point of a gun, he had made his desperate plunge, buying Vortz off on the wild chance that he might win the money today, and redeem his ranch.

"Kelly"—tensely he told her of his plan—"I'm goin' to run Firefly in the Blue Buttes Classic this afternoon."

This impressed the girl as the most hopeless thing yet! Silently she listened to the rest. How he had made Vortz dig up twenty-five in cash to put with the seventy-five Storrs had held for him, and so obtained the hundred dollars necessary to enter Firefly in the race. How, when this was done, everything he had in the world would be at stake—except his horse, and she belonged to a Chinaman. Silently she stood, when he was through and waiting, she knew, for some word of encouragement. She was aching to give it, as she looked up at him, so thin, strained, and tragic. Unable to do it, in honesty, able only to cry in her bitter resentment at the cowardly advantage Vortz had taken of him: "Oh, Jase, I hate that man! He's absolutely heartless. He hasn't a scruple on earth! He's caused me more worry. . . ."

"You, Kelly?" Jase bent to her searchingly.

"And Dad," she said, turning her eyes from him to the crowd going by, as light-hearted and carefree as if the end of the world wasn't coming today. "We've had a bad year at the Bar Bell. The worst ever. Vortz is after Dad about that note. He swears he'll sell us out to collect. He won't give us a single day of grace. Dad's almost crazy! He's raised every cent he can, but it's less than half enough. Vortz has a corner on all the money in Blue Buttes. Oh, you'll find that out, when you try to raise it to pay him back. A mortgage on a place is the same as a deed with Sam Vortz."

That the Shanes must pay for having befriended him was, to Jase Kress, the crowning touch. "It's all my fault," bitterly he blamed himself. "It's all because you tried to buy Firefly at the auction. That made him mad. . . ."

"It's not your fault the crop failed," Kelly smiled through her tears. "But let's not talk of my troubles. We'll have plenty of time for that . . . after the race. Where were you going so fast, when I met you, Jase?"

Remembering with a guilty pang—"To get Firefly!"—he cried worriedly.

"Then I'll go with you," Kelly proposed, adding, as she sensed some opposition in him, "if you want me."

Want her? The look Jase gave her was eloquent answer. But, he explained, he might be in for a bad time while accounting for Firefly's being in that car to the train men. After that nothing could have kept Kelly from going.

Together they hastened to Firefly's rescue, to find, on rounding the dépôt corner, that she had been unloaded with the other horses and tied hard and fast to the shipping pen, where she stood, looking wistfully off at the open range. But before Jase could loose her tie rope, the train crew came running up, swearing that he had a government mule beat for nerve. They had dealt with hobos before, but he was the first who bummed his way with a horse, and so forth.

Then Firefly stepped back, and they saw Kelly Shane, and their voices trailed off before the mirth in her blue eyes. No hobo ever had a girl like that to back him up. Looking at her, even the feeble explanation Jase was making, of having been accidentally locked in the car, seemed perfectly logical. When Kelly said, with a gravity belied by her dancing eyes—"I'll try to persuade him not to bring suit against the road for forced transportation."—the men fell into the spirit of the thing, pretending great alarm and promising: "We'll pass all three of you to the end of the road an' back, if you'll keep it under your hat."

273

So, followed by the good wishes of the entire crew, they led Firefly triumphantly uptown, to the hitching rail where the Bar Bell horses were. And there—Jase halted, transfixed by sight of a horse that looked like Firefly even yet, but without that something that made Firefly different.

"Prairie Lass!" he breathed, a tumult of emotions in his breast, keenest of which was remorse.

For, going slowly up to the colt of the old cayuse Molly, which he had substituted for Firefly—the changeling that had created consternation in the White Rocks stables—it was suddenly borne on Jase how he had spoiled her life. She would have made good as a cayuse. But she fell so far short of what was expected of a daughter of Sacajawea that she had been hated and despised. But why was she here with the Bar Bell horses? Why was Kelly's . . . ? Wonderingly, he turned to the girl, who was watching him with sparkling eyes. "She's wearin' your saddle, Kelly!" he cried.

"But she belongs to me, Jase. Dad bought her. When I told him how you had traded her for Firefly, he thought the best thing he could do was to. . . ."

"Buy up the evidence," a deep voice struck in.

Jase swung to see Pat Shane regarding him with a grin. As they shook hands, he saw, despite Shane's broad smile, worry deeply etched in his genial face, and heard it ring in the wrathful pathos of his tone whenever he mentioned the White Rocks man. "You're safe now, Jase, even if the story comes out," Shane assured him. "For I bought Sacajawea's colt accordin' to the books. So Vortz can't accuse anyone of stealin' her . . . anyhow, not without admittin' he gypped me. An' if he does, I'll go after damages. I don't know how ethical it was . . . but ethics don't worry me none, when I deal with a moral eel like him."

But ethics did worry Jase—some. Although he had paid a

thousand dollars for Firefly, his conscience still hurt. He didn't want her by a trick. He hoped someday to own Firefly honestly.

"Vortz has no claim on Firefly, either," Kelly was telling her father. "He's just sold her to Jase."

"The deuce!" Shane was amazed. "How did that happen?" And he went up in blue smoke when he heard the price Vortz had exacted from Jase. "Why, the graspin' shorthorn. He knew he had you. He knew Lass wasn't a runner, but he swore she was, an' he soaked me seventeen prices."

"An' you paid them!" cried Jase gratefully. "You done it to help me out, when you was short."

"Tut, tut." Shane grinned sheepishly. "What's friends for, boy?" But his face quickly fell back in the old lines of worry as he thought of the efforts he had made, was still making, to save his ranch, and how, for all of them, his purse still lacked enough by half. "I hope," he said grimly, "that you're luckier than me, an' see a way to raise the money."

Right then Jase saw more hope for it than when Storrs had asked him, less when he saw how coldly solemn his plan to run Firefly in the Classic left Pat Shane.

"Boy"—Shane was sincere—"you haven't a chance. Did you ever see Sacajawea run? No? Waal, if you had, you'd see why none of the horses they bring in have a chance against her. Sure, an' she's more than a horse. She's wind, fire, an electric flash . . . something elemental. She's nine parts nerve. . . ."

"That's just what Firefly is," Jase broke in excitedly, "wind, fire . . . a flash of lightning!" But when Shane kept on, shaking his head, looking sorry for him, the boy seized his arms, crying: "Why wouldn't Firefly stand a better chance than any horse they bring in . . . an' their owners must think they got some chance? She's Sacajawea's own daughter. She's made up of the same stuff . . . mebbe better, for her father was Sachem, remember? For all I know, or anyone knows, she may be faster than her mother."

It was true. Pat Shane turned to look at Firefly, really seeing her for the first time. She was rougher-looking than when she had raced Blue Buttes range, but, with her head up eagerly to sniff the free grass on the wind, trembling in every dainty limb with the joy of homecoming, she promised enough to make Shane suddenly thoughtful.

"By glory," he exclaimed, "she might have a show!" And the more he studied her, the more he thought so. He was a born plunger. It did not take a sure thing to arouse his enthusiasm. All Pat Shane ever asked was a show for his money, and, enthusiastically, he looked back at Jase. "Son," he begged, "let me help you on this. We've got a couple of hours to get ready for the Classic. We'll make them pay, an'. . . ." Abruptly he slapped his thigh, as an idea came to him. "Let's enter her under her own name . . . Prairie Lass . . . an' see just what the Honorable Sam Vortz thinks of that!"

Jase stared at him, thrilling at the mere thought of it. But it was such a radical departure from his practice of keeping Firefly under cover, a habit that had become second nature, that he could not reply.

"But, Dad," interposed Kelly, seeing the risk, "Vortz will know she isn't Lass. He'll protest the race."

Shane's laugh had a rollicking ring. "That's the best part of it . . . Vortz can't do a thing! The Classic's a free-for-all. No horse is barred. An' no horse has a monopoly on the name of Prairie Lass. Let's give her something to live up to, Jase. Why can't she put in her best licks as a cayuse?"

Jase felt that way, too. He had not liked being called a cultus, a cayuse himself—when maybe he was. But he had made Firefly wear that cayuse brand her whole life long—when she was a princess. He looked at the people chattering on their way to the races. He looked at poor little Firefly, still wearing, although faintly, the stripes of her servitude—the impress of that degrading old harness, and his heart was swept by a wild desire to bring her out on her own range, under her true colors.

"We'll do it!" he recklessly agreed. "We'll go one better . . . an' enter her as a Shane horse."

And Pat, anticipating the jolt that would give Vortz, gave his grinning consent. "Only, remember," he hastened to assure Jase, "I'm layin' no claims to that mare . . . now, or ever."

A remark Jase ignored. For Firefly's ownership was already involved to such an extent that it made him dizzy to think of it, and, with the Classic but two hours off, he needed a mighty clear head.

XIII

"A dead game sport"

Unflecked by any cloud, the blue sky stretched above the Santo stampede grounds, over the broken buttes in all their savage grandeur. The air crashed with the sounding brass of bands, the pound of hoofs, the clasp of hands, and the hum of the crowd that had broken all previous attendance records by a full thousand. Outlaw horses and wild steers—star performers of preceding days—watched with rolling eyes from their in-

field corrals. Broncho-busters, bulldoggers, ropers in soiled re-
galia took a back seat to "spectate," giving jockeys, in
glistening fresh raiment, their place in the limelight. For this
afternoon was dedicated to the sport of kings—horse racing.

Continuously, since noon, horseflesh had strained
against itself on the track, fanning the crowd's enthusiasm
to white heat as the hour approached for the great race—the
Blue Buttes Classic.

"No guess about it," ran the comment through the
grandstand. "Vortz will drag down another thousand."

"What's the odds," it rolled back, "if he's got the best
horse?"

Spoken like a true fan. The race was the thing. Let the
best horse win. If it was a cayuse, well and good. Ditto, if it
was a Thoroughbred. If their race wasn't run according to
big track rules—as these outside owners sometimes complained—why, it was their race, and they ran it to suit themselves, and it did suit them from the ground up. So the
throng buzzed, while out by the fences men were running in
circles with their fists full of greenbacks, shouting their will-
ingness to bet on Sacajawea, and being taunted laughingly.

"Oh, you gambler!"

"That's no bet . . . it's a sure thing!"

"If you find somebody with more money than brains, let
me in!"

For Blue Buttes knew Sacajawea too well to bet against
her. But many were betting on the horse to come in second,
a favorite for this being Bluebird, belonging to the Carter
string, but—a difference of opinion is what makes horse
racing—and, while men bet, and horses run.

Up in the judges' stand a few favored mortals, of whom
Sam Vortz—having made a last inspection of his racer,
given his last order to her rider—was first and foremost,

watched the proceedings. Owners kept the steps up to it hot, making tardy entries and inquiries, driving the over-worked clerk to the verge of nervous prostration.

Saved from utterly toppling by the lull in which the horses were brought up for the pony race that preceded the Classic, the clerk seized his first chance to run an eye down the entries for the big event. He halted at one almost at the end that had puzzled him all afternoon, and, swinging about, he beckoned to Vortz.

"Sam," he asked, pointing to it, "can you enlighten me on this?"

Importantly Vortz bent over the paper and read the name with a stunned expression. And then, as the meaning of that name here dawned on him, he threw back his head with a roar of mirth that drew the eyes of the grandstand. He laughed himself purple in the face and, with difficulty getting control of himself, read it aloud: "Prairie Lass, entered by Pat Shane." That set him off again. "That's rich," he gasped, when articulation was possible. "That's the best yet!"

"Then don't be stingy," begged another favored mortal, grinning in sympathy.

Vortz wouldn't. No, indeed. It was too good to keep.

"Boys," he chortled, "you know that scrub colt of mine . . . Sacajawea's, but the disgrace of the stables? Well, I sold her to Pat Shane last spring. An' that crazy loon had the nerve to enter her in the Classic!" Then he broke out in a new place. "Pr-rairie Lass," he gasped, mopping his eyes. "Why, men, she couldn't head a cow in a line. What? Did I tell Shane that? Am I crazy?" This in reply to a dry inquiry. "You can bet your copper-toed boots I didn't! I wanted to unload too bad. An' I sure did. I asked Shane two hundred bucks, an' . . . got it. Almost keeled over with heart failure. I wondered why he paid it, for I've got reasons to know he's runnin' mighty close to the cushion. Now it's plain. He's had this on his mind. Thinks that dub can run on her mother's name. Run? That's the joke! I got cayuses out to White Rocks that could choke her to death with a hundred foot of rope."

This time they thought *he* would choke, and hoped he would, although they laughed with him, of course—for he was Sam Vortz. But in their hearts they hated him for cheating Pat Shane, who was every man's friend. Although the ponies got off just then, they forgot to watch them, and roasted Vortz behind his back, as one of his trainers popped up the steps, calling him out.

"Boss," panted the fellow, popeyed, "there's a lunatic down there takin' up bets on Sacajawea! I figgered you might want to place some. . . ."

"Who?" roared the White Rocks man.

"Pat Shane! He's down there now braggin' how he's goin' to send Sacajawea back to the plow. An' he's backin' his talk with a roll that would choke a calf."

Although this should have struck Vortz as the funniest yet, he did not laugh. How could Pat Shane afford to throw money away like that? He'd asked for time on that note. He wasn't a plumb fool. He'd have clocked Lass before this. What was his game? Well, whatever it was, Vortz thought with vengeful satisfaction, it would break Shane and save him the job. Pat Shane had bucked him over once too often, when he stepped between him and that cayuse at the auction. Nevertheless, there was a scowl on his forehead, as he leaned over the clerk again. "Say," he had to shout, for the ponies were coming in amid the wild tumult, "will you look at that entry again an' see who's ridin' for Shane?"

The clerk, glad to oblige him, read it out: "Jase Kress up."

Again Vortz had the strange feeling that the Kress kid was having the laugh on him, this time, however, with the double horror that Pat Shane was in on it. He dismissed it as too ridiculous. But his face was anxious as he rushed back to his man and, flinging a roll of bills at him, he snapped: "Hop down there. Take every cent that fool has to bet. An' hurry." For the gong was ringing.

But he was too late, The hungry horde of Sacajawea fans had found a man with more money than brains, and every cent Shane had offered had been covered so quickly it made his head ache. Yes—made him so sick with remorse and guilt that he went off by himself to look the worst in the face. After which his mercurial spirits rose, so that he had himself pretty well in hand, when the megaphone bawled to the paddocks: "Horses up for the Classic!"

At last. Music crashed with fresh impetus. Thousands of eager eyes strained up the track, down which the burnished, mettlesome, fleet-limbed racers were waltzing, half dragging their attendants in their zest to perform. As each proudly postured before the grandstand, it was announced by the megaphone to wild applause. Deafening was the tumult when Sacajawea—crowned queen of a hundred races, flamingly regal, exquisite, and knowing it—took her bow. Plaudits that Sam Vortz took to himself, so puffing him up that it seemed the judges' stand could not contain him. Jealously he eyed her rivals prancing up to the wire, above which, suspended from a red ribbon strung over the track, was a little bag containing one thousand dollars in gold. The grand prize. There it was. The magnet that drew every jockey's eyes.

More horses piled up, filling the track, until the craning crowd had trouble fitting the horse to the name as it was announced, and wholly unable to when the megaphone threw this bomb among them: "Prairie Lass, by Pat Shane. Jase Kress up!"

The Kress kid. Then he was back. Yes. For in sharp contrast to the other riders, resplendent in shimmering colors, the slim, boyish figure their eyes rested on was clad in what might have been the same bleached-out, weather-beaten garments he had worn on the day he had made his break at the auction. But his still face, out of which burned unforgettable eyes, blazed white, as if he'd seen a ghost. No—like old Cultus after a periodical drunk. He was here, worthless as ever, good for nothing . . . but, no! There was one thing Jase Kress could do. He could ride. Not on Prairie Lass, they laughed. Entered by Pat Shane? Had Pat gone out of his mind? No, he was just a dead game sport, betting every cent he had on Lass to win. Hey, get those horses back! They wanted a look at the White Rocks scrub!

Just then the other horses went back from Firefly, and Blue Buttes had it. Just about what they had expected. But they might have been taken in, if they hadn't been hearing for years what a fizzle she was. The little filly looked likely enough. A little rougher than the other quick bloods, but she compared fine with any of them. Just showed how a horse could fool you sometimes.

But up in the judges' stand was a man who wasn't fooled for an instant. One who recognized this horse the minute she came on the track, and stared down at her like a man turned to stone, staring as hypnotically at her as he had stared at the auction. But, seeing now the points he had noted then intensified, as with flanks drawn in, limbs aquiver, her whole slim, sinewy being made taut, vibrant, with the quickening instincts come down to her from generations of racing forebears, she pranced to the music, looking—under the regulation racing saddle borrowed by

Pat Shane for the occasion—every bit as much the racer as Sacajawea.

Excitedly a neighbor yelled to the watcher. "Beats all how Lass shows up on the track!"

Purple in the face, and not from mirth, Vortz whirled on him. "That ain't Lass! It's the Kress kid's cayuse! By heaven, I knew. . . ."

"If that horse is a cayuse," the other came back, "I'm an Eskimo!"

Again Vortz stared, stricken, seeing Firefly running from him that starlit night, feeling that pound in his pulse, that determination to have her at any price, that hunch forgotten in subsequent pulse-pounding times when he had seen other horses run. The kid had lied to him. Led him to believe the horse was in Spokane. Why? Why was Pat Shane entering him? Why under the name of Prairie Lass? By mighty, he'd protest this race!

But, swinging his burly shoulders to do it, he lapsed back, knowing well he could not. Galling was the reflection that he had only himself to blame for it. For he had drawn up the rules for the Classic, and made them easy, insisting on the one that barred no horse, thinking it necessary to create interest in the race, for there were few Thoroughbreds in the country. But what was he getting worried for? They had no chance against Sacajawea.

Below him, the track was a bedlam, with willing helpers trying to restrain the turbulent racers, while their riders drew for place. Pat Shane was having his hands full with Firefly, when Jase came back, pleased to have drawn second.

"That's lucky!" cried Shane. "Who got the pole?"

"Bluebird . . . a Carter horse. She came in with me on the train."

"I'm sure glad it wasn't Sacajawea," declared Shane fervently.

So was Jase. "Gee, I wish it was over," he said in a tense voice. "When I think what this race means. . . ."

"Boy," Shane said steadily, "it means more than you think. I bet every cent of that money I raised on Firefly."

Speechless, Jase stared at him. Then he burst out in fierce negation: "Not that money you borrowed toward the note? Why, you said yourself we hardly had a show."

"I know," Shane confessed wearily, "but I felt lucky. They was offerin' four to one! I figgered that if, by some fluke, we did win, I could settle everything, an' I might as well be hung for a sheep as a lamb. Waal, I'll probably be hung . . . but it won't be for mutton. But, forget it, Jase. Cheer up, we ain't licked yet."

Cheer up? When he was responsible not only for the Jingle Bob but for the Bar Bell. When he stood to lose not only his own home, but Kelly's.

Jase was too crushed to know how Kelly got there. But there she was, in all the turmoil and dust, pinning his number to his arm, whispering: "Jase, don't think about us."

"Then, you heard . . . ?"

"If you'd been in the grandstand . . . ," she smiled. Dead game, like her dad. "But I knew he would. Dad never goes into anything half-hearted that. . . ."

"Line up!" bellowed the starter.

Jase sprang to the saddle. Bending to hand Kelly his sombrero, he said, his face set and purposeful: "Girl, I'll do my best. Firefly never fell down on me yet."

XIV

"Against the best"

The track was cleared. Firefly was caught in the froth of horses fighting for place. All was endless, seemingly inextricable confusion that struck Jase as the most hopeless thing he had ever been up against. These horses were trained to this. They knew all the ropes. And so did their riders. It was new to him and Firefly. She would do her best, but much might depend on luck, and she wouldn't know how to take advantage of any break.

About him, rattling him to the point of panic, frantic owners were telling jockeys their business. Jockeys were cussing out other riders and calming their horses, while the starter was bawling out all concerned, and getting back as good as he sent.

"Hey you . . . Number One! If you can't handle that blue, get her off the track!"

"Aw, chase yourself!"

"Here! Bring up that black!"

"You get the rest off . . . I'll tend to my horse!"

It was borne in on Jase how cold-nerved these riders were, while he was shaking all over. He had more at stake than any of them. That's what was the matter—he had so much. He must shake it off—be cool—like the rest. It was these men he was fighting. And he was communicating to Firefly his same panic. Her flanks were afoam. She was wearing herself out before the race even began.

Pressed in by surging horses, in momentary expectation

of the gong, Jase shut out every thought but to get started out with them. He became as desperately calm, as this morning he had been under Vortz's gun.

"Steady, girl," soothingly he talked to her. "It's nothin' . . . just a run. Twice around this track . . . that's all. Just do your best, girl."

Through all the uproar of action and sound his voice reached her, and steadied her somewhat, although it was all Jase could do to control her. But he had her headed right and well to the fore, when, loud on his raw nerves, the gong rang.

Firefly all but leaped from under him! The mass of straining horseflesh broke under the wire. But several jumps down the track, Jase heard the *clang! clang! clang!* of the gong, calling them back. Two horses had been left at the post. All that soul-trying strain had to be lived over again, and this time in threefold the confusion, for all nerves were raw, the horses all but unmanageable, and the crowd— scarcely less nervous—clamorously impatient. But through it all Jase was sustained by the lightning flash of love and confidence that Kelly sent him from the fence.

Clang! The seething jam shot forward again! They were off!

Jase never knew how it came about. Firefly managed it, for all that he had thought she did not know, because she had never been taught it, was instinctive with her. And instinct, or luck, had got them off to a good start. The first thing Jase could ever remember for sure was that he was pounding neck to neck with the blue mare that was hugging the pole, and that the track ahead was clear, then thinking that he must always see the track clear like that, keeping the other horses behind, to get that thousand in gold that would settle everything.

Then came agony, to see the blue draw ahead almost a

length, and the hopeless feeling that Firefly had never run so slow, labored so, been so sluggish, as if she were dragging the dead weight of all at stake. Then glimpsing the grassy stretch inside the rail, he could tell by the way it flashed past that she had never run so fast—that it was only his eagerness that made her seem slow. But run as she did, she could not catch that blue will-o-the-wisp! No—although the wind seemed tearing Jase from her back, and he bent low on her neck to cut down its resistance.

The quarter was passed, with no change in their positions, with Firefly drawing on that reserve of power he thought she had plumbed in Oregon, but which he knew now she had not even tapped. But she had to go down to its very dregs this time. She was not racing range-bred horses now, but the best. She had to run like this, beat this, he did not know how much—a whole mile. For the horses, hammering behind, were not sprinters. They were being held back—their best saved for the end of the race. Would Firefly have any best left? Wasn't she drawing on all she had? A thrill shot through him to see that she was creeping up on the blue! Inch by inch, she gained, until her nose stretched at the blue's stirrup.

Then, out of the tail of his eye, Jase saw a red nose come up to his side. Sacajawea! Inexorably, as he gained on the blue, Sacajawea gained on him! On the back stretch he passed the blue, and Firefly had the rail, leaning to it as if she knew the advantage of being there, and Sacajawea was running breast to breast with her.

Locked, breast to breast, they held the turns, and flashed into the stretch. Now, piercing even the tumult of hoofs, deafening as a hundred tom-toms beating, came the roar from the grandstand. Still breast to breast—Sacajawea and her daughter flashed under the ribbon on the first round.

And the frenzied thousands roared as one voice: "Prairie Lass!"

They were crazy to see her win—to see Vortz beaten for once. To take the conceit out of him. Crazy as people are when a belittled beginner shows champion stuff. Crazily, Pat Shane hugged his daughter—who had seen only Jase, with his dark hair streaming, and the stamp of agony on his face.

"Win or lose," wildly cried Shane, his voice husky from emotion, "she's true to her blood!"

It was in that hope that the throng was splitting its throat.

"Hear the fools rave!" snarled Sam Vortz in thunderous fury. "They think Sacajawea's runnin'! Her rider knows his business! He's holdin' her in all right for the stretch . . . where the money is!"

But he knew in his heart, and the glass his eyes were glued on, told him that his prize racer was being run off her legs by a cayuse. No! He knew better than that now! He thought the glass lied, and with a curse he flung it aside, when it showed him the Kress kid's horse in the lead.

"He skinned me . . . the cur!" he raved. "He knew that was a race horse!"

Wes Storrs, stampede manager and one of the judges, said in a voice straight off the ice: "It's plumb legitimate to skin a man in a horse deal! I have your word for it!"

Vortz closed up like a trap—and quickly forgot all this in the valiant fight that was going on before his eyes. For, scoundrel that he was, there was hidden deeply in his nature one redeeming trait—a sporting instinct! And he was, through and through, a race horse man. The race was the thing!

He thrilled to the flight of the red racers—so alike at that distance that only the purple worn by his rider enabled him to distinguish between them. He beat the rail with hoarse, senseless cheers, when the purple gained a hard-earned half-length, and held it until, making the turn into the homestretch, the advantage of having the inside track enabled Firefly to regain her loss. Together the two ran, breast to breast, and less than an eighth of the mile was left!

Did any other horse run in the Blue Buttes Classic that afternoon? Ask anyone! Not a soul saw them! They saw only those two, made up of the same stuff—wind, fire, an electric flash—fighting the age-old battle of mature experience against young, untried blood that dares all and refuses to recognize the impossible, straining against each other, as no horseflesh ever strained on that track!

Although it might mean his ruin, Jase's heart swelled with admiration for Sacajawea, putting up such a battle against her own colt. It almost burst with worship for Firefly—shamefully yoked to a huckster's wagon but yesterday, now holding her own against the fastest horse in the state. No! Not holding her own. For he suddenly saw she was losing ground, felt, with black despair, the all but imperceptible falter in her stride. She had run herself out! She was weakening! And—as once more that human roar reached him in a long-drawn, continuous, wail that gradually swelled into a tidal wave of sound—he saw Sacajawea pulling away from him, filling the track before him, looming between him and the prize that he must have!

Stretched flat on Firefly's neck, over the whizzing, yellow track, the boy pleaded with her, as he never had: "Faster, girl! Just a little . . . faster! So we can go home! So we won't ever have to run wild again! So we can go back to the Jingle Bob! Firefly, do it . . . this once!"

The effect was instantaneous. He felt new strength surge to her straining limbs. For, as if she would make up to Jase for the years of love and care lavished on her, Firefly flattened beneath him, and—ran! Her pace was the wind's pace—a low, fluid motion, bred true from generations of runners As he saw the red ribbon flash fatally near, he poured mad entreaties into her ear.

Slowly, surely Firefly inched up on Sacajawea, whose jockey turned a dazed, scared face at Jase, and bent himself to get a little more out of the mare. For Firefly was closing that gap of daylight! She was running with her nose at her mother's hip—stirrup—neck—breast to breast!

Then the blur of sounds, of humanity gone stark, staring crazy, came at Jase with a rush. The tidal wave broke over him, overwhelming. And the horses flashed past! In what position?

Jase did not know. Suddenly it did not seem to matter. For, slowing Firefly, while the other racers overtook him, thundering on, his nerves broke from the long strain. Coming to a stop, two hundred yards down the track, he was too weak to ride back and see if he had lost the Jingle Bob. He was too faint to sit in the saddle, and, half falling from it, he collapsed against the heaving little filly, dimly conscious that people were running down the track, that the mob up there was cheering someone. . . . It wouldn't be him. They wouldn't even give his horse a hand when she was announced. He dropped his face against Firefly's hot neck, with a dry, racking sob.

Someone lifted his head, and he read the truth in the truest eyes on earth. In Kelly's eyes—full of tears.

Dully he said: "Vortz won?"

She could not answer him. But Pat Shane did, grabbing him in a grizzly embrace: "Vortz . . . your granny! Firefly won by a nose . . . in the gamest race that was ever won on this track."

XV

"Paid in full"

Rose and gold, sunset's afterglow, burned in the west. The hills and vales were swathed in their bluest mist. It was an hour of peace and quiet. Kelly Shane was waiting for Jase. She knew he was coming tonight, for he hadn't been over for two whole days. And, curled up there on the bench under the whispering hedge that bordered the Bar Bell drive, she wondered what was taking his time. Also, she was reviewing things. Not the happenings of today, nor yet the big day of the Classic—two weeks gone—when the end of the world had not come, but a new world had begun. She was reviewing the whole year since Jase had found her crying here, and Vortz had found him before he could tell her something she wanted to hear.

In a way, it seemed to Kelly a wasted year. Jase was just where he had been. The first theft of Firefly haunted him, marring his pleasure in being home and going ahead with his plans. She knew he would never be happy until the whole truth was told. And she feared his troubles would start all over again, on a larger scale, if he confessed to Sam Vortz.

For the White Rocks man had not taken his beating with very good grace. He was sullen, suspicious—openly curious about Firefly, telling Jase bluntly that he knew the mare was a Thoroughbred, and demanding her history, for Cultus Kress hadn't indulged in blooded stock. It had not sweetened his disposition either to lose his hold on the Jingle

Bob. He took that hard. Sooner or later, he would stumble onto the truth, and. . . .

She sprang up at the clatter of hoofs, to see a little horse, red as a harvest sunset, and his rider, a handsome, up-and-coming young fellow, whom nobody would dream of calling a cayuse. Hereafter, Blue Buttes would see Jase by himself—see him making that game race for his ranch. For, there and forever, he had outrun the shadow of old Cultus. As he flung himself down beside her, it seemed to the girl that he had outrun every shadow. His face was so shining—cloudless.

"Kelly!" he literally sang, "behold a man with a clean conscience!"

Her face was a contrast of expressions. "Jase, you didn't tell Vortz, did you?"

"I did . . . right from the minute I swapped colts. It didn't surprise him much. He bucked all over the lot, an' it looked for a time like I was goin' to get piled again. But there's something he wants worse than Firefly. . . ."

"The Jingle Bob!" cried Kelly, in so much alarm that Jase laughed happily.

"I didn't give it to him . . . not all, anyway. But you know that forty borderin' his ranch? It wouldn't make a garden patch"—Jase winced—"for White Rocks, but it has two rattlin' good springs on it, an' the creek runs through it. Plenty of water to supply him. An' I'll never miss it. Well, I offered to deed that forty to him for the mortgage he holds an' the difference in what Firefly's worth . . . now we know she's a race horse."

"He took it?" Kelly could not believe it.

"Not right off," Jase grinned. "He went home an' slept on it. But I guess he saw how your buyin' Prairie Lass tangled up things . . . so maybe she'd go to your dad, if he did prosecute me an' win. Anyhow, he came over this mornin', an' we settled my way. He got the water, an' I got Firefly. An' I've still got that thousand I won for a start. I guess it eased Vortz's sting a lot to learn Sacajawea was beat by her own colt."

He sighed from sheer happiness. "Gee, Kelly, it's great to be home. It's great to work for yourself. Just think, last week I had enough grief to sink a ship. Now, I ain't got a trouble on earth."

She looked at him strangely. How could he forget? There was one trouble left. And it was worrying her much more than Vortz was. For while it would take an unusually clever lawyer to untangle that case, this would appear a real theft. Although disliking to, she reminded him: "You're forgetting Wu Fong."

Exultantly he drew her to him, not wanting to miss a shade of expression on her face when he told her this: "I was just waitin' for you to bring up Fong! I'll say I ain't forgettin' him . . . an', if ever I do, I hope to be shot. But, Kelly, that's all fixed!"

"Honest?" Her eyes were like stars. "Oh, Jase, how was that?"

"You'd never guess! That very night, after the race, I went down to the placer camp to see my old friend, Lo Wing. An' I told him all my tribulations . . . never dreamin' he could do anything, but just like you tell things to a dead-sure friend. Today, I rode down again, an' he met me at the door of his shack with a grin a mile broad. An' he told me . . . guess, Kelly, guess what he told me?"

"Jase Kress, if you don't tell me quick. . . ."

"Kelly," he laughed at her eagerness, "he told me he'd been to Spokane, an' he hunted up Wu Fong. It seems they belonged to the same . . . tong, or something. An' when he told Fong how things was between me an' Firefly, Fong said he'd sell her to me for just what he paid . . . fifty bucks. An' he wouldn't take a cent for all that truck I ditched by the wayside."

Every shadow was gone. The breeze whispered in the shrubs. A coyote made wild music from the hills above. Firefly—his—theirs!—amused herself, while Jase told Kelly what he had tried to say before leaving the Blue Buttes country. All of which she knew already but listened to as thrillingly, for it was the old, sweet story.

Jon Tuska is the author of numerous books about the American West as well as the editor of several short story collections, *Billy the Kid: His Life and Legend* (Greenwood Press, 1994) and *The Western Story: A Chronological Treasury* (University of Nebraska Press, 1995) among them. Together with his wife Vicki Piekarski, Tuska co-founded the Golden West Literary Agency that primarily represents authors of Western fiction and Western Americana. They edit and co-publish twenty-five titles a year in two prestigious series of new hardcover Western novels and story collections. They also co-edited the *Encyclopaedia of Frontier and Western Fiction* (McGraw-Hill, 1983), *The Max Brand Companion* (Greenwood Press, 1996). *The Morrow Anthology of Great Western Short Stories* (Morrow, 1997), and *The First Five Star Western Corral* (Five Star Westerns, 2000). Tuska has also edited a series of short novel collections, *Stories of the Golden West*, of which there have been seven volumes.